THE RETURN OF
"THE NIGHT WIND"

THE RETURN OF "THE NIGHT WIND"

THE NIGHT WIND SAGA, VOLUME II

BY

VARICK VANARDY

Edited by Christopher R. Yates
Foreword by Peter Coogan

The Borgo Press
An Imprint of Wildside Press

MMVII

CONTENTS

A NOTE ON THE TEXT

The text of this novel was reproduced from the 1913 bound edition of *The Return of the Night Wind* published by G. W. Dillingham Company, New York, through The Frank A. Munsey Co., 1913. Other than correcting for obvious, unintentional grammatical or typographical errors, this reproduction remains true to the letter and spirit of the 1913 G. W. Dillingham bound text.

ACKNOWLEDGMENTS

The generous assistance from the following persons and institutions made this reproduction possible: My sincere thanks go to Steve Miller for the original cover scan that graces this book and to Bill Thom and Phil Stephenson-Payne for introductions to Mr. Miller. This cover is a digital copy of the cover of *The Cavalier* magazine, October 4, 1913, wherein the first installment of *The Return of the Night Wind* originally appeared. Also, "thank you" to Stanford University, Stanford, California and Polly Armstrong, Public Services Manager, Special Collections and University Archives for permission to use and reproduce the covers of the "Nick Carter Detective Library" in the Foreword of this book.

FOREWORD

Bingham Harvard is an anomaly. Both in his fictional world and in literary history, he is nearly unique. Physically, he is the only person in the Night Wind series to display extraordinary abilities—no one else manifests superhuman capacities of any sort. Harvard's physical power—he is four times as strong and six times as agile as a normal man—make him unique in his world. He can ignore the police force and maim its officers at will. He flees New York for Europe at the end of *Alias "The Night Wind"* not because he fears the law, but because he fears he will be forced to kill the police detective who has framed him if he stays in the States, and this crime and the moral stain it will leave upon him will unfit him for marriage to Kate Maxwilton, late of the police herself.

Socially, he is a misfit. He has no family backing; he was a foundling orphan. This lack of social standing is part of the reason police Lieutenant Rodney Rushton picks him as a mark to frame for a bank robbery. Rushton believes that Harvard's lack of family will make him an easy victim, that his guardian, bank president Sterling Chester, will fold on him—which he does—and that Harvard himself will, in Rushton's idiom, "weaken and confess when the professional gaff was thrown into him" and go to jail, and well the young bank clerk might have except for his abnormal physiology. Rushton's view exemplifies the "before" side of the large social and cultural shift that Robert Wiebe traces in *The Search for Order*. According to Wiebe, the norm for American life in the 1870s was the small-town "island community," homogeneous agricultural communities that saw themselves as largely self-sufficient and disconnected from the urban centers to which they looked for "markets and supplies, credit and news." The people of these communities knew their neighbors directly and valued thrift, hard work, and sobriety—a "version of Scottish common-sense doctrines." Power, in what Wiebe calls "the distended society," was dispersed; industry, banking, and commerce were still conducted on a small scale. Overall the nation's focus was on the local and small, and this focus was mirrored in the upper reaches of urban society in which family and connection counted, in essence an island community in the midst of the metropolis. The great forces of the twentieth century—bureaucratization, urbanization, immigration, professionalization, standardization, centralization, commercialization, and specialization—were waiting, on the verge of transforming the country. Wiebe traces this transformation, focusing on the way the emerging and growing middle class worked to harness these forces through a "bureaucratic orientation" that valued regularity, functionality, and rationality. By the 1920s, these forces had been largely established and, in a general sense, "the nation had found its direction," which would be played over the next half century.

Rushton held to the older view and felt he could manipulate the small upper-crust of New York into rejecting Harvard as a born criminal, one without the character that came from being born into the proper sort of family. Harvard lacks the social connections and backing that were necessary for success in the island communities of the nineteenth century. He was part of the anonymous, college-educated, urban professional class that was emerging in this period of transition, but, anomalously, he owes no allegiance to that class, nor does he use its forces to clear himself of the false charges against him. Harvard does not symbolize the new professional, bureaucratic orientation, nor does he harness the forces of urban rationality to overturn the prejudice of the old order; instead he mercilessly and aggressively attacks and maims police officers and flees to the continent with the female police officer whom he has won over romantically.

In literary history, he is anomalous as well. It is rare that a pulp series introduces a fantastic element in its debut, only to bury it in its sequels. Harvard's strength plays almost no role in the sequels to *Alias "The Night Wind."* In *Return of "The Night Wind"*, he vows to stop maiming police officers. In *"The Night Wind"'s Promise*, his strength occasionally hangs over the action like threatening storm clouds, but he never deploys it. And in *Lady of the Night Wind*, he attacks the villain once, but does not seriously harm him, though his wife keeps a secret from him about the villain because she fears that his anger and strength will lead him to murder and thence to prison.

The Night Wind does not fit into either of the pulp fictional character types that he logically should, the science-fiction superman and the avenger vigilante. Unlike every other super-strong hero, no explanation is offered for his enhanced abilities. He is merely deemed a prodigy, and that is that. The science-fiction superman appeared at the beginning of science fiction with Frankenstein's creature. In "From Menace to Messiah: The Prehistory of the Superman in Science Fiction Literature," Thomas Andrae finds a common thread in most stories of physical supermen: "Whether savior or destroyer the superman cannot be permitted to exist." The stories of *Homo superior* of the nineteenth and early twentieth centuries end in tragedy and futility because of the threat the superman poses to humanity. Andrae writes, "Whether he becomes an outcast, a pathetically lonely creature who is ostracized, or a tyrannical monster so dangerous that he threatens to enslave the world, convention dictates that he either die or be robbed of his power." Bingham Harvard poses no such threat and suffers no destruction. And he does not escape the fate of the *Homo superior* by taking any of the paths that emerged for the character. He does not become a hermit, as in Upton Sinclair's *The Overman* (1907), in which a shipwrecked musician contemplates the universe in his enforced solitude and comes thereby into contact with a race of people living in a utopian spiritual union in an alternate dimension. His hero refuses rescue, preferring his miraculous new understanding of the universe to exile in empty civilization. Nor does he become a savior figure, as Edgar Rice Burroughs' John Carter does in *A Princess of Mars* (1911) by saving the red planet Barsoom from asphyxiation when its atmosphere plant fails, but seemingly dying in the process, only to return, Christ-like, and unify the planet as the King of Kings (or Jeddak of Jeddak in Barsoomian). Finally, he does not become a hero, like Doc Savage or E. E. "Doc" Smith's Lensmen. Harvard's superhumanity has no larger social purpose—he is a protagonist, but not a hero. He does not learn the lesson of Peter Parker, that with great power comes great responsibility. He views his physical abilities as his alone; society has no claim on his strength. He does not use his power to help others, only to free himself and assert his innocence. The Night Wind's power moves him into the realm of the superhuman, but without a philosophical backing. His extraordinary strength is extrinsic to the story; a skilled fighter could cripple an equal number of policemen without such great strength, and in fact most of his adventures do not depend upon its possession. To some degree he fights against the evil of a corrupt police force, but he is not a hero in the line of Doc Savage. Most of his battles arise out of being framed for embezzlement, so he mostly fights to regain his reputation. This fight is not prosocial, selfless, or heroic. This treatment is completely anomalous in the tradition of the superman.

Nor does Bingham Harvard exemplify the traits of the other major figure of his age, the avenger-vigilante. The avenger-vigilante figure typically acts outside the law to critique society and to avenge wrongs done upon the helpless, either by the powerful or by outside malefactors whose evil the socially powerful are unable to prevent. But always the avenger-vigilante works for the benefit of others. The Night Wind, on the contrary, has no social mission. He seeks to avenge the wrongs done upon himself, not those visited upon innocent victims.

The avenger-vigilante figure appeared in dime novels primarily through the avenger-detective archetype. As explained in *The Dime Novel Detective*, edited by Gary Hoppenstand, the avenger-detective of the dime novels possessed eight major traits:

> 1) he is a vigilante who often works outside traditional law-enforcement agencies; 2) he utilizes iconic weaponry (almost always a gun); 3) he possesses great strength, superb training and determination, coupled with courage; 4) he is a master of disguise; 5) he is a man of great wealth; 6) he combats crime with a dedicated group of assistants; 7) he maintains a sanctum sanctorum for his personal use; and 8) he is strongly nationalistic.

The character who best exemplifies the avenger-detective is Nick Carter, whose adventures Frederic Van Rensselaer Dey, author of the Night Wind series, also penned. Carter is supremely physically superior; has been trained by his father to be a detective; lives by his father's dictum to keep his body, clothing, and conscience clean; and so on, embodying the traits of the avenger-vigilante detective figure. The dime novel avenger-detective is essentially conservative, socially and politically. The city and its institutions, and the people who represent them, are presented as good. The hero "is himself a member-in-good-standing with the WASPs" and neatly embodies a positive vision of society through his personal characteristics of strength, intelligence, moral probity, and wealth. His opponents represent the forces posited as opposing the utopian WASP city, the immigrant and socialist lower classes who seek to change society to their benefit. Hoppenstand sums up the ultimate laissez-faire message of the avenger-detective dime novels as "leave well enough alone and everything will turn out perfect."

"Nick Carter, Detective: The Solution of a Remarkable Case," Issue No. 1, Aug., 1891, Street & Smith, Publishers. The "Celebrated Author," although not credited, is likely Frederic Van Rensselaer Dey, a.k.a. Varick Vanardy of the Night Wind series.

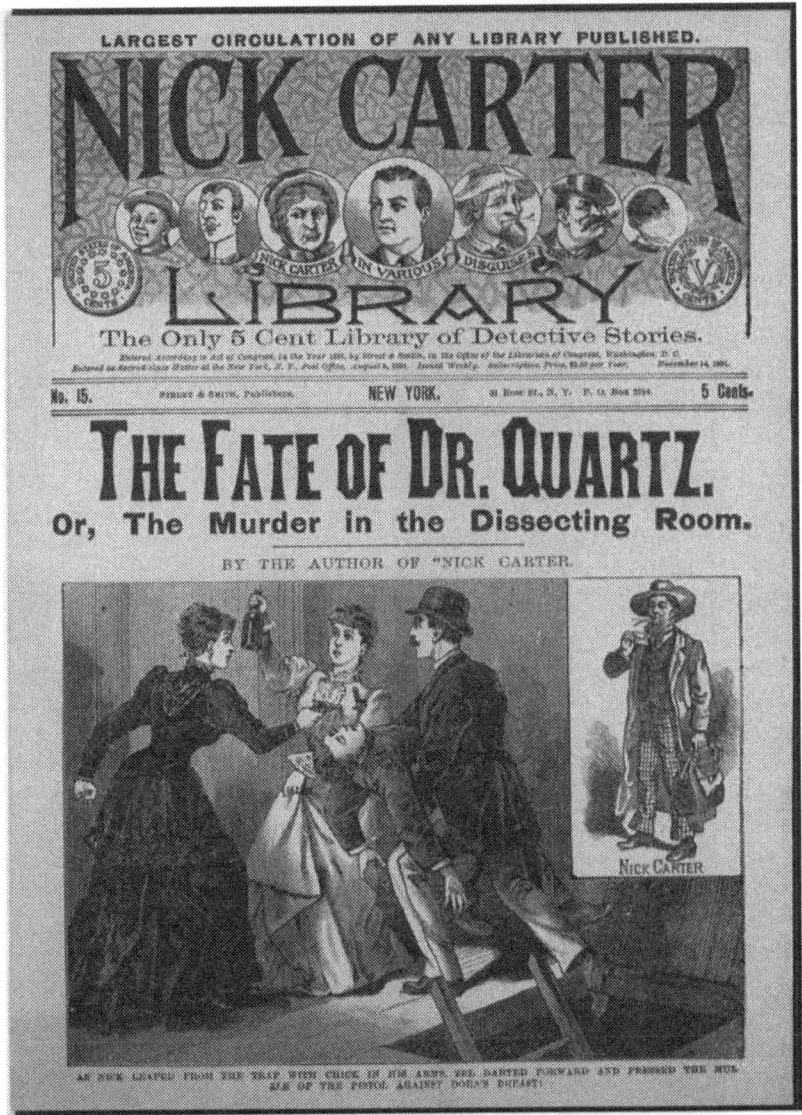

"The Fate of Dr. Quartz: The Murder in the Dissecting Room," Issue No. 15, Nov., 1895, Street & Smith, Publishers. "Dr. Jack Quartz" is the foremost of the Nick Carter series villains and thought to be the prototype for fictional arch-villains, predating Sherlock Holmes' Professor Moriarty by two years.

15

But with the exception of great physical strength, none of this fits Bingham Harvard. Though one expects this formula to intrude into *Alias "The Night Wind,"* anomalously it does not. Harvard does not work outside the law—he actively attacks its agents, but only to assert his innocence. He uses no iconic weaponry; his hands are deadly enough as is. He has no training, though he is stubbornly determined to prove his innocence, and somewhat courageous, and he never doubts his ability to overwhelm and escape all opponents because of his unique physical superiority. He affects no disguise, but is well known by the police and the public on sight. He has enough money to live on the run, but unlike most avenger-vigilantes, his source of wealth is quite prosaic—he happened to have sold a few real estate properties for cash shortly before he was falsely accused, and so he has a large bundle of money to support himself while he works to clear his name. He fights no crime—even in his later novels, he or his bank is the primary victim of the criminals he combats. He does, though, have a small circle of respectable friends who aid him in his cause. He has no secret hideout and expresses no political or social opinions.

His final anomaly comes in the title of this debut novel, *Alias "The Night Wind."* Bingham Harvard is unlike any other dual-identity figure in pulp literature. In the first place, he does not use a secret identity to fight crime. His "Night Wind" alias is pinned on him by a police official as a descriptive for his ability to vanish into the night and to escape police attempts to take him into custody. Unlike his dual-identity predecessor the Scarlet Pimpernel, contemporary the Gray Seal, or follower Zorro, he does not use his second identity to stand in opposition to official authority and fight to right wrongs; he is not, as they are, positioned as enemies of their states because they oppose official government policy and often commit crimes, or seem to. The Night Wind identity does not serve to protect Harvard from discovery or to maintain his social status while he rights wrongs in disguise.

Perhaps this series of anomalies helps to explain why the Night Wind series was forgotten. The series and its hero did not fit into the standard literary categories. Though he is rich, his tales are not social melodramas or critiques of high society. Though he is a fugitive, the authorities present no real danger to him, either physical or legal. He is virtuous—overwhelmingly, placidly, stolidly virtuous—but he is not tempted toward the gutter and never suffers moral qualms over his actions; he knows he is in the right and never doubts his cause. That Dey could create enough material for four novels within these confines speaks more to Dey's professionalism as a one-man fiction factory than to Bingham Harvard's appeal as a character. That such a character is interesting enough to return to over four novels or after nearly a century is perhaps the final anomaly of Bingham Harvard.

—Peter Coogan
September, 2006

Dr. Peter Coogan is the writing specialist for the Kinkel Center for Academic Resources at Fontbonne University in St. Louis, Missouri. In 2002 he completed his dissertation, *The Secret Origin of the Superhero: The Emergence of the Superhero Genre in America from Daniel Boone to Batman*, for his doctorate in American Studies at Michigan State University. In July 2006, MonkeyBrain Books published *Superhero: The Secret Origin of a Genre*, an adaptation of Dr. Coogan's doctoral dissertation and considered by many to be THE book on superheroes.

Quoting Amazon.com, Dr. Coogan's work is "An entertaining and exhaustive history, tracing the superhero's roots in mythology, science fiction, and pulps, which follows the genre's development to its current renaissance in film, literature, and graphic novels."

In 1992 he co-founded and continues to co-chair the Comics Arts Conference, an academic conference held at the San Diego Comic-Con International designed to bring comics scholars and professionals together to discuss comics in a public venue.

17

CHAPTER I

LADY KATE OF THE POLICE

"What are you doing here? How did you get in? Who are you?"

Lady Kate lifted a pair of inscrutable, fathomless eyes to meet the perplexed, half-angry gaze of Banker Chester, and she replied with utter calm, while the ghost of a smile flitted across her perfect features. She answered each of the questions in their order.

"I have been," she said, "waiting for you. I entered with a key. I am—or was—Lady Kate of the Police."

Another suggestion of a smile glowed for the briefest instant upon her face, and was gone as soon as it appeared. She did not alter her attitude of relaxed ease by so much as the movement of a finger. She continued to lean back comfortably in the depths of the huge, leather-upholstered chair she occupied.

The banker looked down upon her with a frown upon his face and growing anger in his eyes. The multitudinous affairs of his daily life in the world of finance had crowded out all recollection of the name she had used; and yet it stirred something of memory within him, too.

And her face? He knew that somewhere he had seen it before, and the vague acknowledgment of the fact to himself stirred him uneasily.

Of the three replies she made to his three questions, only one sank into his understanding as being of paramount and immediate importance; and he replied instantly:

18

"You entered with a key! Whose key? What key?"

"With a key; yes. A latch-key to the front door of this house. Whose key, you ask, Mr. Chester? I came in with the key which you had made expressly for, and gave to—Bingham Harvard."

She straightened and stiffened in her chair when she uttered the name, bending slightly forward toward the man who stood before her. Her eyes, half quizzical, partly smiling until then, were suddenly hard as flint; and her mobile lips, without apparent motion, seemed also to harden.

And the banker!

The mention of that name shocked him into impotency. He stood like a statue while the blood slowly receded from his face, leaving it white and drawn—and frightened.

Lady Kate watched him with the calmness of a stoic; waited for him to recover from the shock of the announcement, which had been even more severe than she had anticipated.

She saw him put out a hand toward the library table, which occupied the middle of the room, to steady himself. She saw him moisten his lips with the tip of his tongue and thrust out his chin, as if the intaking of his breath were an effort. She relaxed into the depths of the chair again, but the hardness that had come into her exquisite face remained.

"Bingham—Harvard!" the banker gasped in a shrill whisper when it was given him again to articulate.

"Yes," Lady Kate said calmly.

"Where—where is he?"

"At least he is not here—now, Mr. Chester. Of that you may be sure."

Then the blood surged back into Chester's face with apoplectic force, changing it from white to a lesser tint of purple.

His wrath mounted with it like boiling water in a kettle over a hot fire. He forgot his dignity, his gentility, his native courtesy. He stormed at her in an outburst of passion that was like the popping of a safety-valve of a locomotive; and Lady Kate listened without a change of expression, without comment, without resentment, until the storm had passed.

19

"How dare you enter my house in the middle of the night, like a thief, and with a key that I once gave to a thief, not knowing that he was one? How dare you sit here in my library?"

"Your insolence, your effrontery, and your presence here are alike insufferable—intolerable. And how dare you—you, whoever you are—utter that name in my presence?"

He sprang to the door and threw it open. "Out, woman! Out, I say, while there is time—while I can retain some measure of control over myself. Be off with you before I use the telephone to summon the police and send you where I have no doubt you belong—where you most certainly do belong if you are, as you imply, hand in glove with that despicable and consummate scoundrel whose name you have spoken! Begone! Leave this house at once, and never dare to enter it again! And—give me that! *Now*!"

This is not all that he said—but it is enough of it. There was much more like it, save only that it was worse. But the effect of it all boomeranged upon himself.

At the end of his tirade, his passion spent, his face became livid again. His head bent forward until his chin touched the bosom of his shirt. He tottered where he stood, and clung desperately to the door that he had opened for Lady Kate's egress.

Involuntarily he closed it again. Then, weakly, with uncertain steps, he half crossed the room and sank down upon a chair opposite her, with the library table between them.

Throughout all of it Lady Kate neither moved nor spoke; and now she did not when he seated himself beyond the table.

But her eyes never left his face; and when, coweringly, half fearfully, he ventured to lift his own, they encountered hers, fixed full upon him, with a calm, judicial scrutiny that was contemptuous beyond words, but, above all else, dismaying.

Lady Kate did not offer to speak; she waited for the banker to do so, knowing that presently he would.

Gradually, and with apparent effort, Chester recovered his mental equilibrium. Behind the narrowness and hardness of his mathematical life as a banker, outside the limited environment of his two-plus-two existence, beyond the horizon of the sordid dollar and what a dollar could earn, he was gentle and kind and good.

His instincts and aspirations were of the highest order; and—he had loved Bingham Harvard as a father loves a favorite son. He loved him still, although he did not know it.

Little by little he recovered his normal poise, and at last, in a tone that was entirely calm and composed—in the tone that he would have used in his private office at the bank—he asked:

"Why are you here, madam? What is the purpose of this midnight call upon me?"

She left the deep chair in which she had been seated and drew up a straight-backed one at the opposite side of the table. She seated herself upon it, and bending slightly forward with her elbows on the table and her hands clasped together just beneath her shapely chin, replied:

"I came here in the interest of Bingham Harvard, Mr. Chester. The purpose of my call upon you is to insist that you make an earnest effort now at once to discover the identity of the thief who robbed your bank, and by doing so establish forever the innocence of Bingham Harvard. That is why I am here."

"I will make no such effort as you demand," was the banker's calm reply. "It would be utterly useless. Bingham Harvard is guilty."

"That," Lady Kate replied slowly and without emphasis, "is a falsehood, and you know in your heart that it is one."

"Madam!"

"Mr. Chester, I did not come here to mince words or to paraphrase with facts. Whosoever says unequivocally that Bingham Harvard was guilty of that theft at your bank lies!"

She waited an instant. "But somewhere there *is* a guilty man, and that guilty man *must* be found; and you, sir, must help with all the power and force that you possess to find him. The innocence of Bingham Harvard must be—shall

21

be—established. His birthright of integrity and honesty must be restored to him."

"His birthright!" The contempt which the banker managed to inject into the utterance of those two words brought a hot flush for the first time to Lady Kate's cheeks. But she replied with the same absence of all emotion, nevertheless:

"Yes, his birthright, for whoever his unknown parents might have been, they endowed him with a lofty soul, a sterling character, a strong heart, and an upright, unsullible mind. You, Mr. Chester, more than any other man, should know all that."

"I know," the banker replied, coldly calm—in another man his manner might have been called coldly insolent— "that I played the part of a father to him from his early youth until the hour came when he turned upon me and bit the hand that had fed him; and, of all despicable things on earth, that is the most base and unforgivable. I would not—no, *I will not lift one finger in any effort to establish an innocence which would be a lie.* Bingham Harvard is guilty."

"And you are, Mr. Chester, content to accept the word of such a creature as Lieutenant Rodney Rushton in preference to the word of my—of Bingham Harvard?"

"Yes. Or the word of any other man, no matter whom— rather than his. And, madam"—the banker glanced at his watch—"permit me to suggest that the hour is late. It is now a quarter to one. No possible good can come by prolonging this interview, which, I must insist, is distinctly abominable to me. I must ask you to restore that latch-key and to go away."

Lady Kate pinched open her mesh-bag and laid the key on the table. Chester started to rise; but she spoke again, in that same calm tone she had been using: "One moment, please."

Chester resumed his seat and Lady Kate picked up the telephone, which was within reach of her hand. "With your permission, sir," she added, as if it were the most natural thing in the world that she should do what she did do. And then, before he could reply or offer an objection, she called for a number. There was a short wait, and then:

"Has Mr. Clancy returned? Thank you. Will you please ask him to come to the telephone? He must have found a letter from me awaiting him when he returned. Say that the person calling is Mrs. Bingham Harvard."

There was a crash at the opposite side of the table as the banker in starting to his feet overturned his chair.

"*What?*" he cried out. "You—you are that man's *wife?* His *wife? You?*"

"Even I," she replied smilingly, putting one small palm over the transmitter while she raised her eyes to his across the table. "I am Bingham Harvard's wife, and I find time every day I live to thank the good God for it."

"And that—that man you are calling now is Tom Clancy? His friend? And the son of my friend? Is it Tom Clancy whom you are calling?"

"Yes, Mr. Chester—one moment, please. Hello, Mr. Clancy! This is Mrs. Harvard. Did you receive my letter? I am with Mr. Chester now—at his home. How soon do you think you can get here? Thank you." Lady Kate hung up the receiver.

"Do you mean to tell me that that man is coming here to my house now and by your invitation?" the banker demanded, beside himself with rage for the second time that night; and, without waiting for her reply, he almost shouted: "It is an outrage! I will not permit it! You must go—now, at once!"

"Mr. Chester," she replied calmly—"Mr. Clancy will be here within ten minutes and you will admit him. You would scarcely use force to eject me from your house, would you? For, unless you do that, we will wait here together until Mr. Clancy arrives."

CHAPTER II

THE GAUNTLET THROWN DOWN

The banker did not admit Thomas Clancy.

When the bell rang he sat stubbornly immovable; and Lady Kate, after regarding him in silence for a brief moment, went calmly to the outer door herself and admitted her friend—the only friend that had been left to Bingham Harvard, alias the Night Wind, when all the world had turned against him and he had been hunted like a wild thing with a price upon his head, dead or alive.

"My dear Mrs. Harvard—" Clancy began impulsively the instant he crossed the threshold, for they had not seen each other until that moment since her return; but she put a finger quickly to her lips, commanding silence, and, turning abruptly after one brief hand-clasp, led the way into the library.

Apparently the banker had not moved a finger, and he did not when Tom Clancy entered the room. He did not raise his eyes or offer anything at all in the way of a greeting to the son of his old friend.

"How are you, Chester?" Clancy remarked genially, and then smiled grimly at the banker's attitude.

"Mr. Chester," said Lady Kate, "I will make a short explanation of the present circumstance so that you may quite understand how it has come about. My husband and I have been abroad since the happening of the unpleasant incidents with which you are familiar. It is approximately six months

24

since we went away. During that time we have sent brief messages infrequently to Mr. Clancy. For obvious reasons we gave him no address whereby he might have communicated with us. He did not know of my intention to return, and had no knowledge of my presence in the city until he received and read a letter which I sent to his home late this afternoon by a messenger. I hope you are heeding what I say; it would be more comprehensive possibly if you would raise your eyes occasionally—unless, indeed, you are ashamed to do so."

Chester raised his eyes with a jerk, opened his mouth as if to speak, but closed his jaws like a trap. Nevertheless, after that moment he kept his gaze fixed upon the Night Wind's wife with more or less intensity—although he could not avoid shifting them at times when her own regard became too scrutinizing for his comfort. She continued:

"In that letter I told Mr. Clancy of my return and of the purpose that brought me here. I came ashore soon after one o'clock this afternoon. I explained to him that my first duty was to talk with you, and that it was imperative that the interview should be private and devoid of the possibility of an interruption. In a word, I told him of my possession of a key to this house, and that I had decided to be here in your library, awaiting you when you should return from a banquet which you were to attend to-night."

"Then it was you who telephoned to the bank this afternoon?" the banker exclaimed, speaking for the first time since Clancy's entrance.

"The telephoning was done at my direction. It was necessary that I should know of your plans for to-night. I was determined to see you before I slept, and in such a manner that there could be no interruption."

Chester did not reply, and after a moment Lady Kate went on:

"In my letter to Mr. Clancy I asked him to hold himself in readiness to come to me—and to you, sir—here, when I should telephone."

For the first time Chester turned his eyes upon Clancy. Tom's father had been his closest business associate, and his life-long friend; and he had been fond of Tom since the latter's infancy.

The banker's eyes were cold and hard. His lips were drawn into firm, unyielding lines. There was no sign or indication of compromise, or even of kindness, about him. His entire attitude was one of utter relentlessness. His voice, when he spoke, was his most austere "banker's voice," cold, distant, expressionless, leaving naught but the naked words he uttered to express what he wished his companions to know.

"Tom Clancy," he said, "you have intruded here without invitation and without permission. When I have finished with what I have to say I want you to leave my house and never to enter it again; and when you go, you must take this woman with you."

Clancy started and bent forward as if to interrupt, but at a sign from Lady Kate he relaxed again, and waited. The banker continued:

"One hundred and thirty-six thousand dollars disappeared from the paying teller's cage at my bank almost a year ago. Bingham Harvard, my foster son, although I never adopted him legally, thank God, was the paying teller. A detective from police headquarters whom I called in, and who had done much good service for me before that, succeeded in fastening the theft of that money upon him. When Harvard was called upon to surrender to the law—right here in this room—he changed into a wild man on the instant; he used great strength to maim and cripple the three officers who were here to take him—and he made his escape. After that he continued to defy the law until he became a terror to the whole city, and an abomination in the sight of every law-abiding citizen."

"You know the history of it all as well as I do. I mention it now because I want you and this woman who says she is his wife—"

"Chester, by—"

Another quick gesture from Lady Kate silenced Clancy's hot anger at the slur. The banker went on imperturbably in the same colorless voice:

"—to understand my attitude thoroughly. Until that thing happened I loved Bingham Harvard as if he were my own son. After it happened, after what he did, and *now and forevermore*, he has ceased to exist so far as I am concerned. There can be no compromise." Chester got suddenly upon his feet and stepped backward, away from the chair he had been occupying.

"And now I want you to go. If you do not—" He took a quick step forward and reached for the telephone.

But Lady Kate was quicker than he. She bent forward and seized it, then leaned back in her chair again with an odd little smile in her eyes as she looked up at the banker across the table.

Clancy was on his feet now, facing the thoroughly incensed Chester; and he was scarcely less angry than the older man, because of those slurs which the latter had dared to cast upon the wife of his friend.

"You contemptible little money-grub!" he exclaimed hotly. "Why, Chester, I am ashamed to remember that my father ever called you his friend. You are not even a friend to yourself. Your soul is so small that it wouldn't weigh in the balance against a fleck of fog."

"Get out of my house!" the banker ordered. "Both of you."

"Oh, we will go in a moment. We'll be glad to go. You needn't worry. But first I have got something to say to you, and I'm going to say it if I have to adopt Bing Harvard's methods to compel you to listen. Do you understand that?"

"Say it, then, and be gone."

"I haven't been idle since the Night Wind blew away, six months ago. I haven't accomplished very much as yet, but I'm going to accomplish everything that I set out to do then. That is, *we* are. And I want to tell you one thing: there is not a move you make or a thing you do that is not reported to me; and as sure as there is justice in Heaven, Bing Harvard and Bing Harvard's wife and I will nail you and your smooth unctuousness to the cross of bitter retribution before we have done with you. And by Heaven, Chester!"—he came a step nearer, pounding his left hand with his right one as he did so—"we'll make you get down on your knees and grovel to the man you have wronged before we are done with you. Come, Katherine, let's get out of here. I'm nauseated."

"Wait," she replied quickly. "Just one more word. Mr. Chester, think once more, please. Help us to right this great wrong that has been done to my husband."

"Not by so much as the turning of a finger," the banker replied in an even tone.

"Listen: Bingham did not wish to return here, ever. He wanted to go far away, to the other side of the world, and begin his life anew. Being his wife, I would not consent to that. I forced him to consent to return, to clear himself of that horrible stigma that you and Rodney Rushton put upon him, and I promise you, now that I am here, it shall be done to the very last balance in the scales of justice and right. With your willing assistance it might be accomplished much more quickly and easily than otherwise. So, Mr. Chester, once more I plead with you: won't you help us?"

"No. Do I understand you to say that Bingham Harvard has returned also? That he is here in the city now? Rest assured, madam, that I shall lose no time in acquainting the police with that interesting bit of news." The banker made a grimace which he intended to be a smile of derision.

"Oh, how unspeakable you are," Katherine returned evenly, but with somber, burning eyes. "No. He is not here. I came alone; came to take up this work with the assistance of Mr. Clancy."

"Where is he? Perhaps you will tell me that."

"He is on the other side; let us say that he is in London, if that interests you. When I have need of him I will cable him, and he will come. I think, when he does come, that you, Mr. Chester, will be the first man he will seek—even as I sought you. But he might not be as gentle with you as I have been."

A deathlike pallor spread slowly over the face of the banker, and he caught his breath in a sharp gasp that had in it something akin to terror.

"Do you dare to threaten me—in his name?" Chester demanded huskily.

28

"Yes. But with exposure; not with violence."

"He will not dare to come here again. He will not dare!" the banker cried out.

Lady Kate smiled at him across the table.

"Did you ever know of anything that Bingham Harvard wanted to do that he did not *dare* to do?" she asked evenly. "Did he hesitate to go about, at his own pleasure and will, when the entire police force of this city was seeking him? Did he hesitate to defend himself when he was attacked? Did the men who attacked him once venture to do so a second time? Did those men drive him away, or did he go away of his own free will and accord? Oh, you miserably little man, how impossible it is for you to understand or to comprehend a man who is big and great, and good, and honest! I am here to find the thief who stole that money, Mr. Chester, and I am beginning to believe that I have not far to look."

"Indeed no, madam. You have only to look at the man you call hus—"

"Stop where you are, sir. I have only to look across this table at *you* to see the real thief. *You* are that thief! *You*! Even though you did not steal the actual cash, *you* are the thief! *You are the real thief*!"

"Yes, by Heaven, and we'll brand it on your forehead, Chester, before we have done with you!" Clancy exclaimed. "Come on, Lady Kate, let's get out of this."

She left her place beside the table and drew nearer to Clancy. Chester sprang forward suddenly and seized upon the telephone. Clancy darted after him and would have torn it from his grasp, but Katherine seized his arm and held him back.

"Wait," she said calmly. "Let him telephone to police headquarters now, if he so desires. He would do so in any event as soon as we are gone. But he does not know (neither do you, Mr. Clancy) of other things I have done in preparation for this moment. I shall not wait for the police to seek me. I shall seek them. They shall know of the Night Wind's return when he shall have returned."

Lady Kate and Thomas Clancy passed out of the house together, leaving Chester at the telephone, wildly calling for police headquarters.

CHAPTER III

THE INSPECTOR'S PRIVATE OFFICE

Tom Clancy had been inside his own home but a few moments when there came a peremptory summons at his front door, and he went in person to open it, knowing well that the police would have lost no time in seeking him, after the announcement that Chester had doubtless made to them over the telephone.

It was Lieutenant Rodney Rushton who confronted him when he did throw the door ajar; and beside Rushton, at the top of the steps, was Coniglio, one of the two headquarters men who had accompanied Rushton on that memorable occasion to which the banker had referred, when the attempt was made, approximately nine months before, to arrest Bingham Harvard at Chester's house.

Rushton thrust himself forward with the same aggressive air he always adopted; belligerent, insolent of tone and manner.

"Where is she?" he demanded without preface, stepping over the threshold. "We want her, Clancy, and we want her right now. Hedging won't go this trip." Coniglio followed him into the house.

Clancy moved backward a pace and gestured toward the parlor door, and with a queer little half smile upon his face.

"Step into the parlor, gentlemen, and be seated," he said. "I was expecting you. In fact I was awaiting you; although"—he let his glance rest for an instant upon Rushton's

31

pig-eyes—"I hardly anticipated that *you* would come, Rushton."

"You didn't, eh? Why not?" Rushton demanded in reply as they passed through the open doorway into the parlor.

"Oh well"—Clancy permitted himself a broad smile this time—"I have always given you credit for plenty of gall, Rushton; but, on the level, I *didn't* think it was quite equal to this."

"That will be about all from you, Mr. Clancy," the lieutenant replied savagely. "We are officers of the law, and as such—"

"As such, you have no more privilege inside of this house than a pan-handler of the streets. Don't forget that. Now, what do you want?"

Clancy's apparently easy-going manner was suddenly changed to sharp directness.

"We want Lady Kate. That's what we want," Rushton retorted, standing with one hand grasping the back of the chair upon which he had been about to seat himself. "We're going to get her, too."

"Did you expect to find the lady here, at my house?" Clancy inquired.

"Well, why not? She was with you less than three-quarters of an hour ago, at Chester's, and you came away from there together. That's what he told the inspector over the telephone. Ain't she here?"

"Certainly not. These are bachelor quarters, lieutenant. The only woman in the house is Scipio's—he is my valet—grandmother; and even she is a late importation; but I found that I needed a house-keeper and cook. Won't you sit down?"

"No, I won't. If Lady Kate isn't here, where is she?" Rushton answered angrily. He knew that Clancy was taunting him and making silent fun of him—and he hated Tom Clancy almost as much as he did the Night Wind.

"Really, lieutenant, I haven't the least idea where she is," Clancy replied.

"That's a—a likely story, that is. If she ain't here you know where she went to after you parted with her."

"On the contrary, I do not know. She was quite willing to tell me, and started to do so, but I stopped her, because I was quite well aware that inquiries would be made of me. So, I don't know, any more than you do, Rushton."

"Say, Clancy, I've got more'n half a notion to clap the irons onto you and take—"

"Oh, no you haven't. Don't bluff, Rushton—not with me. I'm more than seven, and am quite able to walk alone."

"Say, Clancy"—Rushton came a step nearer and thrust out his chin aggressively—"Miss Katherine Maxwell is in the city, an' the inspector wants to see her, right now. If you don't tell us where to find her—"

"If that is all," Clancy interrupted, "you are only wasting your time seeking her."

"What do you mean by that?"

"It is quite as much her desire to see the inspector as it is his to see her," Tom replied. "That is what I mean, exactly."

"Huh! Tell it to Sweeney."

"I am telling it to you. It is the present intention of Lady Kate to call at police headquarters in the morning. You might convey that message to the inspector and to all whom it may concern, lieutenant."

"Say, do you mean that, Clancy? Is that on the level?"

"Certainly."

"Blowed if it ain't just like her, at that. What time? Huh!"

"The lady did not admit me that far into her confidence," Clancy replied.

"Anyhow, I believe you. Say?"

"Well, lieutenant?"

"Where is *he* at? The Night Wind, I mean. That's what *we* want to know."

"Naturally. It is, at least, what *you* want to know, Rushton, and what you are a little bit afraid to hear told, too. To the best of my belief, lieutenant, Mr. Bingham Harvard is somewhere in the city of London awaiting a message which will summon him here, *and you can play it a hundred to one that it won't take him long to get here when he receives that message.*"

Rushton left the chair where he had been standing and started for the front door, uttering a curt command to his companion to follow. At the front door he turned.

"When the Night Wind does come here we'll get him, good and plenty; you take it from me, Clancy. If he pokes his nose into little old New York just once more he'll get what is coming to him, and then some; and so, if you've got any means of sendin' word to him, you'd better advise him to travel in the other direction. There won't be any foolin', if *he* shows up here again," he said. "Besides bein' a thief, he has done enough other acts to send him away for a century."

The lieutenant passed through the doorway toward the street, and Clancy's pleasantly derisive voice followed him, and the sting of the words that Clancy uttered made him halt at the top of the steps outside.

"I think, Rushton," the young broker said, "that you and Coniglio, and the others who have suffered at the hands of Bing Harvard, should organize a secret order for the purpose of hunting him down. Don't you? You might call it 'The Society of Crippled Cops.' Eh? What? Good night, or, rather, good morning to you." Clancy closed the door before Rushton could reply.

* * * * * * *

The air of subdued excitement which pervaded police headquarters the following morning might be likened to that breathless interval of elemental suspense which obtains just before the descent of a tropical tornado.

Information had somehow gone forth and had been passed from lip to ear throughout the department that the Night Wind had returned; or, if he had not actually returned as yet, he was on the point of coming back; *and, anyhow, Lady Kate was back.*

And Lady Kate was due to arrive at headquarters during the forenoon by her own invitation. She intended to face all of them, from the inspector down; and, while it was not known for a fact, it was nevertheless generally believed Lady Kate had gone away with the Night Wind when he disappeared. (Banker Chester had not informed headquarters that Miss Katherine Maxwell had become Mrs. Bingham Harvard. He had kept that bit of information to himself, either because he deemed it unimportant, or because he did not believe it.)

She arrived at precisely eleven o'clock.

In the big room of the detective bureau there fell a decided hush upon all who were present the moment she entered it; and there was an unusual gathering in that same big room. Excuses and actual permission to be present had been sought by many of the men, uniformed and otherwise, who had in the past been in more or less violent contact with the dreaded Night Wind.

The coming of Lady Kate portended something, and nobody could guess what that something might be.

She halted for an instant just outside the door. Her eyes, with the swiftness of a humming bird, flew from face to face. An inscrutable smile lingered in her expression. Then she crossed the room to one of the flat-topped desks and said to the officer who was seated behind it:

"How do you do, Lieutenant Courtleigh? I wish to see the inspector. Will you tell him that I am here?"

"It isn't necessary," was the quick reply, as Courtleigh started to his feet and extended his right hand which Lady Kate accepted with hearty good will. Courtleigh was one of several for whom she retained a respectful and personal liking. "He is expecting you. The deputy commissioner is with him. You may go right inside, Lady Kate."

"Thank you," she said; and did so.

Both men got upon their feet when Lady Kate entered the private office, although neither had intended to do so. But there was some indefinite compelling force in her presence that made them rise involuntarily. Each, also, one after the other, extended a hand in greeting. She accepted each one gravely, then relaxed upon a chair which the deputy commissioner pulled forward for her accommodation.

"This is an unexpected pleasure, Miss Maxwell," the inspector announced, also with gravity. And Katherine permitted the name to pass without correction while she replied:

"Are you quite sure that it is a pleasure, inspector?"

"Yes. Or, at least, it can easily be made so if you are prepared to return to us and to aid us in the dearest wish we have. I assume that both of those reasons will account for your presence here to-day."

She smiled into his eyes enigmatically. "The assumption of conditions that are not established is the beam in the eye of the detective bureau, is it not?" she asked whimsically. "I have returned; I am here as the personal representative of Mr. Bingham Harvard, alias the Night Wind, whom, I believe, you will remember, inspector. I have no idea of returning to the bureau, if that is what you mean."

"Where is Bingham Harvard now, Miss Maxwell?" the deputy commissioner interposed.

"It is perhaps sufficient answer to reply that he is not here," she responded coolly.

"Mr. Chester, the banker, informed this department last night that the man is in London awaiting a summons from you to come here. Is that correct?"

"This department is so in the habit of accepting Mr. Chester's statements without a question that it would ill become me to add to or detract from any statement that he might make," she retorted with easy irony.

"We play with words, Miss Maxwell."

"No; *you* play with truth, which can never be successfully denied for long. *I* am here, Mr. Commissioner, as the agent of destiny, in the person of Bingham Harvard, alias the Night Wind."

"Are we to understand that he has sent you here to interpose for him—to make terms with us—with this department?" the inspector interjected.

Lady Kate lifted her chin and turned her eyes coolly upon the chief of the bureau.

"I am here as much in your own interests as in his," she replied; "to demand that justice be done to a man who has been foully wronged. I am here to insist that this department take up the case of the year-old theft at Chester's bank as if it happened yesterday; to compel you, in one way or another, to seek and find the real thief, so that the name of Bingham Harvard may be cleansed of the stigma that rests upon it."

"That is a pretty big order, isn't it?" the deputy inquired with half a sneer.

"No. It is a simple one. You both know in your hearts that he is innocent, and that Rushton deliberately framed the whole case against him," she replied.

"One moment, Lady Kate!" The inspector bent forward in his chair. "That is a serious charge for you to make in this office. We won't stand for it."

She bent forward, too, toward him. "You will have to stand for it, inspector, just as you will have to take the consequences of what you have already stood for in this matter. I am not here to supplicate. I came to offer you an opportunity to escape from a serious difficulty in which you and every man connected with this bureau are involved. And you had better accept that opportunity before it is too late, for as surely as you are *you*, every man among you who has aided and abetted the outrage that has been done will be made to pay, *pay, pay*!"

"Your statement has the sound of a threat, Miss Maxwell," said the deputy.

"It is a prophecy, Mr. Commissioner."

"Do I understand that you went abroad with this man whom we call the Night Wind?"

"Yes," she replied.

"And that he is over there on the other side now, awaiting a message from you?"

"You may assume that if you like."

"Are you aware that in the light of that confession you are liable to arrest?"

She only smiled at him in reply. He continued:

"You have given aid and succor and sustenance to a man who stands indicted for a felony—to a fugitive from justice; and as such—"

Lady Kate got slowly upon her feet, and her manner was such that the deputy commissioner paused without completing the sentence.

"It is you who threaten, not I," she said deliberately; "but you do not realize how helpless you are when you make that threat. Did you suppose that Katherine Maxwell went abroad with Bingham Harvard as his companion, merely; as his mistress, perhaps? Shame on you both for harboring such a thought! I have given you ample opportunity to address me by my right name, and you have chosen to ignore it. Very well. Know, then, that I am Bingham Harvard's wife; that we were married in the State of Connecticut two weeks before we left this country together. Put me under arrest now, if you like, and see what comes of it. But you will not! You dare not! Therefore, know this: I shall send a cable to my husband this very day, summoning him to return—and he will come. You may figure it out for yourselves when he is due to arrive, and you may meet the incoming steamships in the hope of getting him."

"But, gentlemen, you will not get him. *He will get you.*"

CHAPTER IV

THE NIGHT WIND'S PROPHECY

Six and one-half days later, that is to say at eleven o'clock at night of the sixth day after Lady Kate made her call at police headquarters, something happened.

The inspector left his chair in his private office, seized his hat, and with a curt nod here and there as he passed through the big room, went outside. In the corridor he encountered the deputy commissioner. Both came to a halt. The deputy commissioner said:

"Well?"

"The *Golgotha* has passed Fire Island light. She'll dock in the morning," was the reply of the inspector. "I have sent two men down on the pilot-boat that will pick her up: two others will meet her at quarantine. I have let Rushton pick his own men to meet the ship at the pier—and I shall be there myself, of course."

"Perhaps the Night Wind isn't aboard of the *Golgotha*. Maybe he didn't obey the summons of Lady Kate," the commissioner suggested.

"That is possible, of course—though I doubt it. If he isn't aboard the *Golgotha*, he will come on the next ship, or by another one, later. The *Golgotha* is the first one he could have caught after the receipt of her cable."

"It's strange that Scotland Yard wasn't able to spot him going aboard of the ship, after our urgent messages," the commissioner grumbled.

"He's too slick for that bunch," the inspector replied.

"You are, then, of the opinion that he *is* on the *Golgotha*?"

"It is the very first ship he could have taken. Yes; I've got a hunch that he is aboard of her."

"Your wireless messages haven't uncovered him, inspector."

"Oh, well, he's disguised, of course—and he wouldn't do such a thing unless he did it thoroughly. Harvard isn't an ordinary man, commissioner; he's a marvel, with a big M."

The commissioner shook his head as if still in doubt, said "Good night," swung about, and departed. The inspector gazed after him grimly for a moment, then went on his own way.

His destination was home, and he was tired. The strain of the past week in preparing for the possible event of to-morrow had told upon him. He wished above all things to be fresh and clear-headed for the possible ordeal of the coming day.

He boarded a Broadway car and rode to Columbus Circle. From there he strode briskly up Central Park West for several blocks, then turned into a side street, and mounted the brown-stone steps of his own residence.

He had inserted the latch-key and was about to turn it when he heard the sound of his own name uttered in a low tone, close behind him, and he wheeled around with surprising suddenness while his right hand flew to the pocket where he carried his gun.

His wrist was seized and held before he could draw; then the grasp that held it was slowly relaxed. A pair of earnest eyes, half smiling but infinitely serious, looked calmly into his own startled ones. His hands dropped to his sides.

"Good God!" he breathed, but not profanely, and scarcely above a whisper.

"You have not forgotten me, I see," said the other man. "The Night Wind has returned, inspector. Are you—perhaps—pleased to see me? Don't tremble so, man alive! You are not afraid. I know that. You are only knocked out of your natural orbit. Besides, I did not come here to hurt you—

40

unless you attempt to hurt me; and I don't believe you will do that now."

"How in—How the—How'd you get here, Harvard? Have you got wings?" the inspector managed to articulate. His surprise was profound. It had overwhelmed him for the moment.

"My wife summoned me. I came. That is all. It is enough, isn't it?"

"But—the *Golgotha*! She was the first ship you could have taken after that cable was sent. Bah! You have been here all the time."

"Oh, no, I have not; and no, I did not. Look at this, inspector, if you would be convinced."

The Night Wind produced a folded message from one of his pockets and passed it to the inspector. It was dated six days back—the day of Lady Kate's call at headquarters, and it read:

Come now. Catch *Golgotha* if possible.

KATHERINE.

"Do you mean to tell me that you sailed from Southampton on board the *Golgotha*?" the inspector demanded hotly.

The Night Wind shrugged his shoulders. "It isn't necessary to reply to that question, is it?" he made answer. "At all events, I am here, as you see. Knowing that you would have a couple of men on the pilot-boat to meet the *Golgotha*, and that there would be others at quarantine, and still others— probably including yourself—at the pier, I chose to anticipate them. I had an intense longing to see you and to talk with you, inspector. That explains why I am standing with you now on your own door-step. Odd, isn't it, that we should meet in this friendly manner at this time?"

"What do you want?" the inspector demanded gruffly.

"Justice. Nothing more nor less; but full and complete justice. That is what I have come here to get, and that is what I am going to have," was the slow and carefully worded but emphatic reply.

"You'll get it, all right; more than you want of it."

"Thank you. I will accept that prophecy as it sounds, not as you imply it."

"What do you want of me?"

"First, that you quell the itching of that right palm of yours, which seems to have a tendency to glide closer to the pocket where you carry a weapon. Shall I relieve you of the gun, inspector—you know that I can do so—or shall we talk together amicably?"

The officer grinned in spite of himself. The situation was not without its humorous aspects, and he was quite conscious of it.

"We'll declare a truce for the present meeting, Harvard," he said. "Will you come inside? I can offer you a cigar and a swallow of Scotch."

"I neither smoke nor drink, thank you. We will talk here. Shall we sit down on the steps?"

"Yes. That brings me back to my last question, Harvard. What do you want of me?"

"Inspector, I came here to ask a manly favor at your hands; but one which you will probably deny. If you do deny it, then to give you a warning—not a threat, understand. If you decline to heed the warning, it will become my duty in that case to read you a short prophecy which will not be pleasant to hear, nor in its fulfillment."

They were seated side by side on the top step by then. The inspector had lighted a cigar and was puffing vigorously upon it. He shrugged his shoulders.

"What's the favor?" he demanded briefly.

"That you grant me six weeks' immunity—or truce, if you prefer that word—from outlawry, during which time I shall be free to go and come as I see fit, unmolested; and that you assist me with all the power of your department to find the man who stole the one hundred and thirty-six thousand dollars from Chester's bank; and that, in the mean time, and during those six weeks, Lieutenant Rodney Rushton be relieved from duty," was the calm reply.

The inspector removed the cigar from his mouth and turned to stare at the man beside him. Then he laughed aloud derisively, but with genuine amusement, too.

"Is *that* all?" he exclaimed. "You don't want much, do you? Why don't you demand *my* job during those six weeks, while you are about it? That isn't gall, Harvard; that's gizzard; no less; and it's full of gravel at that. What's the warning?"

"The warning is this: if you deny me the favor I ask, it will mean that you, and others who are near to you downtown, will be compelled, before very long, to hand in your resignations from the police department in order to avoid summary dismissal."

The inspector chuckled audibly.

"Bully!" he exclaimed. "You're a corker, Harvard. No wonder they called you the Night Wind; although it strikes me that Hot Air would have been more appropriate. Now—and be as gentle as you can about it—what's the prophecy?"

"This: There will be, within the year in your department, and throughout the entire service which you, and men like Rushton, do so much to discredit, the greatest upheaval in its history. I have been absent six months, but I have not been idle—nor have my best friends been inactive; and I have four such friends."

"Is that all?"

"No. Some among you will be indicted, tried, convicted, and sent to prison. Some will be dismissed. Some will resign. Are you so blind, inspector, that you cannot see the writing on the wall? Or *won't* you see it?"

"Does that end the prophecy?" the inspector inquired, ignoring the questions.

"Yes. And now I have a short statement to make."

"Fine. What is it? A confession of guilt? It is time for that, I think."

Harvard got upon his feet and stood four steps lower down, facing the inspector. His back was toward the street; but he had seen, before he changed his position, that a patrolman on his beat had turned the corner and was slowly approaching them. Nevertheless, he gave no sign that he had

43

seen, although he knew that the inspector had made the same discovery—or had been anticipating it.

"I am going to the root of things, inspector," the Night Wind said with slow emphasis. "I am not the only victim of a frame-up. There are others—hundreds of them; there have been thousands. I have come back here to fight you with your own weapons, and to a finish. Your 'system' denied to my wife the favor she sought, and you have denied me; so henceforth there shall be no favors asked or granted."

"Your men named me the Night Wind months ago because I moved swiftly and silently, and because God gave me sinews and muscles greater and stronger than most men's. But I thank God for them, although they are as much a phenomenon to me as they are to you."

"But if I have been a Night Wind in the past I will be a hurricane, a tornado, a veritable tempest, in the future; and so take heed lest you walk blindly into the vortex of it and are destroyed. That is, I believe, all that I have to say. And please understand that these several appeals have been made to you, not with any idea or hope that they would be granted, but solely because I have conceived it to be my duty to make them."

He was silent for a moment, watching the inspector narrowly; and that officer sat immovable upon the step, but with a certain intensity about his pose which indicated plainly enough the nearer approach of the patrolman.

"I know who is coming," the Night Wind said quietly; and the inspector started guiltily. "You will sit very still, inspector, and permit him to pass."

"But he won't pass; that's the trouble. He will see me and he'll stop to talk."

"In that case you will tell him that you don't wish to be interrupted," the Night Wind said quietly.

"Suppose he comes up the steps, and sees you, and recognizes you?"

"So much the worse for him—and for you. But you can prevent it if you will."

The patrolman came nearer. He discovered the inspector seated upon the steps and stopped, calling out a "How are you, inspector?" as he did so. Then he put a foot upon the lowest step, as if to ascend them.

Harvard heard that footfall. His back was toward the policeman, and he could not see him; but he took one step upward and forward, bringing himself beside the inspector, who made no attempt to rise or to speak. Then Harvard turned and faced the newcomer.

It was Compton, an acquaintance of those other days, and the recognition between him and the Night Wind was mutual and instant.

Compton gasped. Then he swore. Then, like the popping of a safety valve, he cried out:

"The Night Wind, by all that's—"

Then, without completing the sentence, he sprang upward.

The inspector, at the same instant, started to his feet.

CHAPTER V

A STRATEGIC VICTORY

The Night Wind's method of meeting this sudden attack upon him was perhaps the most amazing of all his acts.

He inevitably did the surprising thing—the unexpected. He certainly performed one at that trying moment when it was given to him to act quickly and finally, or to be captured. For, be it known here and now, Bingham Harvard, alias the Night Wind, had returned to New York, fully determined to maim no more cops and to break no more bones, as he had done in that former experience of his—unless it should become imperatively necessary in order to escape premature arrest.

It will be recalled that he had spoken to the inspector just at the instant when the officer had inserted the key in the latch of the door, and that the inspector had wheeled about and reached for his gun, startled by hearing a voice so near to him.

And so the officer's key had been left in the door-latch; and Bingham Harvard had taken note of that fact. Not with a thought of making use of it, for that did not occur to him, but merely as an incident. His career as a fugitive from justice had taught him to observe closely the most trivial things.

Patrolman Compton started to mount the steps, Harvard sprang to the top of them and turned half about almost behind the inspector, and the inspector started to his feet all at the selfsame instant.

46

And this is what happened then:

The Night Wind pushed the inspector forward with sudden force into the arms of the patrolman, and in the brief instant while they struggled to free themselves from each other—an instant which could have occupied little more than a natural second of time—he wheeled, turned the latch-key which the inspector had left in the door, withdrew it, and pushed the door open at the same time, closing it swiftly and silently behind him.

Confusion sometimes attacks the most sensible of men; it fell upon both of those police officers then.

The Night Wind had disappeared, and neither of them had seen him go. One of them—Compton—could not even guess where or how he had gone.

A second thought, however, brought the solution of the problem to the inspector's mind, for he remembered that he had left the key in the door; and he smiled firmly at the mingled consternation and fright that was depicted upon the face of the patrolman.

Compton actually gasped.

During this instant that the inspector had struggled in his arms, shutting off his view, the Night Wind had apparently flown away.

"Say, inspector," he breathed hoarsely, "that guy ain't human."

The inspector laughed aloud, and intended the laugh to be as much a reassurance to the Night Wind, who he had no doubt was waiting just inside the vestibule, as a relief to his own emotions of the moment—and Compton's, likewise.

"He's just as human as we are, Compton," he replied, loudly enough for the man inside the vestibule to hear. "He's a little bit quicker in his motions and a good deal stronger in his muscles than most of us; that is all. You beat it now, and see that you forget everything that has happened here tonight; forget even that you saw either of us."

"But"—Compton hesitated—"where is he? Where'd he go to?"

The inspector jerked his thumb toward the house door.

"Beat it," he ordered again, "and don't forget what I said about this affair."

"I—I didn't know that he was back here," Compton replied, still hesitating.

"Nor, I—until less than half an hour ago. I'll phone to your captain to send you down to see me some time tomorrow. See that you keep your mouth shut till then. Duck now, and see how quick you can get around that next corner, out of sight."

A moment or two later, when Compton had turned the corner and disappeared, the inspector addressed the closed vestibule door.

"All right, Harvard," he said. "The truce still goes. My gun remains in my pocket and my arms are folded. Come out."

Harvard opened the door and stepped outside. He was smiling, and there was an unmistakable grin depicted upon the face of the inspector.

"Say," he said, not without enthusiasm at the thought, "I'd give a lot if I had you down at the bureau working with us. You'd make a peach of a man for us."

"Oh, no, I would not!" Harvard replied. "I'm honest."

"Do you think that a man has got to be dishonest in order to be a policeman or a detective?" the inspector demanded. "Do you think every man-jack of us is a crook?"

"By no means. The dishonest cop, the crooked detective—the men like Rushton—are the exceptions, inspector. I believe the rank and file of your department to be about the best and finest men in the world, take them all in all. But the trouble is that when one of them who is not on the level does something like what Rushton did to me, you all stand for him and for his act, even though you know him to be wrong. It is your mistaken sense of loyalty to one another."

"Oh, well, we'll let it go at that. Sit down here for another moment. I want to ask you three or four questions."

"I can reply to them quite as well standing."

"You have made me like you to-night. I never did before."

"That isn't a question."

"How do you suppose that Rushton convinced me and others of your guilt in regard to that missing money at the bank where you were paying-teller?"

"If I should reply frankly to that question you would not consider it complimentary, inspector."

"Nevertheless, reply. We're talking straight from the shoulder now."

"Then you must have been a fool or a knave to have been convinced by so shallow a frame-up as that was; and, inspector, I know that you are not a fool."

"That is plain speaking, at least."

"You asked for it."

"Look here, Harvard, why don't you give yourself up and stand your trial? If you will do that—"

"I will not do it, so save your breath."

"Well, then, I will say this, and I ask you to believe me, for I am in earnest: I accepted the evidence that Rushton supplied in exactly the same way that your banker friend Chester accepted it. If it was a frame-up, which I still doubt, I had no knowledge of it, and have none now. I am only the skipper on the bridge of that big ship that we call the detective bureau—and it is a big ship to handle. I can't always tell if the lookout in the crow's nest is seeing things as they *are*, or as he would *like* to see them. I have to take his word for it and accept the evidence he brings to me; and I'd be a poor officer if I didn't have faith in my men, wouldn't I?"

Harvard looked intently into the eyes of the inspector before he replied. Then he said:

"Do I understand now that you are beginning to be willing to give me the benefit of the doubt?"

"No. I still believe that you are guilty. I've got to. But I want you to understand that I believe it honestly."

"Then—you are a *fool*, after all."

The inspector flushed hotly and did not reply.

"Do you believe, inspector, that Lieutenant Rodney Rushton—Oh, what's the use? We only play with words. Shall I tell you the literal truth regarding your present position in regard to this matter? I will, anyhow. You *dare* not disbelieve Rushton, because the very fact of doing so would lead to the uncovering of certain things connected with your own career which you very much prefer to keep hidden. Your system is so involved that a man like yourself, who would like to be honest and square, can't be; and there are a lot more like you. But, also, there are others who are unlike you, who will keep on the level at any cost; and, inspector, *this now somewhat celebrated case of Bingham Harvard is going to be the indirect means of weeding out every dishonest official from your department."*

Harvard ran down the steps and went swiftly away, without once turning his head to look back; and the inspector sat quite still where he was for several moments before he went into the house.

Down at the corner a black-bodied taxicab awaited the coming of the Night Wind; and there was a black chauffeur seated under the steering-wheel.

Inside of the taxi, patiently waiting, was Lady Kate.

CHAPTER VI

"BREAKING" A COP

Patrolman Compton chose to disobey the inspector.

He believed that the end would justify the means. He figured it out that he could effect the capture of the Night Wind, and that by doing so he would not only win the forgiveness of the chief of the detective bureau, but that he would achieve promotion as well. He took a "chance," and he lost.

Compton knew that, just around the corner, he was due to meet his roundsman, and that only one block away there would be a third man on "peg." Another patrolman was about due at the opposite side of the avenue he was approaching, and that would make four men on the job—if only the Night Wind elected to come that way when he should part with the inspector. It all depended upon that circumstance.

He noticed a black taxi standing near the corner, as he passed hurriedly along, but he gave it no attention. He was too intent upon the working of the plan he had formed.

But the black chauffeur of the taxi noticed him, nevertheless—and kept a wary eye on him without appearing to do so.

The black chauffeur saw him meet the roundsman just around the corner; saw them engage in a hurried and somewhat excited whispered conversation; saw them both start rapidly away toward the nearest peg-post; saw the three return together at the opposite side of the avenue and meet still another patrolman, with whom there was another whispered exchange of confidence.

The chauffeur was Lady Kate's loyal servant, Black Julius, and the taxicab was not a taxicab at all, but Lady Kate's own powerful car, which had been long ago transformed into an imitation of one.

Julius lost no time in reporting to his mistress all that he had seen and noted.

"We will wait as we are," she told him. "Those policemen will cross over to this side when they see Mr. Harvard coming, but they will wait just around the corner, to avoid being seen by him. Evidently they do not suspect us."

It was Lady Kate's perfect knowledge of police methods which enabled her to prophesy so correctly, and she figured it out to her own satisfaction that Harvard would have ample time to leap into the car before any of the policemen could get near enough to lay a hand upon him.

Once he was inside the car Julius could be trusted to do the rest. There might be a bullet or two fired at them, as they made their escape, but such bullets usually went wild.

She held the door slightly ajar, when she saw her husband approaching, and she waited until he was almost at the corner before she threw it wide open and called to him:

"Quick, Bingham! On guard!"

The policemen who waited behind the corner heard her, and started forward.

But Harvard had also heard her, and understood exactly what was meant.

That wonderful swiftness of motion of which he was a master did not desert him—nor his customary clear-headed perception of things.

The men were a trifle closer to the corner than Katherine had anticipated, and they moved more quickly than she had believed possible. Compton was in the lead, with his weapon drawn, ready for use.

But he was a trifle too much in the lead; and the Night Wind had moved forward more quickly than he had expected. Then, it all happened in the briefest interval; and it was over and the Night Wind had gone before the other three amazed cops realized what had happened.

Harvard, warned by Katherine's call to him, knowing from his knowledge of Compton what to expect, met that officer face to face as he rounded the corner, seized the wrist of the hand that held the gun that was already pointed at him and tore the weapon from Compton's grasp with the other hand. Then he wheeled Compton sharply around, and held him hugged tightly against his own body, while he backed swiftly toward the open door of the car, pointing Compton's own weapon over Compton's shoulder at the other three cops as he did so.

And they stopped in their tracks, outgeneraled.

They could not shoot at the Night Wind without hitting their comrade—and they knew that he would not shoot at them—unless, perchance, they should force him to do so.

So Harvard backed in at the open doorway of the car, pulling Compton in after him; and he laughed aloud as he tossed Compton's gun to the pavement in front of the other three officers.

Then the door was slammed shut and the car, driven by Black Julius, shot swiftly away, bearing the now utterly discomfited Compton a sorry prisoner inside of it.

"For the love of Mike!" the roundsman who had been left at the corner with the remaining two policemen, exclaimed. "What do you know about that! Say! It's him all right. I'd give up three months' pay rather than have had this happen."

Inside the imitation taxicab, Compton found himself to be extremely uncomfortable.

Harvard forced him down upon the small front seat, facing himself and Katherine. Then deliberately, he removed Compton's belt and shield.

"You disobeyed orders, Compton," the Night Wind said with mock gravity. "I heard the inspector direct you to forget what you had seen and heard."

"I wish to the Lord I had," Compton replied dubiously. "Say, let me out of this, won't you? I'm off my post."

"Certainly; and you are going to remain off it for quite some time. I'm done with breaking bones, Compton; henceforth I shall give my attention to 'breaking' cops, when they interfere with me as you have done. We will take you for a little ride, and we will leave you, presently, minus your belt and shield, to make your way back as best you can, to report;" and Harvard called an order to Julius through the open window.

"I'll be 'broke' for this!" Compton muttered miserably.

"Maybe not—if you go directly to the inspector with your story. I shall send the belt and shield to him in the morning. I rather liked you—until this thing happened to-night, Compton. Do you remember when you last saw me?"

"Sure I do."

"Well, I saw you, too; and officer Casey was with you; and two plainclothes men from headquarters. It was down at the pier, when I went away, six months ago. I thought, at the time, that you and Casey held those two plainclothes men back when they would have attempted to stop me. Is that right?"

"Sure it is."

"Well, I rather liked you for that. It is too bad that you disobeyed the inspector's specific orders to-night. You would have avoided all this."

"Say, Mr. Harvard, on the level, won't you let me out of this and give me back my belt and shield, and let me go? I'll be—"

"No. If you had succeeded in capturing me, would you have let me go? Swallow a little of your own medicine, Compton. It will be good for you."

Compton became sullen after that. Half an hour later they dropped him at an isolated point in the Bronx, a mile or more from the nearest trolley line; and still later when Julius had driven them back into the city, they stopped for a moment before an all-night district messenger office where Julius left a neatly wrapped package addressed to the inspector, and bearing the legend, "to be delivered immediately." It contained Compton's belt and stick and shield.

"What about the inspector, Bingham?" Katherine asked her husband while they were on their way back.

"Oh, it turned out exactly as we thought it would," he replied. "Still, I am not sorry that I made the effort. I have had the satisfaction of doing what I considered to be my duty. I have given the 'system' its chance. Now, it is war."

"Still," she said slowly, "I regret just a little, that you would not consent to work it without letting them know that you were back."

"I don't, Katherine. I'd much rather fight it in the open—or as near to the open as I can arrive, under the circumstances. They know what they are up against now."

"Tom Clancy thinks—"

"Oh, I know perfectly well that Tom thinks—God bless him! He is what you might call single-thoughted, if I may coin a word. There are two things certain, my dear: we are going to find the man who stole that hundred and thirty-six thousand dollars, and we are going to put the 'system' that tried to fasten the crime on me, everlastingly on the blink. But that is not what concerns me most at the present moment."

"What is, then?"

"Your own safety, dear. They will hound the life out of you now, if you give them half a chance."

"I'm not going to give them half a chance, or a tenth part of one—if you will adhere to your agreement that we shall see each other only rarely while this problem is being worked out."

"I will stick to it, Katherine, if only for your own sake—although it will be hard; but it won't be long."

"No, dear, it won't be long; and I have selected my own method and plans for working. You and Tom can work together as you see fit, and see as much of each other as you both deem wise. All that I ask is that you will both leave me entirely to my own resources, and that you will not seek to see me, unless I send word to you. I must work alone. Only, don't forget that I will always have Julius near me."

Harvard nodded in acquiescence, and was silent. Presently she asked:

"How did you explain your presence here to the inspector, with the fact that the *Golgotha* will not arrive for many hours yet?"

"I didn't explain it. He thinks I came ashore in a flying machine, or that I have been here all the time—or that I came on the same steamer with you. It doesn't matter what he thinks."

"You have not seen Rushton yet?"

"No, dear."

"You intend to see him?"

"Yes; before I sleep again," was the decided reply.

"You—you will not do anything to—to—"

Harvard smiled reassuringly into her eyes while he put an arm around her and drew her closer to him.

"No, little mascot," he said. "Rushton is merely the personification of the charge against me; nothing more. Once, I intended to kill him, but your love for me has crowded all thoughts of hatred out of my heart and soul. Rushton will work out his own condemnation;" and the Night Wind bent forward and called to Julius to stop.

"I will get down here," he told his wife. "I am going to see Tom Clancy. He is expecting me, and I have the key to his house that you gave me. In the morning the actual campaign begins. Remember, sweetheart, that I must hear from you every day, through Tom, or Julius, or by letter, as agreed. In a fortnight, more or less, within a month at most, we will be able to face the world together—for I have a plan or two, also, which I have not disclosed."

We will draw the curtain over their parting, after which Julius drove the car away, while the Night Wind stood quite still and watched it go from him, bearing the woman he loved with all his heart and soul—and who loved him.

Then he hurried away to seek his friend Tom Clancy.

CHAPTER VII

A MIDNIGHT CALL

Clancy had given Katherine a key to his home, to be delivered to Harvard at the first opportunity, and the message that went with the key was:

> Tell Bing to come to me the moment he has
> that key in his possession, no matter what
> hour of the day or night it may happen to be.
> If it is daylight, he can go to the house and
> wait there till I get home; if it is night—well,
> he knows the location of my room.

Thus Thomas Clancy was awakened during the small hours of the morning to discover that his room was brilliantly alight, and that a man was seated on the bed beside him.

"You sleep like a dead man, Tom," was Harvard's greeting. "I could have taken the furniture out of the room without rousing you."

"Hell, Bing! Gee, but it's good to see you again;" and the two friends grasped hands in the manner that only real friendship knows and feels. Then Tom tumbled out of bed and began to clothe himself. "I can't think properly unless I've got a bale or two of dry goods wrapped around me, Bing!" he exclaimed cheerily. "Habit, I suppose; and habit is the greatest slave-driver in the world. Where have you been?

57

What have you been doing all this time? And—*say!*" He paused with one shoe suspended in the air preparatory to pulling it on his foot. "How the devil did you get here, anyhow? Did I get a false report? Did the *Golgotha* come up the bay last night, after all?"

"No, Tom. I believe that she is somewhere outside of Sandy Hook, right now."

"H-m! Well, I don't care, so long as you *are* here. There! Now I am human again; and being clothed, I'm also in my right mind. Have you seen Ka—? Of course you have—otherwise you would not have had the key."

"Oh, I have had a comfortably busy night, Tom," Harvard replied, laughing lightly. His heart felt very light just then, for it seemed as if there was at last a rift in the clouds that had enveloped him so long.

Clancy bent forward in his chair.

"I want to tell you one thing, Bingham Harvard," he remarked solemnly. "You are the luckiest felon that ever fell; you're the guy that put the hap in happiness. Why, say, I would be willing to have a murder charge framed up against me if I was dead certain that it would bring me a wife like yours. It's lucky for you that I'm your 'buzzim' friend, so to speak—I'll tell you that. Talk about women! Why, Bing, Katherine is just the apex of the most splendid womanhood that has been created."

Harvard laughed softly and happily.

"I don't suppose you have seen Rushton yet, have you?" Clancy asked.

"No; but I have seen and talked with the inspector and with an officer named Compton. I waited for the inspector at his own door," Harvard replied; and then, rapidly, he related the incidents of the night as we already know them; and the room rang with Tom Clancy's laughter while the story was being told.

"They won't call you the bone-breaker any more, after this incident!" he exclaimed, when Harvard had finished. "They will call you the heart-breaker, for if you didn't break that cop's heart—and the inspector's, too, for that matter—

I'm a Dutchman. Now, it is time to get down to business. Have you got any plans?"

"I have got one general one upon which all the lesser ones depend, of course," Harvard replied; "to find the thief who stole that money. But the great difficulty is—" He paused.

"Is what, Bing?"

"Well, it is the same as if you hid something in that other room and then came outside of it and locked the door so that I couldn't get in, and told me to find it. The thief is inside of that bank, Tom. If I could get into it again and stay in it for a week or so—"

"Go on. You haven't finished."

"Oh, yes, I have, for, of course, it is utterly impossible for me to do that. Say, Tom, I wonder if it is true that some of those theatrical guys can disguise a fellow so that his best friends won't recognize him. Is it?"

"Hardly. Anyhow, *you* couldn't disguise yourself so that a blind man wouldn't know you. You've got too much 'presence' about you—too much Bing Harvard. But you needn't worry about that. I have had a man working inside of Chester's bank for the last three months," Clancy concluded coolly.

"You have? You have done that?"

"Surest thing you know, Bing."

"And for the last three months! Then nothing has turned up as yet, or you would have told me of it the first shot out of the box."

"Nope. Nothing has materialized, so far. You see, we needed you here, to tell us what to do, and where to look, and all that. We can accomplish more in three weeks, with you close at hand to make suggestions, than in three years without you. That's what!"

"Who else do you mean by that word 'we,' Tom?"

"My friend whom I call Mr. Redhead, because that isn't his name; the main guy of the only bunch of real detectives in this glorious country; the head and front of the one great detective agency that *does things*. He is just itching to see you, too."

"Do you mean Bu—?"

"I mean Mr. Redhead. I told you that."

"Is it one of his men that is at the bank?"

"You betcher life it is."

"What is he doing there? What is his position?"

"Oh, he is one of the bookkeepers."

"I should like to have a talk with that man."

"You will have the opportunity before you are twenty-four hours older, Bing. And now I want to drop that part of the subject for a few minutes. What are you going to do about Rushton?"

"Put that question a little plainer, Tom."

"Have you still got a bug that you want to get his gore—or anything like that?"

"No, Tom. There is no room for hate of any sort where love like mine abounds. My attitude toward Rushton now is one of sorrow—mingled, perhaps, with a grain of contempt."

"Well, maybe that is all right. I cannot deny, though, that I'd rather like to see you break him in two and throw the pieces away. However, you're not going to let up on him, are you, when the time comes to give him what's coming to him?"

"I think he will get it without its being given to him. But—I am going to see him, Tom, and give him *his* chance, just the same as I saw and gave it to the inspector. I have promised myself that much."

"Good! When are you going to see him, and *how* are you going to see him?"

Harvard looked at his watch.

"It is just two o'clock in the morning," he said. "I want to be ready for work to-morrow. I shall go to see him now—at his own home. I'll give him his chance."

"Well—I'll—be—Say! You will kill him, Bing. You will scare him to death. You don't really mean it, do you?"

"Of course I mean it."

"Then I'm going with you."

"Oh, no, you're not. I am not going to permit you to destroy your usefulness to me by any such foolishness. I know the way to his house. It won't be the first time I have seen the inside of it, for I did go there to kill him once. I promised myself that I would give him *his* chance, Tom. It won't do any good, of course, but it will satisfy my own ideas of what is right."

"Won't you let me go as far as the door with you and wait there till you come out?" Tom Clancy pleaded; but Harvard shook his head emphatically while he got out of his chair and reached for his hat.

"I'll meet you anywhere you say, at any time you choose, to-morrow night, Tom," he said; "and I would like to see your friend Redhead, too. During the day I will have certain small things to attend to—"

"And one very big thing, Bing; which is, to keep yourself out of sight. Don't forget who you are, and that you have already pretty well advertised the fact that you have returned. Every cop in New York will be on the lookout for you in the morning."

"I know. I am prepared for that, too."

Clancy crossed the room toward his desk. He returned in a moment with an envelope in his hand, which he gave to Harvard.

"You will find in this full written directions concerning where you are to go and what you are to do to-morrow night, in order to meet me—and Redhead. But say, I wish you would pass up this Rushton call; anyhow, for to-night."

"It can't be done, Tom," Harvard replied, smiling. "I am going there—*now.*"

CHAPTER VIII

RODNEY RUSHTON'S ORDEAL

The Night Wind paused for a moment at the bottom of the steps that led to the door of the house where Lieutenant Rodney Rushton lived. He looked at his watch and saw that the hour was half past two.

Lights gleamed from the windows of the top floor—it was a three-story house—and announced that the headquarters man was still awake. They suggested also that he might not be alone.

Harvard thought over that possibility for a moment, then shrugged his shoulders indifferently, mounted the steps, selected the electric button which would ring the bell in Rushton's quarters, and pressed upon it. Then he stood quite close to the inner door and waited. The house was Rushton's own property, and he reserved the top floor of it for his own uses, letting out the others.

Harvard could hear heavy footsteps descending the stairs inside. Then the door was jerked open, and Rushton, with an angry scowl upon his forehead, stood just beyond it.

He could not see Harvard's face distinctly in the half light, and certainly Bingham Harvard was the last man on earth that he might have expected to find there, so there was no instant recognition on his part.

The Night Wind, being prepared, stepped inside the doorway the instant it was opened.

62

Every muscle, every sinew and nerve, every energy he possessed, was tense, and ready for action if he should be called upon to make use of any of them.

He stepped inside the hallway so quickly, with that unaccountable swiftness of action that was his characteristic, that he had passed the threshold and had closed the door behind him before Rushton could blurt out the profane question that he had determined to put to the person who had dared to disturb him at that hour, after he had been on duty all the day and part of the night.

"The Night Wind has returned, Rushton," was Harvard's greeting; "and I did not come here to hurt you unless you attempt to hurt me."

It was said coolly enough, but with unmistakable emphasis, nevertheless. Rushton started backward, almost staggering, and caught at the post of the balustrade for support. His face went gray, his eyes widened, and the pupils dilated. Although he was called a man who was unafraid, he was frightened then for an instant.

"*You!*" he managed to say in a hoarse whisper. "They said—they said that you were on the *Golgotha*. She hasn't docked yet. I telephoned the very last thing before—*Say!* You've got a gall, comin' here, you have!" He sought to gain a little courage by bluster.

"Softly, Rushton, softly. Lead the way upstairs. I want to talk to you."

"I won't. You beat it outa here."

The Night Wind bent forward nearer to the frightened man, boring him with his eyes.

"Lead the way to your rooms, Rushton," he said quietly. "I'm not going to hurt you, unless you force me to it. When I have had my say I will go away as I came, quietly, and you will be none the worse for my call upon you. You may be some better. That is up to you. You are not hankering after any more broken bones, are you?"

Rushton still hesitated, glaring into the eyes of the man he so hated and feared.

"You are unarmed just now, Rushton," the Night Wind said, with a half smile. "I am always armed—with these."

And he stretched out his arms toward the man from head-quarters until his fingers were so close to Rushton's throat that the man shrank away from them in terror.

Then, without further objection or hesitation, he began slowly to mount the stairs; and Harvard followed after him.

So they entered the front room of the top floor, where two lights were burning brightly.

Upon a couch at one side were Rushton's weapons—a police revolver, a Colt automatic, and a loaded "billy." Rushton would have made a leap toward them had not the Night Wind's hand fallen heavily upon his shoulder just as he was about to do so. The man knew himself to be helpless then.

Harvard stepped past him, appropriated the weapons, and dropped them inside the table drawer, which he pulled open. There was a key in the lock of the drawer, and he turned it, after which he threw it behind the couch.

"Now, Rushton," he said coldly, "I don't think you will try to get gay with me. I am not in the mood to be gay just now. Sit down—over there—in that chair. You will be away from the temptations of guns and telephones and such things over there."

"Say, Harvard, what do you mean by this highhanded business, anyhow?" Rushton had found his voice at last. He had assured himself that the Night Wind had not come there to kill him, as he had at first surmised—for he remembered how near to death he had been on one occasion at this man's hands.

"I am here to fulfill a promise that I made to myself some time ago, lieutenant," Harvard replied.

"Oh, you are, are you? It's a good thing to keep your word with somebody, I suppose."

"I promised myself that I would give you a chance—an opportunity to redeem yourself—and the last one, Rushton."

Rushton sneered openly. "I ain't in the redeemin' business, Mister Harvard," he said.

Harvard bent forward, studying the man before him much as he might have given curious attention to a gila monster or to any poisonous reptile. Then he shook his head and murmured, more to himself than to the officer:

"You are not even human. Something—I wonder what it was—was left out of you when you were made. Rushton, don't you know what a simple fool you are? Haven't you any idea of it? Is your crooked conceit so great that you cannot see your own reflection?"

"I think I'll smoke, if you don't mind," Rushton said, half rising from his chair; but Harvard interrupted him sharply, and he dropped back upon it again.

"You will sit where you are. You can do your smoking after I have gone away," Harvard announced coldly.

"Well, you can't go any too soon to suit me, mister. You know the way out," was the sneering reply. "Say, what did you come here for, anyhow?"

"Pay close attention for a moment and I will tell you. I told you a moment ago that I came here to give you a chance. I meant that. The chance is this: If you will admit, in the presence of the inspector in charge of the detective bureau, of Mr. Chester, Mr. Clancy, and myself, that I am innocent of that theft at the bank, and that the evidence which you produced against me was a frame-up, you will probably be given an opportunity to redeem yourself at headquarters, and you will have the satisfaction of knowing that you have performed at least one good deed—of knowing that for once you have done what is right." Harvard chose his words carefully and slowly. He said them earnestly. Rushton laughed outright and brutally.

"Now whadda you know about that!" he ejaculated derisively. "Little Bingie Harvard, who never had no father nor mother—"

Rushton got thus far and stopped. His jaw fell open. His eyes started and stared. He trembled with sudden cold. He huddled down into the depths of the chair, more frightened than he had ever been in all his crooked life before.

The Night Wind had leaped to his feet and was standing over the man who had taunted him with his unknown birth. His eyes were blazing. His face had gone white with rage. His furious temper, ungovernable when roused, was nearly loosed.

But he controlled himself, and after a moment returned to his chair; and for several moments after that there was utter silence between the two men. There would be no danger that Rushton would again transgress in the manner he had done.

"I did not expect that you would consider what I had to offer," the Night Wind said colorlessly after a time. "It takes a big man to admit that he has done wrong, and you are the littlest man that ever lived. Well, so be it. I have done my part, and you will have to take the consequences, Rushton."

"Huh! Consequences! What consequences?"

"Dismissal from the force, for one thing. Prison, for another. Utter and entire ostracism at the hands of all decent men, for still another. Restitution, reprisal, ignominy, self-scorn, the contempt of others will go to make of the sum total."

"You make me tired, Harvard. What do you think I am, anyhow? A boob? Even if all that you say was so, do you think I would be fool enough to admit it?"

"It *is* so, and you are fool enough *not* to admit it."

"Well, if that is all that you came here to say to me, you'd better chase yourself."

"Rushton"—Harvard bent forward again, with a sudden thought that came into his understanding like a flash of light—"I believe that you know—have known all the time—*who did take that money*."

"Of course I know. Of course I have known all the time. *You* took it."

"You know that that is not what I mean."

"I ain't no mind-reader, Harvard. If you have come back to this burg with any idea that you're going to throw it into me, you've got another guess comin', that's all. I suppose you think you're smart, comin' here to my house in the dead of night an' givin' me all this hot air. I s'pose you think that you can go around this old town the same way you done the act once before, breakin' bones an' raisin' hell generally; but you can't. The net'll be out for you in the morning, and it will be put out in such a way that you will wish before you're twenty-four hours older that you'd stayed where you was."

"And there's another thing, too, that you can put into your pipe and smoke. We ain't goin' to take no foolishness from Lady Kate. They tell me down-town that she has married *you*. Well, that fact ain't goin' to protect her none; it's goin' to do her a lot of harm, if anybody should ask you."

"There's more'n one way to kill a cat, Mr. Bingham Harvard, as you'll find out, and I'll tell you right now (and I ain't sayin' it for myself alone; I'm sayin' it for the whole bunch down at headquarters), if that wife of yours don't walk in a mighty straight and narrow path she'll find herself up against it so hard that she won't know what has happened to her when it does happen."

"You talk about frame-ups. Say! You ain't the only guy that has made that yell, and you ain't likely to be, either. You take it from me, you'd better send *her* back to where you've been stayin', unless you want to see her takin' a trip up the river for an extended stay. And that warnin' ain't no idle dream, either."

"Rushton, are you threatening to 'frame' something on my wife?" There was deadly menace in the tone in which that question was asked.

"No, I ain't. I ain't threatenin' nothin'. I'm givin' you warning."

Harvard was silent for a moment after that, thinking.

That flash of light that had fallen upon him a moment ago when he charged Rushton with having known from the beginning who was the real thief called up other flashes by sequences.

A new idea possessed him now. One that had never even remotely occurred to him before that night. But it was a promising one; and, if there were promise in it, the search for substantiation must be begun in that very room. He knew that.

Harvard produced a pair of handcuffs. Then he crossed again to Rushton.

"Lean forward," he ordered, "and put your hands together, behind you."

"Say, what are you up to, anyhow? I ain't—"

"You had better do as I tell you, Rushton," was the quiet interruption; and Rushton did. Then he leaned backward again with his wrists locked tightly together behind his back, and with an ugly scowl on his face and a furious gleaming in his eyes.

Next, Harvard jerked a rope from the curtains at one end of the room and tied Rushton securely to the chair.

"That won't render you uncomfortable, Rushton, unless you attempt to get up—in which case you will find that it will choke you a little," he said. "The notion has seized me to go through your desk and the papers it contains, and I want you to be quiet while I do so."

Rushton's face turned livid. Then the blood rushed into it again, until it was nearly purple in hue. He ground his teeth together, and he swore frightfully; and to not one of the things he said did Harvard pay the slightest attention—until the language became utterly intolerable. Then he turned from his occupation at the desk long enough to say, with calm decision:

"If I hear you utter one more word, Rushton, I will put a gag between your jaws."

There was silence after that, save for the flutter and rattle of paper as Harvard searched the desk.

From time to time he glanced at his watch, and then each time the search went forward again, for he had already discovered enough to establish the importance of making it a thorough one; and Harvard had no doubt that there were other places than the desk to be examined also before he completed the task he had set himself.

Then a startling thing happened. The telephone bell rang out sharply.

For a moment the Night Wind hesitated, glancing at Rushton while he did so. And then, with sudden decision, he went to the telephone and lifted the receiver from the hook.

CHAPTER IX

PLAYING THE GAME

Rushton gave an eager start when the telephone call rang out. Then, as the Night Wind lifted the receiver from the hook and put it against his ear, the lieutenant, with an assumption of carelessness that was plainly evident, remarked:

"I guess maybe you'd better let me answer that call, if you'll bring the phone over here. More'n likely they'll recognize your voice, Harvard."

But Harvard paid no attention to the suggestion.

And then Bingham Harvard smiled broadly, for he recognized the voice at the other end of the wire; and he was mentally glad that he had been sufficiently thoughtful in the "Hello" he had given to render his own voice as low and guttural as possible.

The following conversation followed, it being remembered that Rodney Rushton could hear only that part of it uttered by Harvard.

The voice at the other telephone was unmistakably the voice of the inspector.

"That you, Rushton?" he inquired; and without waiting for a reply to the question, continued: "I called you up to tell you that the Night Wind is back. He's in town now. As likely as not he's been here some time. That was all rot about his coming on the *Golgotha*, because she is outside of Sandy Hook yet. Do you get me?"

"Sure," said Harvard.

69

"What's the matter? Got a cold?"

"A little;" and Harvard coughed. The inspector continued:

"I know he is here, because I saw him and spoke to him. He's looking for blood, too, so you had best keep an eye out. I wasn't going to say anything about it until morning, but about half an hour ago a messenger came to my house bringing a belt and stick and shield that belong to Compton; and a few minutes later Compton telephoned to me from somewhere out in the Bronx to say that the Night Wind took them away from him and then dropped him out there among the goats."

"Uh-huh," said Harvard, noncommittally.

"It doesn't seem to interest you very much, Rushton. Or, are you scared stiff?"

"Both," Harvard replied. And he coughed again badly.

"You *have* got a cold, haven't you?" the inspector said sympathetically. "Well, forget it. You won't have any time to nurse colds now. You slip on your clothes and beat it up here to my house as soon as you can make it. I want to see you now."

"What for?" Harvard trusted himself to say.

There was a moment of hesitation at the other end of the wire. Then:

"I can't talk it over the wire—that is why I want you to come here to see me before we meet down at the office. But I'll say this much—we've got to separate that bunch of busybodies—Clancy, Lady Kate, and the Night Wind. We've got to get *her*, anyhow, and send her away—and Clancy, too, if possible."

"Frame something?" Harvard asked suggestively.

"We've got to get rid of them somehow."

Just then Rushton took a large chance. Driven to desperation by hearing only one end of a conversation that he knew was intended for himself, he yelled at the top of his voice:

"That ain't me talkin'—it's the Night Wind!"

Harvard knew that the inspector must have heard that shout and the words that were uttered; and he smiled broadly when he heard the inspector swear; then, before the choice selection of words was quite finished, he said in his natural tones:

"Hello, inspector—how are you feeling about now?"

"Curse you, Harvard—I wish I could get at you," came the reply.

"Oh, I shall be gone from here long before you could get here or send others, inspector. I am nearly through for the night. That was very kind of you to give me that bit of information in regard to Mrs. Harvard and my friend Clancy."

"Say, what are you doing in Rushton's rooms?"

"Searching his papers and so forth."

"Where's Rushton?"

"He is here, sitting with his hands behind his back like a good little boy that has been naughty. He is harmless. Would you like to have me deliver that message of yours to him?"

"I would like to speak to him if you will let me do it."

"Certainly—on the condition that you will speak loud enough for both of us to hear what you say. If you do not, I shall hold the receiver so that he can't hear."

"All right," came the reply; and Harvard stepped across to the chair where Rushton was seated, stretching the telephone cord to its full length in doing so. Then he held the receiver down so that both of them could hear what might be said through it.

"Hello, inspector," Rushton called hoarsely. "This—"

Harvard lifted the transmitter and receiver out of his reach. "None of that, Rushton," he said. Then he put them down again for Rushton to talk.

"Tell me what has happened, Rushton," the inspector said. "He will let you do that."

"Aw, he rung my bell an' I went down like a jackass, with nothin' on me—that is, no gun 'r nothin'; an' he got me dead to rights down in the lower hall. And now he's got my own irons onto me, and he's goin' through my papers. It ain't nice to tell, but it's so."

"Tell Rushton about that idea of yours for a new frame-up, inspector," Harvard interposed; and the inspector replied:

"I'll tell him all right, Harvard, only I will go down there to do it. Just now I prefer to talk with you a little more. You see——"

That was all that Harvard heard, for he hung the receiver upon the hook instantly. The thought struck him suddenly that the inspector was talking to kill time, and that if he did that it was not without a purpose.

It was not unlikely that another person was in the room with the inspector when he called Rushton's number, and if that happened to be true, signs and signals would have sufficed to send that second person into the street to find another telephone. If that were the case, headquarters and then the nearest station house would be speedily notified.

The fact of the matter was even more ominous, if Harvard had but known it; for, in addition to the regular telephone service, the inspector had a private, direct wire between his house and his own office at headquarters, and that private wire was working even while the inspector was talking with Harvard.

For one brief interval Bingham Harvard thought deeply when he replaced the receiver on the hook.

He had not completed his search of Rushton's papers, and there might never be another opportunity. He decided that he would allow himself ten minutes more.

He sprang to the desk again and pulled out the contents of the two remaining pigeonholes that he had not searched, and stuffed them into his pockets regardless of what they might be. Then he pulled out the drawers, one after another, and fumbled rapidly among the contents of them.

There was a package of small memorandum books, held together by a rubber band, and a glance into one of them told him that they might possibly be of value, so he dropped the entire package into his side pocket.

He looked into a closet and discovered a very small iron safe, but it was locked, and he did not care to search Rushton's pockets for the key.

Then he snapped off the lights, leaving Rushton in darkness, and passed into the hall, and thence into the rear room; but a quick search around it was unfruitful of results.

He knew that time was passing—that it would not be long, after headquarters was once notified of what was happening, before officers would come a-running from the nearest precinct station house, so he abandoned the idea of further search, and started down the stairs.

It had been an adventurous night thus far, and he did not care to have it end disastrously. He was assured, too, that he had collected some valuable information from Rushton's desk—or, at least, the beginning of things that would prove to be of value.

As he opened the street door and stepped into the vestibule he could hear the sound of running feet approaching the house, and he had no doubts about what that meant.

But he paused an instant, nevertheless, for his trained ear told him that men were running toward him from either direction; and then, too, the rumble of a heavy wagon and the pounding of horses' hoofs on the pavement announced the rapid approach of the patrol wagon.

It did not occur to him that he would be unable to get through them and escape; the thought that was uppermost in his mind at that moment was one of dread lest he should be compelled to hurt somebody before he would be able to do so—for he had determined, if it were possible, to carry out the task he had set himself to do in clearing his own name, without injuring anybody.

The noise of running feet came nearer from both directions, and with sudden resolution the Night Wind stepped outside of the door and closed it tightly after him.

Then, perceiving that he had no time to make a getaway, he turned about and began to shake the door, apparently with all his strength, although he really used but little of it—and then half a dozen cops dashed up the steps behind him.

He did not wait for them to question him; he shouted orders at them; and he did it in a manner so peremptory that they very naturally mistook him for a plain clothes man who had "beat them to it."

"Quick, now. All together," he ordered. "Smash in the door. One, two—there you are!"

There was a rending crash. The door gave way before the onslaught of the several men who threw themselves against it. There was a smashing splintering of wood, the clinking of broken glass, the harsh rending of iron—and the Night Wind passed into the darkness of the hall in the very forefront of those uniformed men.

It was then that he managed to step to one side while they passed him and stumbled and ran up the stairway.

Somebody shouted an order for somebody else to remain on guard at the door, and for still another somebody or two to perform the same service outside on the pavement. The people who lived on the parlor floor of the house, and on the second floor also, opened their doors in affright, yelled murder and fire and other things, and slammed them shut again.

The patrol wagon deposited its quota of men at the curb, and they came tumbling into the house—and just as the major part of them passed him the Night Wind stepped outside and ran quickly down the steps.

One of the uniformed men who was on guard stepped toward him, and the Night Wind seized him by the arm and dragged him rapidly along the sidewalk, exclaiming as he did so:

"Come here a moment! I've got something to say to you! You other fellows stay where you are!"

It worked.

A few doors farther along the street the Night Wind seized his man and dexterously relieved him of his gun, which he threw into the middle of the street; and as he did so he said smilingly:

"I am the Night Wind, my friend. You can go back there now and tell them that you saw me. They will be pleased to hear it."

CHAPTER X

A "SYSTEM" AND A "KEY"

There was a small and select gathering of police officials in the private office of the inspector the following day at noon. It is a notable fact, and one worthy of record, that the deputy commissioner was not among them.

The inspector had summoned them one by one, and when the few were present whom he desired orders were given that he was not to be disturbed on any account for half an hour, and the door was locked to make sure.

Just how we know about that conference in order to report it at this time of the story should be explained as demonstrative of the thoroughness with which Tom Clancy was working in the interests of his friend Harvard, and as showing how wisely he had made his selection of the detective agency that was to perform much of the work—that agency which was directed by the master mind to whom Tom referred as "Redhead."

There were present, besides the inspector, Lieutenants Rushton, Coniglio, and Masters; and Detective-sergeants Boynton, Potowski, and Connor; and please don't forget Connor, for, as it happens, he had worked side by side with Redhead in a Western State long before he became a member of the New York police department, and was still working for him. Are we wise now? Redhead had long ago found it important that he should keep posted concerning the inside

75

workings of police departments in various cities, and hence—

Rushton delivered a short speech. He said (condensed):

"You guys all know enough about the Night Wind an' what he has done to us, an' what he's likely to *do* to us unless we put the kibosh onto him, so it ain't necessary for me to go into particulars." Rushton looked from face to face in that gathering to make sure that they each appreciated the significance of what he had said; then he continued:

"The Night Wind has come back, and he's worse than ever—take it from me; and from the skipper, too. Both of us saw him last night, and both times *he* saw *us first*. Some of you know by experience what that means; some of you know only by hearsay, but you may as well put it down in your memoranda that when the Night Wind sees you first there ain't nothin' doin' for *you*."

"The skipper 'n me ain't personally ashamed of what happened to us last night, because this Bing Harvard ain't really human. He is something supernatural. He's chain lightning in his motions, a panther in his tread on the streets, the tongue of a toad in his agility, and a veritable Samson in strength. He's the strongest and the quickest man I ever heard of. There ain't no man livin' that can stand up against him, so it ain't no dishonor to have him get the best of you. Them that's been up against him know that."

"He says he has stopped breaking bones an' maiming us cops, an' maybe he has. But it wouldn't be safe to bank too heavily on the proposition if one or two of you should undertake to tackle him. It's a cinch that if he had to do it in order to make a getaway he'd be right there on the job."

"When he moves he don't make no more noise than a shadow—and how he does it I don't know. He says he has come back here to clear his name, but I happen to be the guy that got the goods on him for that Centropolis bank affair, and so I know that unless he frames something on somebody else he's the guilty man. Anyhow, there's an indictment out against him, and we've got to get him. We've got to or go out of business."

"Now I'm comin' to the point of this here statement."

"The Night Wind didn't come back to New York alone. He brought Lady Kate—her that used to be down here with us—back with him. She *says* she's his wife now; and *he* says so, too; but I ain't seen no marriage certificate, and, so whether it's true 'r not, *we* ain't got no call to take official notice of it."

"And that ain't all. He has got a friend in this burg who is some friend—name of Tom Clancy—a down-town stock broker, comfortably rich, and willin' to spend his last dollar for Bing Harvard. He is something of a sport, as slick as grease, ain't afraid of nothin', and as busy as a cat that has been smeared over with lard.

"Well, *we've got to get them two, an' get 'em good and plenty!*"

"That is what you guys are here to be told. It don't make much difference how we get 'em, so long as we do it, for the skipper and me are about agreed that we ain't likely to put the irons onto the Night Wind's wrists as long as them two are runnin' around loose."

"There are seven of us here in this bunch, and what passes between us seven don't go no farther—see? We've got to work together for the good of the community and for the force, and the one thing that we've got to do right off the reel is to find some means of sendin' them two—Lady Kate and Clancy—away."

"I ain't askin' you to frame nothin'. That ain't my way. But it's a cinch that if you look close enough into the history of any man 'r woman you'll find *something* that will do the trick. I guess that's all, inspector."

The inspector took his feet from the desk and brought them down solidly upon the floor.

"I guess you understand Lieutenant Rushton well enough so that I need add nothing to what he has said," he told them. "Coniglio, you and Masters, with Boynton and Potowski on the side, are assigned to Clancy. The rest of us will take care of the girl. I want quick action if I can get it. That is all—only I want to be kept thoroughly posted all the time."

* * * * * * *

Behind closed doors in another private office farther down-town there was also a consultation. It took place at approximately the same hour, and was between two persons, of whom one was Redhead and the other Lady Kate.

It was the first meeting between these two; but Clancy had arranged for it, and Katherine was expected, when Black Julius drove her there in the imitation taxicab.

There was some preliminary talk between them which need not be recorded, and then:

"It might have been better, Mrs. Harvard, if you had returned directly to your old job at headquarters instead of going to Chester as you did. No doubt the inspector would have taken you back, and—well, there might have been possibilities—eh?"

"Perhaps. But they never would have trusted me again. They were morally certain that I went away with Mr. Harvard; indeed, some of them *knew* the fact. Bingham and I saw and recognized four members of the force at the pier the day we sailed, and we were reasonably certain that they saw and recognized us. No; I think I did right, chief."

"Are you aware that under the circumstances, as they now exist, you are in constant danger, Mrs. Harvard?" he asked her.

"Quite so," she smiled back at him.

"They will want to get you out of the way, and at once; and Clancy, too. But you, even more than he. You are an active menace to them and to every thing that they stand for. Rushton and a few of his cronies will not hesitate to frame something on you, and the very fact that you have been one of them will render that an easy task. Really, Mrs. Harvard, you should keep out of sight. This is a man's job, not a woman's."

"I shall pass out of sight, chief, the moment I leave this office. I determined upon that much, and exactly how I would accomplish it, before I landed in New York. And that is the real reason for my presence here, to consult with you. I used to think, when I was connected with headquarters, that I would rather have been here with you than there."

"I heartily wish you had been," he replied earnestly.

"And now I want your promise of secrecy concerning me. I mean that I do not wish my husband to know where I may be, or what I am doing. I wish him to be kept in entire ignorance. Is that agreed upon?"

"Certainly."

"I will report directly to you from time to time, and you will make such use as you see fit of what I may be able to tell you. Only, I wanted to be sure of your approval and your coöperation."

"Of my coöperation, surely. Of my approval—I will first have to know something more about what you think of undertaking."

"Chief, I have thought and dreamed and planned for this opportunity constantly, ever since I left New York. I have worked out countless ideas, only to dismiss each one as being, for one reason or another, impracticable. I will tell you what I have decided upon presently, but, first, will you reply to a few questions that I wish to ask?"

"Gladly—if I can."

"Who took that money? I do not mean, what person took it. But was it an inside job, or was it accomplished from the outside, in some inexplicable manner? What is your opinion as to that? Mr. Clancy has told me that you have had one of your men acting as an employee at the bank for some time."

"That is true, Mrs. Harvard. I cannot answer your question, however, more than to say that I am personally satisfied that neither of the two assistant tellers was the thief. My operative at the bank has accomplished absolutely nothing. I have kept every man who is employed there (who might have stolen the money) under rigid surveillance—with no result whatever. And if one of those men *had* taken it, there *would* have been a result."

"So you incline to the theory of an outside job?"

"If there *was* a job. But one confronts greater difficulties in the theory of an outside worker than in the other one."

"What do you mean when you say 'if there *was* a job'?"

"Sometimes I am on the point of believing that the money was never stolen at all."

"But that is absurd. Don't forget that it was Bingham who discovered the loss."

"Precisely. You have made use of the right word—loss. Was the money stolen or was it lost?"

"But it couldn't have been lost, chief, inside of that cage. Of course it was stolen. And I believe it was stolen from the outside. And—I believe that Rodney Rushton knows who stole it, and has appropriated a very large portion of it to his own uses since he found out that interesting fact. And, also, what Rodney Rushton was able to find out you can discover as well as he—unless—"

"Unless what, Mrs. Harvard?" The chief was suddenly interested in her suggestions.

"*Unless Rushton knew, before the money disappeared, that it would disappear,*" she replied with slow emphasis.

"By Jove!" he exclaimed, and leaned back in his chair. "A double frame-up, eh? The idea is worth a lot of careful thought, Mrs. Harvard. But an outsider could not have taken the packages of money from the paying teller's cage without help from the inside."

"Certainly not. And expert help, at that."

"Which fact brings us up against it just as hard as we were before. We are backed up into the same corner."

Katherine took a folded sheet of paper from her mesh bag and spread it open on the desk between them, and the chief bent down over it.

"This," she said, "is a detailed plan of the inside of that cage, drawn to a scale, and by my husband. And here"—she produced a second paper—"is a floor plan of the bank itself prepared in the same manner. The red cross on this one shows the spot from which the packages of bills actually disappeared. The black circles with numbers inside of them, on both plans, indicate the positions of the various workers in the bank at the time of the theft, or approximating it as nearly as possible. Below, and against each of the numbers, are the names and occupations of the workers. Chief, I have studied those plans until I can close my eyes and see each of them or both of them as plainly as you see them now."

"I have no doubt of it. They make an interesting study, too."

Katherine leaned back in her chair again.

"Ever since the first day of my association with the New York police," she said, "I have heard the word 'system' dinned into my ears. Also, in studying over those plans so constantly, I was reminded that there never was a mathematical problem to be worked out for which a system was not necessary. And—a 'key.' And so I have searched my intelligence to discover the system by which those packages of money were stolen and to find the key that would open that system and make it available. *I think, chief, that I have discovered both.*"

"You do?"

"Yes."

"Then the task is already accomplished, Mrs. Harvard."

"No. It must yet be proven. My theories—and there are nothing more than theories as yet—must be established; and there is the possibility that I may be utterly in error."

"But, tell me—"

"Please do not ask me to do that, chief; not yet. You see, I haven't the courage of my own convictions in this matter— and that is why I wish to work alone, unaided and unimpeded, until I have discovered something to uphold and sustain my opinions. I have seen one innocent man terribly wronged; and the man inside of that bank who is, I believe, the key to this mystery may be as innocent as my husband was and is. I utterly refuse to cast even the shadow of a doubt upon him until I have satisfied myself that I have a fairly good reason for doing so."

"But you may keep the plans, and you can study them as I have done. If you should arrive at the same solution that appeals to me—well, then, we will consult together in regard to it. In the mean time, I shall probably have established it or shattered it."

"And your method? That is what you came here to consult with me about, isn't it?"

"Yes." Katherine hesitated a moment, and then, with a whimsical smile, said: "I am perfectly well aware, chief, that the detective in disguise is largely a creature of romance; but nevertheless I have determined upon a disguise which I believe will be effective. It is absolutely necessary that I should find a place inside of that bank, and I have found a way to accomplish it, with your aid."

She leaned forward and laid a card upon the desk before him. It bore a name (not her own) and an address.

"Will you come to that address at ten o'clock tonight, and ask for that person?" Katherine continued.

He glanced at the card, then uttered a low whistle. "Will that person be you, Mrs. Harvard?" he asked; and when she nodded her head brightly in assent he added:

"You will be obliged to sacrifice something in order to play that part; and I am afraid that you will find it more difficult than you imagine. However, if you have decided, there is nothing more to be said, I suppose. I will be there, Mrs. Harvard, and I will give you an hour."

As Lady Kate descended to the street in one of the elevators Detective-Sergeant Connor, fresh from that conference at headquarters, ascended in another. He was on his way to report to his real chief, Redhead; but he did not know that Rodney Rushton had followed him, and was, even then, waiting outside of the building.

Still less did Lady Kate, on her way to the street, anticipate the possible proximity of Lieutenant Rushton.

CHAPTER XI

LADY KATE'S MISFORTUNE

Rushton saw Lady Kate. Lady Kate did not see Rushton.

If Black Julius had been there with his car, waiting at the curb where his mistress left him, the things that happened so quickly after Katherine emerged from the entrance to the tall building might have been avoided; but the traffic regulations had forced Julius to take his car around the corner to wait.

Only a moment before Lady Kate came out of the building Rushton met and spoke to one of the regular plain clothes men who were attached to that precinct, and they were still talking together when she appeared.

Rushton could think quickly on occasion. He did it then, and acted with the thought.

"Quick, Hardner!" he exclaimed under his breath with sudden inspiration. "If you'll do what I tell you to now, and do it right, I'll get you a promotion—and I know what I am talking about. D'ye see that woman there, at the curb? Looks as though she was lookin' f'r a cab 'r something. I want her pinched now, quick! Y'understand? Here; take this"—and he shoved something that he took from one of his own pockets into Hardner's hand—"an' plant it on her before she is searched. She's a dip—see? Run her around to your own station house an' hold her there. Stay with her yourself, an' don't let anybody talk to her or her talk to anybody—an' no telephonin', either. And you stay right on the job with her till further orders. Hurry! She is moving off. You'll have the big chief stuck on you if you do this job right."

Rushton withdrew into a doorway behind a standing show case and watched.

Hardner, a big brute of a man who had "bull" and plain clothes man written all over him, and who had been "bouncer" in a dance hall before he became a cop, did not hesitate.

He shoved himself forward through the throng of people who were moving in either direction, and he dropped a great paw roughly upon Katherine's shoulder and whirled her around so that she faced him, before she had taken half a dozen steps toward the corner around which Julius had taken his car.

"I want you, my little lady," Hardner said brutally, with a grin and a leer. "I saw you pinch one leather a minute 'r two ago, and I guess you've got more'n that on you. Gee! But you're a peach, ain't you? With a pair of lamps like yours, you ain't got no call to be a common dip. Not you. Come along."

He seized her roughly by the arm and forced her along the street beside him, in the direction opposite the corner around which Julius was waiting.

Lady Kate was so amazed by the attack and the suddenness of it, so utterly nonplussed, that she had been led along the street twenty feet or more before she recovered her natural wit and poise; and then she sought to wrench her arm free from Hardner's grasp.

But the effort was unavailing. Also, a dozen people had witnessed the arrest, and a crowd was rapidly forming around them; and at that instant Hardner threw back one side of his coat and exhibited his shield of authority.

Katherine thoroughly understood how futile it would be to attempt resistance there; and she realized, also, that she had walked into a trap or had fallen into one. She could see Rushton's hand in what was taking place as plainly as if it had been held before her eyes.

And so she walked along quietly beside Hardner without resistance or announced objection. And presently they arrived at the station house, which was not far distant, where she hoped and believed she would find somebody who knew her, who would identify her, and whom she could persuade to befriend her.

But Rushton anticipated any such event.

No sooner had Hardner started away with her before Rushton hurried to a telephone, and he had that particular station house on the wire long before the plain clothes man and his charge reached there.

The instructions that he gave were explicit and emphatic; and they were accompanied by threats that were not to be doubted in their general character. Thus, when Lady Kate did arrive at the station house, a sergeant whom she did not know had taken the lieutenant's place at the desk, she was roughly questioned, a pretense was made of entering the record of the case in the "blotter," and she was rushed into the captain's room, where Hardner stood guard over her until a patrol wagon came and took her away; for Rushton had done more telephoning than merely to call up the station house.

If anybody supposes that a policeman in New York City cannot do pretty nearly as he pleases with a private citizen, in spite of magistrates and the law and so-called justice, provided that policeman is abetted in his act by one of the men "higher up," Mr. Anybody has got another guess coming; and Lady Kate speedily found herself in a position that was by no means enviable.

The "wagon" did not take her to headquarters, as she had confidently believed it was intended to do—for she surmised that she would have some kind of a frame-up to face, and she was prepared to resort, as a last extremity, to certain influences that she possessed to get her out of her difficulties; influences and associations which she had never revealed even to her husband.

She had reserved that part of her history—the part that had always surrounded her with a cloak of mystery—until such time as Bingham Harvard would be enabled to face the world as an honest man.

That wagon was met by another, and, still later, the second one was met by a third; and in the course of time, after having been driven across Queensboro Bridge, Lady Kate realized that she was to be given no opportunity whatever to escape from the predicament she was in.

When she was at last locked up, guarded by a matron whose face was as hard and uncompromising in a feminine way as Hardner's, she knew only that she was somewhere out in Queens, but she had no idea as to the exact location.

Her cell was comfortable enough—more like a small room than a cell; but she understood perfectly well that she would not have been sent out to that remote place unless the persons who had her sent there knew what they were about.

There would be no hope for her now unless she could manage an actual escape, and that possibility appeared to be exceedingly vague and remote.

In the mean time, Black Julius, always patient where his loved mistress was concerned, became alarmed.

Katherine had implicit faith in her servitor, and usually told him more or less of her plans, whenever he drove her about in the imitation taxicab, so that he could meet her halfway in carrying them into effect.

She had told him that day where she was going, and how long a time she expected to be detained; so, when almost an hour more than that time had elapsed, Julius left his car where it was, entered the tall building, and sought the office where he knew she had gone.

For reasons of his own he adopted, when he entered it, the dialect of a Southern negro; and fortune favored him so far that at the moment he entered the reception office of the suite Redhead came into it through another door at the opposite side.

"I's lookin' fo' de lady what I done druv down yere in ma cab, boss," Julius announced with a bow. "She said she was comin' out mos' an houah ago, an' she ain't come yet. If she's yere, boss, will you jes' tell her that I's waitin'?"

Chief Redhead eyed the negro narrowly, then stepped closer to him.

"Do you know the lady's name?" he asked in a low tone.

86

"Yassir. I's heered her called Mis' Maxwell," Julius replied.

"She left here almost an hour ago. Haven't you seen her?"

"No, sah; an' if she done left de buildin' she'd have come straight as a string to me—unlessen somethin' stopped her." Julius was genuinely alarmed by that time.

"You go into my private office and wait until I—" the chief began; but Julius interrupted.

"No, sah," he said. "I'll go down to my cab an' wait dere—jes' a lil' while. You kin fin' me aroun' de corner."

The chief had no difficulty when he reached the street, and by deft questioning, in discovering what had happened. There were several loiterers about who had seen a young woman arrested about an hour before for picking pockets.

The man at the cigar-stand just inside the entrance to the building had witnessed part of the incident; and there were others also.

The chief hurried around the corner to Julius. He had made a close surmise as to the real character of the negro.

"Are you Mrs. Harvard's servant?" he asked abruptly. "I am her friend and confidant. You need not be afraid to tell me."

"Yes, sir," Julius replied, dropping the assumed dialect.

"I thought so. She was arrested on a false charge when she came out of the building. An officer in plain clothes took her away. I want you to wait here a few moments until I return, and then drive me to the nearest station house."

He hurried away without waiting for an answer.

Inside of his own office he summoned one of his own men aside and rapidly recounted what had happened.

"Find Connor," he added, "and tell him all I have told you. Tell him to get me all the particulars of what has happened, even if he has to queer himself over there to do it. I'm afraid he is queered anyhow. Somebody must have followed him when he came here to report, and while waiting outside for him saw Lady Kate go out. More than likely it was Rushton himself. Tell Connor that if he gets a move on him he can find out what I want to know before Rushton has had time to tell of his suspicions. I am going around to the station house, but I don't expect to get such information there."

Nor did he.

He was permitted to examine the blotter himself. There was no entry concerning such a case as he inquired about. No pickpocket—male or female—had been brought in that day. (He did not make use of her name in making his inquiries.) Every cop at the station house was profoundly ignorant of any such circumstances as he described.

The face of Julius was very grave when the chief returned to him outside.

"I've got to find her, sir, right away, somehow," he said helplessly.

"We *will* find her right away—*somehow*, Julius," was the quick reply. "There is one chance that I may learn where she has been taken within an hour or two. It is almost certain that they would not take her to headquarters, or to a near-by station house."

"I want to help, sir. I've *got* to help."

"You shall help. Take me back to my office, then return for me in two hours. I will have determined upon some course by that time."

"I won't come back, sir. I'll wait, or maybe I'll just drive around the streets and keep my eyes open, and if I happen to see that man Rushton get in my way I'll run over him with the car."

"Why? What do you know about Rushton?" the chief asked quickly.

"I know that he has made Miss Kitty every bit of trouble she's ever had, and I know that I saw him go up the street past me while I was waiting around the corner for her; and if she has been arrested, as you say, it is his doings, and he knows where she is to be found. And if I happen to see him, *he's got to tell me, sir*."

"No, Julius, not that. You would only betray the fact to him that you are her servant, and she doesn't wish him to know that. Do as I have directed, and leave the rest to me. We will find her."

CHAPTER XII

THE LITTLE DOOR

Exactly midnight.

The Night Wind paused in the doorway he had been seeking and looked up and down the street by which he had approached it. There was no person in sight. He turned, then, to look more closely at the building.

It presented every outward aspect of a warehouse. The windows were grimy, and—he assumed—cobwebbed, although it was much too dark just there for him to determine that. They were protected by heavy wire-screens that were almost as effective as bars might have been.

The door was a huge one, through the opening of which truck horses, three abreast, could have passed; but there was a very small door in the middle of it, faintly determinable, which, he assumed, was the one which would be opened for him from the inside at twelve-ten precisely, according to the directions that Tom Clancy had given him.

It was the night following his interview with the inspector and with Rushton; the night that followed upon the day of Katherine's disappearance. But he had, as yet, heard nothing of that.

He turned his back to the little door the better to be watchful for the approach of strangers along the street, and so did not hear it when it was opened—and then Tom Clancy's voice brought him sharply around again.

"Hello, Bing. Come in," was the greeting.

Harvard stepped through the narrow doorway into impenetrable blackness. He felt Tom's grasp upon his arm, and was led blindly forward through a thick wall of darkness until at last a faint glimmer of light could be seen.

It looked as if it were a mile away, but they came to it in another moment, after which they mounted some stairs, traversed another considerable distance (Tom carried the candle now that he had left waiting on the stairs), ascended to a third floor where they presently came to an iron ladder at the top of which there was an opening through which the stars could be seen.

There was a structure on the roof, square and roomy, once a combination of cupola and watch-tower, but now transformed into a place of residence.

The door stood invitingly open, a student-lamp with a green shade was on the center-table of the one room, there were rugs on the floor, a three-quarter bed in one corner, a couch in another, several comfortable chairs, two well-filled bookcases, and a genial air of comfort and hominess.

"Behold your future residence, Mr. Night Wind," Clancy exclaimed as he closed the door. There had not been a word passed between them since the first greetings at the street.

"You are to live here, Bing, until we catch that thief. Wait a minute, now, till I finish. I've got to get this off of my chest."

"Go on, then."

"There are four ways out of the building down on the ground floor, one on each of the four sides. One opens upon the street, as you know; the others give upon narrow alleyways, which in turn will take you to one of the two streets. Up there in the corner is a coil of knotted rope, and out on the cornices, yonder, and yonder"—he pointed in two directions—"are iron hooks, in case you should happen to want to take to the street from the roof. Right there, on the table, is a telephone. It is a private wire into Redhead's office, which nobody but himself and ourselves and the telephone company know about."

"Oh. So this place is his, eh?" Bingham asked.

"Yes. He calls it his think-shop. Whenever the world and worldly things get on his nerves he chucks the world and comes here; and he has put the place at your disposal as long as you may need it. It is better than the fly-by-night existence that you would otherwise have to lead, isn't it?"

"Decidedly. I'm very grateful. But where is he? You said he was to be here, Tom."

"He couldn't make it, Bing. Something else demanded his attention. He sent me word of it at the last moment. But he will be here before daylight, if possible."

"Where is he? What has happened?" Harvard asked suspiciously. Something about Clancy's manner warned him that there was a reason which concerned himself.

"I have got some bad news for you, Bing. The chief told me not to tell you about it till he got here, because he believed there would be no reason for telling it afterward. But I don't think it's right to withhold it."

"Well? Well? What is it?"

"Katherine has been arrested."

Harvard started to his feet, stood still and rigid for a moment, then succeeded in controlling himself and sat down slowly again.

"Tell me about it," he said with forced calm. "Every word of it; all that you know about it."

And so Clancy told him—everything that *he* knew at the time, and Harvard listened in utter silence.

At the end of the recital he was still silent for so long a time that Clancy twice raised his eyes expectantly, but wisely kept still, waiting for his friend to speak.

Then Harvard left his chair, went to the door and passed outside on the roof which covered a considerable area and was dipped toward the rear of the building just enough to allow for drainage; otherwise it was flat.

"I am not going to wait here for the arrival of your friend Redhead," he said to Tom when the latter followed him outside. "I am going to find Katherine."

"But how? Where will you go? How will you find her, Bing?"

91

"I will find her by seeking the men who are responsible for her arrest and compelling them to tell me where she is. Great Heaven, Tom, don't you understand what this move of theirs means? Why, it is even a worse frame-up than Rushton put over on me. Unless I get her out of their clutches, and do it at once, Katherine will be railroaded to prison on a false charge, and there won't be a ghost of a show for her. Don't you see it?"

"Yes; of course I do see it. But the chief—"

"The chief will do everything in his power, of course. Let him keep on doing it. If he succeeds in finding her and rescuing her before I do, so much the better. But I will tell you one thing, Tom. It is this: if those fellows keep up this sort of thing they will force me back again into the condition of mind I was in before I went away, and if that happens I will take the law into my own hands in a manner that won't be good for the several men who are responsible for this business."

"Be careful, Bing."

"Oh, I am cool enough. I haven't lost my temper, and I'm not going to. Take me down to the street and let me out. Then give me the key that will admit me here again when I wish to return."

"Tell me what you are going to do, Bing."

"I don't know—all that I shall do. But I will go, first, to Chester's house to see him. What I may do after that will depend largely upon Chester."

"He won't admit you. Katherine gave up your key to him, you know."

"I have another one. I had a duplicate made of that one long ago. I am going straight from here to Chester's house, and to his bedside. It is high time that I had a personal interview with him, anyhow. I will make him find out for me where they have taken Katherine."

"Do you think you can do that?"

"I will do it, Tom. You may tell the chief, as you call him, to telephone to me, here, at noon tomorrow. Give me his number, and in case I am not here, or able to get here in time I will telephone to him a little before twelve."

At the little door through the big one, which gave upon the street, Clancy put one hand on his friend's shoulder and said:

"I know there is no stopping you, Bing, so I won't try. But there is something more I wish to say to you before you go."

"Well?"

"In the interview that Katherine had with the chief she advanced some sort of a theory—he did not explain it to me so I cannot tell you what it was—which has got him going on an entirely new tack. He said, 'Clancy, that girl is a wonder. She has struck the key-note of the whole thing, I believe'; and that is all he would tell me. Think that over, Bing, while you are on your way to Chester's; that is, if you are going there."

"Oh, I am going there, Tom, right now!" Harvard replied as he stepped through the little doorway to the street.

CHAPTER XIII

PUTTING ONE OVER ON RUSHTON

Sterling Chester, the banker, awoke with a start. The glare of many electric lights in his room where he had been sleeping dazzled him; and then he half started to a sitting posture in the bed, but fell backward upon the pillows again with a cry of amazement and fright when the tall figure of a man stepped into view.

"Bingham! You?" he cried out, and yet his voice was raised but little.

"Yes. It is I, Mr. Chester," Harvard replied calmly. "Stay where you are. You need not leave your bed; and don't attempt to call for help or to give any sort of alarm. It would not avail."

"What—what are you going to do? Why are you here? Don't—please don't do anything that you will be sorry for, Bingham." The banker was beside himself with terror in the presence of this man who had been so grievously wronged.

"I did not come here to injure you in any way, Mr. Chester," Harvard replied slowly. "Do you know me so little that you fear I might do that?"

"How—how did you get in? She—that woman who came here one night and waited for me in the library—gave me the key that you had."

"I had two, sir. I gave her only one of them. And please do remember that '*that woman*' is my wife. She is Mrs.

94

Bingham Harvard, if you have occasion to refer to her again. It is on her account that I am here now."

"On her—on Mrs. Harvard's account, you say?" The banker was endeavoring with all his power to speak composedly; but he was horribly afraid; he did not know what this man might yet do to him. He feared to do or say anything which might try that temper of which he had seen more than one exhibition.

"Yes. Your friends whom you have taken to your bosom, whom you permitted and assisted to perpetrate the foul wrong against me, have turned their attention and their activities against my wife. Failing to 'get' me, they believe that they can reach me through her. She was arrested yesterday, in the early afternoon, and has been spirited away to one of the distant precincts of the city, I imagine. I have come here to ask *you* to find out for me now where they have taken her."

"I? *I*? My dear Bingham, how in the world can I do that?"

"I will tell you presently how you *must* do it, Mr. Chester. Rushton, your chosen coadjutor, instigated her arrest. She is charged with picking pockets. It is another one of his scoundrelly frame-ups. Whatever they found upon her was 'planted,' as they call it. She will not have a ghost of a chance to clear herself. Unless I interfere before she can be taken into some distant magistrate's court this morning a case will be made out against her; she will be arraigned, tried, convicted, sentenced—railroaded to prison before I can do a thing to prevent it."

Harvard hesitated in his speech for just a moment, and while he did so the banker gradually recovered his mental poise. He was still in fear of what Harvard might do if anything should occur to rouse that terrible temper; but—the banker had not seen Bingham Harvard in so long a time that the mere sight of him, whom he had loved so well as child and boy and man, gradually got the better of his fears.

Chester was conscious, in that moment, that he still loved Bingham Harvard; that still, to all intent and purpose, the man who stood beside his bed was the grown-up boy to whom he had given the affection and devotion of a father.

Yet he gave no sign of all this.

He felt less fear, more self-assurance as to the outcome of this mysterious midnight call. And as if in confirmation of that thought, Harvard spoke again, in a changed tone—in a voice that had in it something of the old thrill of respect, esteem, and love that he had always so freely bestowed upon his lifelong benefactor.

"Mr. Chester," he said, bending slightly forward, "cannot you understand why I am here? Don't you see that I *had* to come? Isn't there any of that old love for me left in your heart to bestow at this crucial moment? Don't answer me now. Listen to me, instead. She whom you know as Lady Kate is my wife. She is my world—my *all*. The machinations of Rushton, which began when he first succeeded in convincing you of my guilt, have grown and spread until they have reached out and seized upon her, my wife."

"I was desperate before, sir, when I saw my good name taken from me by the falseness of manufactured evidence— worse than all when I realized that the act had stolen away your love for me; for I will not believe that it was killed."

He straightened himself and took a step farther away from the bedside.

"I know that it was not destroyed, sir. I know now, better than you know it yourself, that in your inmost heart there still glows that father-love which you gave so freely to me through so many years of my life."

"Listen, Mr. Chester—listen, gov'nor, for that is what I used to call you, and what you liked to have me call you—it is to that father-love that you had for me that I appeal now. Won't you help me, sir? But even if you are reluctant to help *me*, won't you help *her* in this extremity?"

"But how, Bingham? I do not understand you at all. How can I be of help?" the banker demanded, with just a little show of petulance. The fear within him was nearly gone by that time, and yet there was a touch of it left, too. Harvard had touched the right cord of memory when he appealed to the father-love. "In what way can I be of assistance? I confess that I do not see how that can be."

"Mr. Chester—gov'nor—you place honesty of purpose and of conduct above all things else, I know. Justice, impartially meted out to all, is your creed. I know that, too. Then, sir—my more than friend in the past—no matter how you may regard me, I ask you in the name of your love of honesty to be just to Katherine."

"Well, well, well, Bingham, what is it that you wish me to do? But, before you tell me that, try to remember that you have no right to be here in my bedroom now. In the name of that justice you talk about I should, by rights, go straight to the telephone, summon the police, and turn you over to—"

Harvard raised a hand in warning. The banker stopped with the sentence unfinished.

"Wait," Harvard said. "I had to come here—to the city first; to you now. If I had followed my own inclinations I would have taken Katherine away to the farthest corner of the world, to start life all over again. I would never have returned here, even to establish my innocence, if *she* had not insisted upon it, if she had not made me do it."

"I *had* to come. My birthright, mysterious and unknown though it is, in so far as my parentage is concerned—my birthright is honesty. That birthright I must not, will not, lose. Whoever gave it to me does not matter; it is none the less my own."

"And I have not come to you to-night to threaten you or to harm you in any way. God forbid. Whatever happened, whatever may yet happen, I love you as a son should love his own father. If you will not help me to do justice to myself, then help me to do justice to another. Can you refuse such a plea as that, sir?"

"But how? How? What do you wish me to do? You have not told me that."

"I have told you Katherine is even now in the power of that scoundrel, Rodney Rushton. I have told you that he has framed up a charge against her of picking pockets. I have told you that in order to make that charge good they have probably not hesitated to 'plant' articles upon her to convict

97

her. I have told you that they have spirited her away to some station-house or jail where I cannot hope to find her in time to save her from this terrible danger. I have told you that Rushton has done this, and that therefore Rushton knows where she is hidden. I want you to make—no, induce is the word—I want you to *induce* Lieutenant Rushton to tell you where she is."

"My dear Bingham"—the banker nearly forgot himself for the moment—"I do not know where Lieutenant Rushton may be now. I cannot dress and go to him at such an hour; and if I did so, he would refuse to give me the information you want."

"I know where Rushton may be found right now."

"But—"

"And there is the telephone. You have only to throw your bath-robe around you and to go down with me to the library."

"To telephone to him? To telephone to Lieutenant Rushton at this hour of the night?"

"Yes. He is barely more than arrived home. More than likely he will not yet have gone to bed. He will answer the telephone. And if you couch your request in the right words and manner he will tell you."

"But I do not know what to say to him," Chester protested, nevertheless rising from the bed and reaching for an elaborately quilted dressing-gown—and by that act Bingham Harvard knew that he had won, although he was not certain whether it was through love or fear that he had done so.

"You will say," said Harvard, speaking rapidly and finding the banker's slippers for him as he did so, "that you have only just now learned of the arrest of Lady Kate. You will say that your information came through Tom Clancy, and that will be the truth, for I got the news from him. Are you listening, sir?"

"Yes, yes. Go on."

"If he should ask you how Clancy came to know about it, say—truthfully—that he did not tell you that. Then, Mr. Chester—and here is the point!—you must congratulate Rushton upon the arrest; you must make him think that you

98

approve of it. You must give him to understand that you consider it the best move he has made yet. You must rub him
metaphorically down the back for all of it. Do you understand?"

"Yes. But I cannot—"

"Mr. Chester, you *must*. There are no two ways about it.
You *must*. And there is more."

"Well? Well?"

"You must tell Rushton that you wish to see Lady Kate
the first thing in the morning. You must make Rushton think
that you believe you can induce her to betray my hiding-
place. Remind him of the fact that she came here to your
home one night and practically forced her way inside. Suggest to him that you will frighten her into telling you what
you wish to know about me by holding over her the threat of
another indictment for burglary. You can do it and you must
do it, Mr. Chester. Come. You are ready. Let us go down."

They did not speak again until they were in the library
and the telephone was before them. But the banker's
thoughts had evidently been upon Harvard's last utterances.

"And then?" he asked. "What then—if he does tell me
where she is now?"

"Then, sir, you must dress yourself and go with me to
find her."

"But—at this hour of the night, and when I do not know
where it may be—"

"Listen once again, sir. I have not ceased to love you.
Even at this moment my filial impulses toward you are uppermost. And yet *you must do what I ask*. It hurts me more
than I can say to seem to threaten—but you *must*. My life,
Katherine's, our whole future and your contented future, too,
sir—depend upon it, and I would be worse than a weakling if
I did not force you to it. Would I not? You know that I
would."

The banker took another step toward the telephone, and
halted again.

"Go ahead, sir." Harvard said. "Take your seat at the
telephone. I will hold the receiver so that we both may hear
what is said. When necessary I will prompt you in what to

say. Have no fear. All will be well. It will not be as difficult
as you think. You will find that he will fall into the trap.
Come, sir; you must do it; and you know that you *can* and
will do it."

Seated at the telephone, before he raised the receiver
from the hook, Chester, more disturbed than he had ever
been in his life before, asked once again:

"Suppose—he—won't—tell me what I want to know,
Bingham?"

"He must tell you. You must make him do it somehow.
For I tell you plainly, Mr. Chester, if this scheme of theirs is
carried out I shall hold you as responsible as the others; and I
will, with these two hands of mine, kill every man who has
been instrumental in bringing disgrace upon my wife. That is
the last word, sir. Remember that you will not be talking half
so much to save *her* as to save *yourself*."

There was an intensity in that last utterance of Bingham
Harvard's that the banker could not mistake.

Harvard lifted the receiver from the hook and asked for
the number; and after a wait of several moments the answer
came.

Harvard was holding the receiver so that both could hear
it. His left cheek was in touch with Chester's left one as he
faced away from the transmitter, while Chester's lips were
close to it.

"Hello, there!" they heard the voice of Rushton exclaim
angrily. "What's the matter with you fellows? Can't you ever
let a fellow sleep?"

"This—this is Mr. Chester speaking—Chester, of the
Centropolis Bank, lieutenant," the banker managed to announce tremblingly. "I—I felt that I had to call you up at
once, on account of some news I have just heard—"

"Some splendid news," Harvard breathed softly.

"Some really splendid news, lieutenant," the banker
added.

"Oh! It's you, is it, Chester?" Rushton growled from the
other end. "What's the matter with you? Your voice sounds
as if you were scared to death."

"You are eager," the Night Wind breathed as softly as before.

"I am only eager—extremely eager, lieutenant. I have just heard, through Clancy, of the—er—arrest of—er—that woman yesterday afternoon. That was a masterly stroke, lieutenant. I—er—"

"You must see her," Harvard prompted.

"—must see her at once, you know, so I want you to tell me where she is, and—"

"You must see her! What for?" Rushton demanded.

"Felonious entrance," Harvard prompted in a whisper.

"Why, don't you see?" Chester went on, remembering his instructions. "She came here to my house one night and forced her way inside. Couldn't that be construed into an attempted burglary? And couldn't I make an additional charge against her when she is arraigned in the morning?"

"Say, Chester," Rushton replied, "I didn't think you had it in you. You're wakin' up, you are. Now, that ain't a bad idea at all. But what do you want to see her about? You don't have to do no talkin' to her first in order to make that charge against her."

"Induce her to betray me," Harvard whispered quickly.

"Why—er—you see, lieutenant, I had an idea about that," the banker continued slowly, choosing his words with care, for he was in dread lest he should offend the man whose left cheek he could feel touching his own. "You see—er—that the charge I shall make against her is a felony. It is quite—er—a serious matter, is it not?"

"Betcher life it is, Chester."

"And—er—she will be correspondingly dismayed by it, I assume; especially coming as it will in addition to the other one."

"Say, Chester, I'm gittin' to be real proud of you!" Rushton exclaimed over the wire.

"Use it as a lever—against me," Harvard prompted in a whisper.

"And—ahem—it has occurred to me, Rushton," the banker continued, "that it may be used as a sort of a cudgel over her head, don't you see, to induce her to tell us some-thing about Harvard, and—er—er—"

"If you had the power to offer her immunity," Harvard whispered.

"Go on, Chester," Rushton demanded impatiently.

"And—well, if I had the power—from you, you know—to offer her immunity; to let her go free, provided she would tell me something about Harvard—why—er—don't you see, Rushton? She is only a woman, after all; and it seems to me that the idea *might* work."

"You would have to see her alone—go there where she is alone," Harvard prompted.

"I think it's a cinch of an idea, Chester," Rushton said. "I'll take you over there the first thing in the—"

"No, no, no, Rushton; that would not do at all. I must go to her alone. She must have no suspicion whatever that you have any knowledge of what I am doing. It would make her suspicious and might spoil everything."

"I guess that's right, too. You're wakin' up, Chester. But how'll she think you got onto the fact of her arrest at all—eh?"

"Why, I'll tell her the truth; that I heard it through Clancy."

"Bully! That'll be an additional lever, at that. What time will you go to see her if I tell you where to find her? You'll have to get there early, you know."

"At seven," Harvard prompted; and Chester repeated the two words over the wire.

"All right. I'll fix it for you," Rushton replied. "I'll tele-phone out there right now. And I'll be there myself along about a quarter past or half past seven, after you have gone inside to talk to her. You will find Lady Kate at the—" And here Rushton gave a clear description of the locality of the place where Katherine was confined and how the banker was to get there by the most direct route; and he added many cau-tions and much advice regarding Chester's methods of pro-cedure when he should see her.

"Say good-by and hang up quickly," Harvard ordered; and the banker obeyed.

102

"And now, Mr. Chester, get into your clothes and be ready to start at once," Harvard directed then. "While you are doing that I will telephone to the garage and order your car, for I will need it badly as soon as we get Katherine. Hurry, now, for there isn't any time to waste."

Thirty minutes later, at exactly two o'clock in the morning, they started.

CHAPTER XIV

INTO JAIL—AND OUT

The new county jail in Queens had not been built when this happened. The old one, since replaced, needs no comment here. Nor were the local officials celebrated for perspicacity or astuteness.

When the banker, accompanied by the Night Wind, arrived at the jail the latter knew that he ran a considerable risk of being recognized, but he counted upon the very boldness of his act to offset that in a great degree; and for the rest, he determined to make constant use of his handkerchief and to keep his head turned away as much as possible while they were passing the guard.

Also, he figured that at that hour in the morning— between three and four o'clock—the turnkey's eyes would be heavy with sleep, and that doubtless his mental capacities would be proportionately stupefied.

Harvard had planned exactly what he would do once they were inside the prison and the door of Katherine's cell had been unlocked—or in case the turnkey should decline to unlock it, as he would be more than apt to do. In furtherance of those plans the Night Wind had provided himself with some stout cord and two of the banker's towels before they started.

There was some difficulty in arousing the guard, who was supposed to be wide awake; but he came to the door presently and glared at Chester a moment before he demanded gruffly:

"Well, what do *you* want?"

"I am Mr. Chester, of the Centropolis Bank," was the prompt and pompous reply, for the banker was quite himself by that time. "No doubt Lieutenant Rushton has already telephoned to you regarding me. I am to be admitted at once—at once, do you understand?—to see the woman who is detained here under the name of Kate Maxwell, alias Lady Kate." Harvard had prompted him exactly what to say at the start.

"Huh!" the turnkey replied. "You ain't due here till seven o'clock, and there wasn't anything said about two of you. You were to come alone."

"Those are mere details, Mr. Turnkey. If you have any doubts about the matter, you can call up Lieutenant Rushton—although I don't think he would thank you for doing it after he has given you explicit orders."

"More'n likely she's undressed and in bed," the turnkey replied, as he admitted them grumblingly.

"In that case she will have to dress again," Chester announced, as he brushed his way inside. It would seem, indeed, as if he was suddenly imbued with something of the spirit of the adventure. But—he did not *fear* the turnkey, while the man who clung so closely beside him and half a pace to the rear inspired him with constant terror lest he should do some act which would provoke Bingham Harvard's wrath.

Katherine's cell was the largest and best one in the women's part of the prison. A screen had been pulled down over the barred doorway, but, nevertheless, Katherine had removed none of her clothing. Nor was she asleep—which is not strange, under the circumstances.

"Two gents to see you, Kate," the turnkey announced with maddening familiarity. Harvard could have choked him then—as he meant to do presently.

"Unlock that door and let her step outside," he commanded, speaking for the first time and careless now whether the turnkey should recognize him or not. But he did want

Katherine to hear his voice, and so to be prepared for what should follow.

He heard her gasp when he did speak. Then she came forward quickly and grasped the bars of the heavy door as she peered out at them. Her astonishment then was profound.

"Why, Mr. Chester—" she exclaimed, and stopped, fearful lest she should say too much.

The turnkey had paid no attention to Harvard's order. Instead, he was studying the Night Wind's face, as if it were faintly suggestive of something that he ought to remember; and Harvard repeated:

"Unlock the door, turnkey."

"Who told you to give orders in this place, mister?" the turnkey demanded with a leer. "I guess you can talk through them all right, and Lieutenant Rushton didn't say nothin' about unlockin' no doors. You'll have to do your—"

His speech ended in a gasp and a gurgle.

Harvard's left hand had seized him by the throat and effectually shut off further utterance. Harvard's right hand forced a towel between his jaws as they fell open because of the choking he was receiving; and one of Harvard's feet tripped him, and he was forced backward and down upon the flagged flooring, with one of Harvard's knees upon his chest and with that merciless hand still clutching at his throat.

He struggled mightily, of course, flaying with his arms, and kicking out with his legs and feet; and he made ineffectual guttural noises as he attempted to cry out for help.

But the struggles soon became spasmodic and almost ceased.

He was very nearly unconscious before Harvard was able to make use of both hands to knot the twisted towel behind the turnkey's head, thus making the gag effectual; and after that it required only a moment to use the cord, and to bind his ankles together and to tie his wrists behind his back.

The turnkey's keys had been in his grasp when he was attacked. Harvard picked them up where they had fallen to the floor and then turned his eyes for an instant upon the banker.

Chester was shaking as if with a palsy. His teeth were chattering and he was mumbling incoherently:

"Don't kill him, Bingham! For God's sake, don't kill him!"

"Shut up!" Harvard ordered peremptorily.

Then he sprang to the cell door, unlocked it, and threw it open, and in another instant Lady Kate was in his arms.

But not for long.

He held her so for a moment, then thrust her aside and turned his attention to the work in hand; and in regard to that, also, he had decided while on the way over exactly what he would do.

He lifted the burly form of the turnkey from the floor and bore him inside of the cell, dropping him upon the cot that was there; and then he turned and spoke sharply to the banker.

"Come here, Chester," he said; and the banker passed inside of the cell.

No sooner had he entered it than Harvard stepped quickly outside, closing the door after him and locking it; and while that was being done, Chester looked on dumbly and apparently without understanding of the fact that it was Harvard's intention to leave him there.

But Katherine understood, and she put one hand upon her husband's arm in protest.

"Is it necessary, Bingham?" she asked softly.

"Yes," he replied shortly. "It will be a lesson to him. He will find out something of what it means to an innocent man to be locked in a cell; and he will have time to do some real thinking under circumstances that may lead him to think straight."

Then he turned to Chester and spoke to him through the bars.

"I am going to leave you here, Mr. Chester," he said calmly. "I do it because I believe it will be good for you. You won't be locked up more than two or three hours, at the most. Somebody will be here by that time. And I don't think they will dare to do anything to you for assisting in the escape of a prisoner—because I believe that as yet there has

107

been no official record made of that prisoner. And, anyhow, it will be best for you to be found here. You can lay it all to me—to the Night Wind," he added coldly.

"Oh, Bingham! Please—"

But Harvard had already grasped Katherine by the arm and was leading her away along the corridor; and because Katherine's cell had been located in an isolated part of the women's section of the prison, as well as on account of the quiet with which the Night Wind had accomplished the coup, they passed outside of the jail without any sort of an alarm being given, unlocking and relocking the several doors they were obliged to pass with the guard's keys.

Harvard dropped them upon the steps outside the building and led his wife to the waiting limousine.

"Mr. Chester will remain here for several hours," he told the chauffeur, who was new in the employ of the banker, and therefore did not know Bingham Harvard. "You are to drive us directly to New York. When you have crossed the bridge I will direct you where to go."

Inside the security of the closed car Katherine threw herself into Bing Harvard's arms and wept—for the first time since the indignity of the arrest, with its false charge, was put upon her. But she recovered very soon and raised a pair of smiling eyes to her husband's face.

"How did you do it?" she asked earnestly.

"Oh, Chester and I just did it; that's all, dear," he replied. "The old gentleman was almost in a state of collapse from abject terror all the time he was with me. I think he was actually relieved to be left in that cell—only I don't think he will enjoy his company if he should venture to remove that turnkey's gag and bonds;" and Harvard chuckled. He was happier at that moment than he had been in a long time.

"Did you ride over here together?" she asked. "And did you try to reason with him, to convince him that you are innocent? He would listen to you and believe you, would he not, dear?"

"No, girlie. We came over together, of course, but the ride was taken in utter silence. Chester was too frightened to talk, and I wanted to think. And I knew how utterly useless it would be to reason with him."

It was very nearly daylight by the time they had crossed Queensboro Bridge, where they were confronted by the problem of where they should go for concealment during the day.

Harvard told Katherine of the retreat on top of the warehouse, to which he held the key, and suggested that they might go there, but she shook her head with emphasis.

"No, dear," she said; "and we must part here. We must not be together, and you must not know where to find me— for I know that if you could do that you would not remain away; and we would both be in constant danger. Remember, you promised me that, Bingham."

"Yes. I know."

"And now we are both outlaws for the time being. And I have my plans, which I am determined to carry out to the end. Besides, I have a safe retreat to go to. And I will find Julius there, awaiting me, I know. Oh, Bingham, isn't it wonderful that you got me out of that terrible place so quickly? Tell the man to drive us to Columbus Circle. I will get down there and take a car. And you—"

"I'll get down, too, and put you on the car. Then—"

"No; you must not."

"—and then I will go to that warehouse over on the East Side."

"Please, Bingham, let me get down alone. See; I have a veil to cover my face, and it is almost light now. I will be perfectly safe. And you have the man drive you to a place somewhere near that warehouse."

There was no resisting her when she pleaded with him like that. With all his great strength of muscle and will, Bingham Harvard was as putty in the hands of Lady Kate.

CHAPTER XV

FRIENDS IN NEED

The Night Wind made use of Chester's car to take him only a part of the distance to his destination, and when he dismissed it he told the chauffeur:

"You may drive back now to that jail in Queens. Wait in front of the door until Mr. Chester comes out. That is all."

He watched it until it disappeared around a corner, then turned abruptly to hasten to the safe refuge for the day on the roof of the old warehouse, and in turning came face to face with a man between whom and himself the recognition was mutual and instant.

"Harvard, by thunder!" the other man exclaimed.

"Hello, Mordaunt!" Bing greeted, and stopped in his tracks.

Of two men whom he had determined to see at the earliest possible moment this man was one—Benton Mordaunt; one of the assistant paying-tellers who had been inside the cage with him that day when the money had so mysteriously disappeared. They had discussed the subject of the lost packages of bills many times immediately after the incident occurred, but they had never seen each other since the framed-up charge was made against Bingham Harvard.

"By Jove, I'm glad to see you, Bing!" Mordaunt said with genuine feeling, reaching out his hand, which Harvard did not hesitate to accept. "Say, you're a crackajack, all right! You didn't do a thing to that bunch of cops that was

110

trying to run you in, did you? But isn't it a little risky for you to be gallivanting around town like this?"

"I suppose so, Ben," Harvard smiled. "The fact is I was just hunting cover."

"Then come around to the house with me. I've moved since I saw you; thought I'd like it better farther down-town. The wife will be tickled to death to see you, Bing. You know neither of us ever took any stock in all that rot about your taking that cash. I live just around the next corner; and you're just in time for breakfast. Come along."

Harvard hesitated, then accepted the invitation, and the two started off together, side by side.

"What got you out of bed so early?" he asked Mordaunt.

"Oh, I have formed the habit of turning out for a long walk before breakfast. It is good for me, too. I get through the day a heap better since I began it."

"Who is teller, now, Ben—you or Atkinson? Which one of you took my place?"

"Atkinson. I kind-a thought I'd land it, but he got around the old man somehow, and so pulled it off."

"Ben, who got those packages of bills? Who stole that money?"

"Search me, Bing. To me it is just as great a mystery as ever. There is only just one thing about that whole business that I'm certain about, and there are a lot more down at the bank just like me."

"What is that?"

"That Bingham Harvard did *not* do it."

"Do you mean that, Ben? And do some of the others agree with you in that opinion?"

"Some of them! There aren't half a dozen employees in the whole place, counting old Chet himself, who have ever thought for a moment that you were guilty. It is a sore subject with most of them, too. It isn't safe to suggest to any of them that you did it."

"Ben, that is the best news I have heard in a long time. Is this your home?"

"Yes. Come along inside. Cora will be just as glad to see you as I am; you can bank on that."

111

"Wait just a moment here at the bottom of the steps. I want to ask two or three questions first."

"Go ahead, then."

"Who are the fellows down there who believe me guilty? Is Jim Atkinson one of them?"

"Well—er—he *says* he isn't. He swears that he doesn't believe you did the act, but I think he is willing to be convinced that you did. Honestly, at heart, I believe he does think so."

Harvard nodded. "Who are the others?" he asked.

"Well, the big watchman outside the screens doesn't make any bones of laying it to you. I'd a punched his jaw for him one day if he wasn't so infernally big, and if I hadn't known that I'd lose my job if I did do it."

"Don't punch anybody's jaw on my account, Ben," Harvard said, smiling. "Tell me the names of the others who believe that I am the guilty man."

"Oh, what's the use? They don't admit it openly; the sentiment there is too strong in your favor for that. They only look it, and think it; but it's easy enough to read them."

"Of course. Who are they? I want to know; and I have got a good reason for wanting to know."

"I won't tell you another word until you are inside the house, Bing. Look yonder, up the street. There is a cop coming this way now. If he should happen to spot you—well, we'd both be in trouble, I reckon. Eh?"

He ran up the steps, and Harvard followed, perforce; but inside the vestibule he seized his friend's arm before the latter could open the door; and he said:

"I had forgotten for the moment the risk that you run in taking me into your home, old fellow. It won't do, you know. Chester would fire you in a minute if he ever heard of it; and that cop may have recognized me even at that distance."

"Tut, tut, and piffle, and fudge, Bing Harvard!" Mordaunt replied, and threw the door ajar. Then, as soon as it was closed again he called loudly for his wife to come down quickly and find out whom he had brought back to breakfast with him.

"Those names, quick, Ben!" Harvard insisted. "You can mention them before your wife gets here; and I *must* know them, provided you are reasonably certain that you are right concerning their attitude."

"Lacey, the note-teller, and Powell, Seixas, and Quinn, bookkeepers." Mordaunt replied rapidly. "Then there is one more. He is non-committal, and doesn't say much, but he is one of that bunch if I am any judge. That's Lucius Graff, the assistant receiving teller. Here she is. Look, Cora! See who I have brought home with me? Do you know him?"

"Why, Bing-ham—Har-vard! Oh! I am *so* glad to see you! So *very* glad. I believe I'm going to cry." And, indeed, there were very palpable tears in the young woman's eyes.

It was, in fact, as much as Harvard could do to keep back his own at this wholly unexpected sympathy and confidence. And there was no mistaking the genuineness of it. He began to realize that the world was not wholly bad and mistrustful, after all.

Breakfast tasted particularly good to Bingham Harvard that morning. He had not felt quite so normal since the awful cataclysm had so shaken the very foundations of his being.

And the one subject under consideration throughout the meal was the lost packages of bills with the theft of which Harvard had been charged.

"Ben and I have thought about it and talked about it ever since it happened," Mrs. Mordaunt said as they left the table. "And we can't agree about it, either; so, whether he likes it or not, I am going to tell you what we each think—that is, if you want to hear our opinions."

"Certainly I do, Mrs. Mordaunt," Harvard replied eagerly. "And for some reason I believe that I would rather have your judgment of the matter than Ben's."

"Now, look here, Cora," her husband started to remonstrate; but she made a funny little face at him, so that he laughed and subsided.

"Ben thinks that Jim Atkinson could tell a lot about the mystery if he chose to do so," she went on, speaking with great seriousness. "But I don't. From what little I have seen of him I should say he is more fool than knave; but maybe

I'm wrong, at that. I don't mean to say that Ben actually thinks that Atkinson took it," she continued hastily; "but—well—it's pretty close to that, when all is said."

"What is your own opinion, Mrs. Mordaunt? Really, I would like to hear it."

"I haven't got a decided opinion; only a general one."

"All the better. We will weed it out by the process of elimination."

"Well, there are a number of the employees down at the bank who either believe that you are guilty or who are willing to believe it. If *I* was a detective *I* would look for the guilty person among *that* lot. And it wouldn't surprise *me* if every one of them had a hand in it, or knows something about it now. The idea that anybody in his right senses could believe that *you* were the guilty man, Bingham Harvard! That very fact speaks a lot against the character of any man who thought it. So, there!"

"You have got a champion in Cora, all right, Bing," Mordaunt said, laughing. "What do you think about her opinion—and mine?"

"I don't know, Ben. I haven't decided yet. But they have offered a suggestion which I shall follow."

"What is that?"

"You have mentioned five names to me—of employees at the bank who are satisfied of my guilt; or, at least, who are not convinced of my innocence."

"Seven, Bing, if you include Atkinson and the watchman—the special officer, outside the screen."

"Six, then—Atkinson, Lacey, Powell, Seixas, Quinn, and Graff. Lon Badger, the watch, hardly counts. He never goes inside of the screen, and he is too big to get into the paying teller's cage unless there was a special door made for him."

"All the same, Bing, he is the most outspoken of the whole bunch."

"That is because he is merely stupid and likes to hear himself express an opinion. Men of his caliber don't often have an opportunity to express one, you know."

"I suppose so. But what is that suggestion you spoke about?"

"This—I am going to seek an interview with each and every one of them, from Atkinson, all the way down the list. I am going to talk with each one, straight from the shoulder, and form my own judgment about them, one by one."

"Look here, Bing. Have you thought about the risk you will run in doing that?"

"No; and I shall not think about it. I will merely do it."

"There isn't one in the whole bunch who wouldn't give you dead away in a holy minute if you gave him half a chance."

"I know that, and I shall be prepared for it—and govern myself accordingly. And now, Mrs. Mordaunt, I must be going. I have remained too long as it is. As a matter of fact I really should not have consented to come here at all. It was putting you both to needless risk. But—the temptation was great. I haven't many friends now."

"More than you think, Mr. Harvard," she replied. "And you must not leave the house in the daytime. You will be seen and recognized. Make yourself comfortable here, for the day; and tonight, when it is dark—My goodness, who do you suppose that is, Ben?"

The front door bell had been rung sharply three times. Mordaunt leaped to his feet before his wife's question was fairly out.

"I'll soon know," he announced; and then, as he left the room, he added, for Harvard's information: "I've got an arrangement of mirrors in the window on the second floor which enables me to see who is at the door when the bell rings."

He was gone only two or three moments, and returned down the stairs, taking two steps at a time, so great was his haste, for the doorbell had been rung twice more while he was gone.

"Bing!" he exclaimed excitedly, "there are two cops in uniform on the front step, and there is another chap with them who looks as if he might be a detective in plain clothes. What do you know about that? What shall we do? Eh? Cora,

115

you suggest something, can't you? I'll bet a hundred to one that the cop we saw on the street knew you. Or—say? I know what's done it. I have been followed everywhere I have gone lately, and I plumb forgot all about it when I met you. Cora, why in the world don't you suggest something? It looks to me as if Bing is up against it, just about now!"

CHAPTER XVI

THE NIGHT WIND'S
INCREDIBLE SWIFTNESS

The Night Wind's decision was instantly taken.

Whatever might happen he could not sacrifice his friends. They should be protected, at all hazards, and he thought he saw a way to accomplish it.

They were in that room, which in an ordinary city house of the old style is called the "back parlor," and there was a large closet, the door of which was standing partly ajar. Harvard could see that the closet was spacious and roomy. Moreover, the key was in the lock of the door.

"Quick!" he said. "Get inside of that closet—both of you;" and he seized upon them, each by an arm, and forced them through the doorway which he kicked wider with one swing of his foot—and he accomplished it before either of them had the least idea of his intention. "I'm going to lock you both in there," he added. "The cops will let you out, if you pound loud enough. It's up to you to make them think that you tried to send a telephone message to betray me."

Then he closed the door with a bang and turned the key.

The telephone was fastened against the wall beside the door, and he seized upon it and tore it from its fastenings.

Surely, he thought, with all that evidence, the police could not but be of the opinion that the Night Wind had discovered that he was being betrayed and had acted with his customary whirlwind energy.

The doorbell was still pealing its summonses, and more insistently than ever, and without hesitation he hurried through the hall toward it.

"There are three of them out there," was his thought. "Surely I must be able to get past them. The only trouble is that I will probably have to hurt somebody."

The men outside were adding loud rappings to their bell ringing by that time, and Harvard had not a doubt that in another moment one of them would thrust his stick through the glass of the door, so that he might reach inside and open it.

But he did not give them an opportunity to do that. Instead, he seized the knob of the door and opened it with a jerk, stepping nimbly aside behind the other half of the door as he did so.

One of the men rushed inside, and Harvard thrust out a foot and tripped him, so that he plunged headlong to the floor, half the length of the hall.

The second man—the one in plain clothes—was close behind the first, but the fate of his companion made him pull himself up when he was just in the act of crossing the threshold.

But Harvard's right hand shot out and seized the detective by the collar, and a mighty jerk forward, given with a whirling motion, sent him sprawling after the first one who was already attempting to get upon his feet. They collided and went to the floor together, and very much mixed as to just how it happened.

The third man—another in uniform—was just inside the vestibule.

He was in the act of rushing forward also, but managed to catch himself in time; and he attempted to reach for his police whistle and his revolver at the same time. He had found the former and was lifting it toward his lips when the Night Wind seized him, pulled him through the doorway, and then actually lifted him off of his feet and threw him bodily at the other two, who were rapidly getting up again.

Harvard did not wait to see what came of that effort.

He sprang outside and pulled the door shut after him, and put one hand upon the iron balustrade to vault it into the areaway, well knowing that bullets would now be sent whizzing after him, since there was no longer any danger of the policemen shooting one of their own number.

There was the sound of a shot from inside the house, followed by the tinkle of breaking glass just as he grasped the iron rail over the steps; and at the same instant a woman, evidently a servant, rushed out upon the front steps from the house adjoining.

There were brownstone ledges before the parlor windows of that next house, and, instead of jumping into the area, Harvard sprang upon one of them, and from that to the next one, and then over the rail to the top of the steps where the servant girl had come to a halt, paralyzed with fright—for two more shots followed the first one, even while the Night Wind crossed over the two ledges to the steps of the adjoining house.

"I am not going to harm you," he said as he grasped her by both of her arms and forced her back again through the open doorway through which she had appeared; and he added, by way of warning: "Unless you make a noise."

He closed the door and waited, still retaining his hold upon the girl.

Just what happened outside after that he could only conjecture, but this is what actually occurred: the two policemen and the plain clothes man followed their bullets into the street with all the speed they could summon.

They dashed from the house and down the steps, glancing up and down the street as they did so in a vain search for a sign of the fugitive. But the street was deserted, save for a few who had heard the shots and had rushed to their doors or windows to discover what was happening—and the Night Wind had moved so quickly, and so soon after the sound of the first shot, that not one of these had seen him cross over the window ledges and enter the house adjoining.

The street corner was quite near.

It seemed impossible to the policemen that the Night Wind could have reached it in that short interval, but nevertheless there was no other way to account for his complete disappearance; and they ran to it and looked each way along the avenue, and questioned persons who were near enough to be questioned. But not a soul had seen a sign of any man running away.

They looked into each other's faces then rather sheepishly. One of them felt of himself tentatively, as if to be assured that none of his bones was broken. Then they shook their heads and returned to the house where Benton Mordaunt made his home.

Once inside of it, they went through the hall into the back parlor—and discovered the wrecked telephone; and then, from behind the closet door beside it they heard the voices of a man and a woman calling for help, and pounding and kicking against the door.

The key was in the lock, and one of the cops turned it and released the two prisoners—and Mordaunt and his wife came forth in a pitiable plight, considering how immaculately and carefully both had been attired when Harvard thrust them so gently inside of their temporary prison.

Mordaunt's collar had been literally torn away from his neck, his hair was rumpled and disheveled (he had done it all himself, of course, during those few moments of waiting—as he had also performed much the same service for his wife); Mrs. Mordaunt's abundant hair was down her back, and she managed to assume a countenance that was thoroughly terrorized.

"What happened here, Mordaunt?" the plain clothes man demanded. "You may as well tell the truth now, 'cause I know part of it already. I've been trailing you for some time, and I suspected that that guy was the Night Wind when I saw you stop and shake hands with him. I wasn't sure—then. But I took a chance, and pulled these two officers along with me to make sure. Now, what happened? Give it to me straight."

"I should think you could tell what has happened without my explaining," Mordaunt retorted with assumed anger. "I guess it was pretty near to being the same thing that happened to you fellows, to judge by the looks of you."

"Cut out the flourishes, Mordaunt. I want to know why you brought that human cyclone home with you the way you did."

120

"Maybe that will answer your question," Mordaunt replied, pointing at the wrecked telephone. "When I left him down in the basement with my wife and came up here to try to use the telephone to get headquarters—Aw, what's the use? Can't you see what happened? Doesn't the condition of that telephone tell you? Look at *me*! Look at my wife. *What happened*? I've been in an earthquake and a house fell on me; that's what happened. Say, why didn't you fellows get him? You were three to one—and he had to get past you, didn't he?"

Then it was that Mrs. Mordaunt staggered, caught hold of a chair back, and called faintly for water. It was quite evident to her that the ruse had worked, and she thought it best to cap the climax with a partial fainting spell.

In the mean time the Night Wind was still standing just inside the closed door of the adjoining house, retaining his hold upon the servant girl's arm. But he questioned her in a kindly voice—and Bingham Harvard could be extremely gentle and persuasive when he chose to exert himself to that end.

"You must not be frightened, really," he told her reassuringly. "I wouldn't harm you for the world; and I am not a robber, nor a thief, nor a bad man at all. Look up at me. Do I look like a desperate character?"

"N-no, sir," she replied falteringly.

"Those men were after me because they thought I had done something that I did not do at all. You have heard of such things, haven't you?"

"Yes, sir."

"Well, that is the case now. I only want to stand here until they go away, and then I will go, too; and—let me see— here is a five-dollar bill for you, for letting me do it. Now shall we be good friends?"

"Please, sir. Yes, sir; and thank you very much. I don't believe you are bad. You don't look bad at all. But, you see, sir, I was all alone in the house. Mr. and Mrs. Tucker went away at daylight this morning to Trenton to see their son, who is sick; and I got awfully scared when I kept hearing that bell ringing next door the way it did. And then when they began to pound and kick against the door, as well as ring, I couldn't stand it any longer, so I rushed out. And then you grabbed me, and—"

"Yes, yes. I understand," Harvard interrupted her. He discovered that she had a tongue, after all. "If one of those policemen should ring the bell at this house, and I should permit you to go to the door to answer it, what would you say to him if he asked you if you had seen me?"

"I'd tell him that I don't know anything at all about you; and no more I do—except that I'd take my oath that you're a gentleman."

"Well, I like your face, too, and I am going to prove it by trusting you. I want you to go outside and stand on the steps so you can tell me when those men go away from the next house. And leave the door open, so I can see you all the time. I don't think they will ask you any questions when they see you standing there, with the door open behind you."

And so it proved when, a little later, the officers came from Mordaunt's house. The Night Wind had made another of his miraculous escapes, due to his incredible swiftness of motion and his superhuman strength; and they were thoroughly crestfallen. But they knew that they would have to make a report of it, because the two uniformed men had been called off of their beats by the plain clothes man; one of them into another precinct, the boundary being through the middle of the avenue.

An hour later the Night Wind opened the little door through the greater one of the old warehouse, and stepped inside into darkness that was the same as night; and he was quite certain that he had succeeded in approaching it unseen.

CHAPTER XVII

RUSHTON SHOWS HIS COLORS

The varied sensations experienced by Sterling Chester, the banker, when he found himself locked inside of a prison cell with the bound and gagged and helpless turnkey, defy description.

Impotent anger and outraged dignity partly overcame the terror that had mastered him ever since the moment when he discovered the Night Wind standing beside his bed—and the absence of that dreaded individual helped.

Nevertheless he kept perfectly still where he was standing, until he felt assured that Harvard and his wife had left the jail; and then, slowly, he turned his gaze upon the prostrate figure on the cot.

He started guiltily and nervously.

The eyes of the turnkey were staring up at him with a savage glare, while behind the gag the man made nonunderstandable noises in his throat, although it was not difficult to imagine the words that those noises were intended to convey.

Chester untied the towel which Harvard had used for a gag, but the minute it was removed he started backward in dismay, for in all his uneventful life Chester had never before heard such a torrent of words, uttered by one man, as poured from the mouth of that thoroughly enraged but still helpless turnkey.

It had been Chester's intention to release the man from his bonds also; but, in the face of the threats that were hurled at him, once those cords should be removed, he dared not do it.

Instead, he went to the barred door and shook it, discovering that it was hopelessly locked; then he returned to a solitary chair which the cell contained, and sat down despondently.

"Say, you blankety-blank-blank, blankety-blank, ain't you going to cut these cords and let me loose?" the turnkey roared at him then, the explosions of his wrath having spent themselves.

"I was intending to do so, of course," Chester returned helplessly, "but you have made such terrible threats against me that I am afraid to. We will remain as we are until somebody comes."

Then the turnkey wheedled and begged, and he swore and threatened again, all to no purpose, Chester had remembered that Lieutenant Rushton was due to arrive at the jail by a little after seven, and he had irrevocably decided to wait for that moment, unless some other person should appear before that.

"What I won't do to you when I do get out of this fix won't be worth mentioning," the turnkey swore at him at last, and lapsed into a sullen silence afterward, nor did he utter another sound until the interruption came.

Rushton had had no intention of permitting the banker to arrive at the jail ahead of him, notwithstanding the agreement made over the telephone; and it never once occurred to him that Chester would seek to go there before the appointed time; rather, it was supposable that he would be late.

It was a quarter to seven when Rushton got there, and for five minutes he rang the bell at the outer door fruitlessly; and then a half-dressed day-guard pulled open the wicket and peered out at him.

He knew Rushton, as it happened, and instantly opened the door; and they both asked the same question at once:

"Where's Mullen?" they demanded of each other as with one voice. (Mullen was, of course, the turnkey, at that moment locked in a cell with Chester.)

"I thought he was here," said the day-guard. "I relieve him at seven. It's most that now."

"He ought to be here. Where is he? Has anybody been here this morning?"

"How do I know? I'm just out of bed, lieutenant."

"There is something wrong," Rushton exclaimed. "Never mind, Mullen. Take me into the women's wing. You've got keys, haven't you?"

"Sure."

The man was in the act of turning to lead the way through the prison when he chanced to glance again through the open doorway, and discovered something lying on the steps. It was the ring of keys that the Night Wind had thrown down outside the door.

Rushton was speechless. He sensed rather than understood what those keys, found outside the prison, might indicate; and there was precious little time lost after that in traversing the corridors and reaching the cell wherein Lady Kate had been locked.

The spectacle that greeted Rushton when he peered through the bars touched his sense of humor, notwithstanding his anger, and he roared with derisive laughter while he unlocked the door, threw it open, and stepped inside.

Chester attempted at once to explain, and had not said a dozen words before Rushton thoroughly comprehended what had happened, and rather correctly how it had happened; and he glared down upon poor Chester so savagely that the latter stopped in the middle of his explanation.

"So you put one over onto me, did you?" Rushton demanded of him. "All the while you was givin' me that guff over the wire the Night Wind was settin' right there beside you tellin' you what to say, and you didn't have sense enough or sand enough to give me the tip! I feel like—" He stopped, and an odd gleam came into his eyes as he added in a different tone: "I'll talk privately with you about this later, Chester."

Then Rushton turned on his heels and cut the cords that held the turnkey captive.

Mullen leaped to his feet with a furious expletive and instantly rushed at Chester, who had risen to his feet and stood beside the chair where he had been seated.

There was no doubt regarding Mullen's intention. The banker would have been knocked senseless in another instant if a smashing blow from Rushton's fist, delivered behind the turnkey's ear, had not prevented it. And Rushton was known as the strongest man on the force.

"None of that, Mullen!" he growled as the turnkey slowly picked himself up, for he dared not fight back against Rushton. "I've a good notion to have you fired for what's happened; and if you ever say a single word about it to anybody, I will. It's *your* fault, every bit of it. You had no call to let anybody but Chester into the jail. Now, what time was it when the Night Wind was here and made that getaway?"

"Maybe about four, or after that. I don't know. I ain't got over the chokin' he gave me yet."

"Served you right. I wish he'd finished the job while he was at it. Come on, Chester."

Chester and Rushton passed outside of the jail together, and found the banker's limousine car awaiting them at the door. It had arrived shortly after Rushton went inside.

The chauffeur, being questioned, could give the lieutenant almost no information at all, as we know; so the two entered the car, and Rushton directed that they be taken directly to headquarters, in Manhattan.

"Say, Chester," the lieutenant remarked, as if casually, after they had ridden in silence for some distance, "I'm needin' a couple uh thousand mighty bad in my business just about now. You don't happen to have that much with you in your clothes, have you?"

"Why, no, lieutenant," the banker responded mildly. "I rarely carry money about with me in sums of more than a few dollars at a time. But I can accommodate you, of course, if you will come around to the bank some time to-day. What—er—what security have you to offer for the loan, Mr. Rushton?"

"*Security*! *Loan*! Say, what do you take me for, anyhow? Oh, never mind. We'll call it that, if you prefer. But the 'loan' 'll be a gift; take it from me, Chester; and the security will be a closed mouth. And I want the two thousand to-day. You ought to be ticklin' yourself under the chin that I didn't ask for five."

"Really, lieutenant, I cannot see why you should expect me to give you that amount of money," the banker expostulated, honestly amazed by the demand.

"You don't, eh? Say! Haven't you got any notion at all what you're up against, and what I'm standin' to save you from? Don't you know what would happen to you if I should make a holler about what happened last night an' this mornin'?"

"I am quite sure that I do not know what you are talking about, lieutenant."

"Well, you *are* young and innocent and guileless. Ain't you helped a prisoner to escape? Ain't you laid yourself liable to the *law*? It would be Sing Sing prison for yours, if I should squeal on you. That's what would happen to *you*."

"Why, lieutenant, I have done nothing—absolutely nothing at all."

"Aw, can it, Chester. You're up against it now as hard as the Night Wind is himself; and if you don't know it, take it from *me*, 'cause I'm tellin' it to you; see? I've got you where I want you now, and you've got to come across—unless you want to find yourself indicted by the grand jury, and standin' trial in General Sessions. That's exactly what'll happen to you if I squeal. Now, do I get that three thousand, or don't I?"

"Why, you said two thousand only a moment ago."

"Did I? Well, I'm sayin' *four* now. Do I get it?"

"Really, Rushton, this is equivalent to blackmail," the now exasperated banker exclaimed. "I protest."

"That makes it five thousand. I don't like to be called names, Chester. Why do you suppose I told that guy of yours out in front to take us to headquarters, unless I intended to leave you there in case you wouldn't come across? Now, which is it goin' to be? Five thousand cash for me or a cell at police headquarters for you? What's the answer?"

"I—I suppose I must submit, if what you say is true," the banker replied weakly.

"You'll find out that it's true, all right, if you go to askin' questions. It's a serious job, helpin' prisoners to escape, 'specially when they're charged with felonies. We had Lady Kate where we wanted her, an' now you've up and set her free. We'd have got the Night Wind in another twenty-four hours if you hadn't interfered, and I wouldn't wonder if that couldn't be held up against you, too. But I can make it all right with the inspector. Fortunately we kept the fact of Lady Kate's arrest a secret. But that won't help you none, once it leaks out. Five thousand is cheap. I'm almost inclined—"

"Lieutenant, if you will come to me at the bank as soon as it opens you shall have it," said the now helpless and thoroughly frightened Chester.

"That's the way to talk. I'll be there. Betcher life on that."

"But—you make me think, lieutenant, that—" The banker hesitated.

"Think what, Chester? Go on. What do I make you think?" Rushton asked with a coarse laugh.

"I—I really don't know, lieutenant."

"I guess you don't. I guess you're right about that. Well, you've got more of them thinks comin' to you."

There were several moments of silence between them after that, and then:

"Lieutenant," the banker asked timidly, "now that there appears to be no longer any necessity for us to go to the police headquarters, will you tell Gustave to take me directly to my home? I would like to go there before I go to the bank. He may drive you down-town afterward if you wish him to do so."

"Sure," was the quick reply. "And I won't need Gustave; and I'll meet you at the bank at ten, to get that money. That is understood, isn't it?"

"Certainly. Certainly."

When, somewhat later, the banker entered his own house he was told that a lady and gentleman were waiting in the library to see him, and, having no idea who it might be, he hurried to that room.

Lady Kate rose to receive him as he entered it. Tom Clancy was standing near one of the windows, with his back toward them, and did not turn around.

CHAPTER XVIII

THE BANKER'S DILEMMA

When Lady Kate confronted Chester so unexpectedly in the library of his own house, and he discovered Tom Clancy standing at his ease and much with the manner of a man who was perfectly at home in that room, the banker was so overcome with utter amazement that he could not speak.

Incidents had fallen so swiftly upon him since he was awakened in the middle of the night by Bingham Harvard, and one disaster after another had so unnerved him, that he could only gasp his astonishment, clinging with heavy hand to the back of the nearest chair to steady his tottering physique.

"Pray be seated, Mr. Chester," Katherine said, much as if she were mistress of the house and the banker an expected guest. "Mr. Clancy and I have been awaiting your return, feeling certain that you would come here before you went to the bank."

Dumbly he complied, sinking upon the chair the back of which he had already grasped.

Clancy swung himself slowly around, came forward to the table in the middle of the room, threw one leg across a corner of it, and, with a countenance as solemn as that of a judge who is about to pronounce sentence, waited.

Katherine's expression was solemnity itself, too. The banker could not guess that these two had entirely agreed between themselves upon the course of procedure they

130

would adopt when Chester arrived and discovered them awaiting him.

For Lady Kate, when she parted with Harvard, earlier that morning, had gone straight to a telephone to call Tom Clancy from his bed, and to ask him to meet her with the least possible delay. She had had an inspiration during that early ride across Queensboro Bridge, beside her husband, that morning, and she lost no time in carrying it into effect the moment it was possible to do so; and it had required only a few words of explanation to Clancy to make him "catch on with every one of his ten fingers," as he expressed it.

Lady Kate had been a woman detective at police head-quarters long enough to understand what the possible consequences might be to a person who assisted in the escape of an important prisoner. She believed that she had at last discovered a leverage by which the banker could be pried out of his state of complacency, and when she explained it to Tom he thought so, too.

So they went together to Chester's house and waited, for both were certain that Chester would not be detained very long at that Queens County jail.

She remained silent for a time, also, after requesting the banker to be seated. He gazed furtively around him, peering this way and that, half expectantly, half timorously.

"Mr. Harvard is not present, Mr. Chester," Katherine announced, reading his thought; and a sigh from the greatly troubled man told her that the assurance had been received gratefully.

"I suppose, sir, that you are wondering why Mr. Clancy and I have sought this interview," she said presently.

Chester nodded his head without words.

"We have come here to have a last word with you before we take a decided action in regard to what happened during the early hours of this morning," she told him, still with that solemn visage—while Tom Clancy wore the expression of a pallbearer at a state funeral.

The banker fidgeted in his chair and raised his head and eyes expectantly to Katherine.

"Of course," she went on slowly, "it is not entirely becoming in me to interest myself in procuring an indictment against you for aiding in the escape of a prisoner who is charged with a felony—particularly since I am the beneficiary in that escape—but, all the same, Mr. Chester, I shall not hesitate to do that very thing, if you force me to it. And Mr. Clancy quite agrees with me in that decision."

"Most certainly I do," said Tom sepulchrally. "It is a grave offense, Chester—most grave, indeed."

"And we are working for very great results, sir," Katherine added.

"Nothing short of complete vindication for Bing Harvard will satisfy *me*," said Tom.

"While all we shall demand of you, sir, is an opportunity—the right kind of an opportunity, of course—to establish his innocence," Lady Kate supplied.

"And that opportunity, Chester, as you should know, is directly inside of the walls of the Centropolis Bank," Tom announced solemnly.

It is doubtful if the banker had a full understanding of these explanatory remarks made by his unwelcome callers; but he did have a most vivid recollection of that last interview with Rodney Rushton, of the lieutenant's threats, of his demand, and of the consequences which might be expected to ensue if he, Chester, were defiant.

And here were two people—the very last in the world from whom he would have been led to expect such an announcement—threatening him with precisely the same sort of dire calamities that Rushton had held over his head—indictment and all the horrors that went with it.

He wondered dumbly what they could want, what they would demand of him.

Then something of the absurdity of the present situation occurred to him—at least it struck him as absurd at the moment—but only for a moment.

"Do you mean to tell me that you, the prisoner who has escaped, can make this nonsensical charge against me—of aiding in that escape?" he demanded of Katherine, with a touch of his old spirit. But it faded very quickly when she replied, with concise calmness:

"Certainly not—for I have no intention of giving myself up. But Mr. Clancy, as a citizen who demands that the laws be upheld, and that justice be done to all alike, can demand that the grand jury shall take cognizance of what you have done. He, as a citizen, can force an indictment against you. You would be brought to trial at General Sessions, and there is not the slightest doubt that you would be convicted. And that, Mr. Sterling Chester, president of the Centropolis Bank, would mean Sing Sing prison for you. Or, even if you should escape the full penalty for your offense, you would find yourself the subject of a great deal of unpleasant notoriety."

Chester drummed upon the arms of the chair where he was seated. He was very pale. Little beads of sweat stood out upon his forehead. His lips were dry, and he attempted to moisten them with the tip of his tongue.

"What do you want?" he managed to cry out, like one who is in pain. "What did you two come here to demand of me?"

"Justice," said Clancy.

"An opportunity to seek full justice," Katherine amended.

"Do you want me to lie to myself and to all the world and announce that I believe in the innocence of Bingham Harvard? Is that what you want?" Chester demanded with more spirit than he had yet shown. "I cannot do that, because I do *not* believe it. That is—" He paused himself and came to a full stop.

Katherine asked mildly: "What were you about to add to that statement, Mr. Chester?"

"I was going to say that I have never once had the slightest doubt of the guilt of Bingham Harvard until—until certain things happened this morning—until certain things were said to me this morning, which have—which have impressed me. You are not the only person who has threatened me since I was forced to go out upon that unfortunate errand this morning, Mrs. Harvard."

Clancy spoke up quickly.

133

"No! Rushton has been threatening you, too, has he?" he demanded.

"Yes; and almost in the words that have been used here," the banker replied.

"I'll bet a brick watch against a whole panful of dough-nuts that he made you pay for it, too, Chester."

"I am to pay him five thousand dollars at the bank at ten o'clock this morning—or as soon as I arrive there," Chester announced without emotion.

"For his silence—eh?"

"Yes."

"And he agreed to make it all right with the inspector—and all that sort of rot, didn't he?"

"Yes."

Tom Clancy looked at his watch. The time was already nearly half past nine. He reached out for the telephone and pulled it across the table toward him. Then he called the number of the Centropolis Bank, which was familiar to him; and Chester looked on in amazement, and kept silent.

"Hello?" Clancy's two companions in the room heard him say. "The Centropolis Bank—I want to speak to the cashier, if he has arrived. Hello—the cashier? I am talking at the home of Mr. Chester—your president. Mr. Chester is not well this morning and wishes me to say that he will not be at the bank until noon to-day. Oh, no, it is not serious at all. Merely a temporary indisposition. His rest was broken last night. He will be down about noon. In the mean time, he asks me to say that he has an appointment with Lieutenant Rushton this morning at ten. You are to see Rushton in person, when he calls, and say to him that if he will return at three o'clock, or a quarter past, this afternoon, the business arrangement between them will be consummated. Who am I? Oh, I quite forgot to tell you that. I am a doctor. Dr. Thomas C—. Good-by."

He put down the telephone and turned to Katherine.

"If I don't get Mr. Rodney Rushton good and plenty, where the hair is mighty short, before this day is over, you may lock me up as an incompetent!" he announced. Then he wheeled toward Chester. "And you've got to help, understand? You have *got* to. You will pay him that five thousand in bills—marked bills, Chester; and Chief Redhead and a few others will do the rest."

"It seems to me," said Katherine, "that we are neglecting the purpose that brought us here."

"So we are. Look here, Chester, this is what we want—provided you *don't* want to face an indictment, a trial, and a prison sentence. We want a chance—just a chance."

"I don't understand you at all, Tom," the banker replied wearily.

"I'll explain. You are shy just one assistant paying teller down at your bank, and you have been shy that one ever since Bing Harvard got out. Oh, I know what I'm talking about. You shove one of your note tellers into the cage during the rush hours and get along with Atkinson and Mordaunt the rest of the time. That's right, isn't it?"

"Yes."

"Well, we want you to put another assistant paying teller to work when the bank opens for business to-morrow morning. You are the whole push down there, and you don't have to consult your directors about it. I know that, too."

"But, who is it, Tom? Who and what is he? I cannot appoint a teller unless I know—"

"Yes you can—and in this case you've got to do it. He is a young man that I am going to send to you, and I will go on his bond for any sum you want. So will the Gibraltar Security Company. I have arranged for that—or will, to-day."

"You must inform me who and what he is, Tom," Chester announced firmly.

"His name"—Tom cast a covert glance toward Katherine out of the corner of his eyes—"is Caton. Erin Caton. That's Irish, of course. He is a paying teller, naturally, or I wouldn't be sending him to you. Incidentally he will be laboring in the interests of Mr. and Mrs. Bingham Harvard, and he is going to stay right there inside of that cage during business hours until he finds out who lifted that one hundred and thirty-six thousand dollars which you have made yourself think that Bing Harvard stole."

"Do you mean that he is a detective?" Chester asked, feeling that he would have to submit.

"He will be one when he gets there, Chester—and the best ever. I'll guarantee that you will be charmed with him, and that you will see the time when you will bless the day that you took him into your employ."

Then Tom Clancy turned slowly around and winked one eye deliberately at Lady Kate—and for some unknown reason she smiled brightly and nodded her head with emphasis.

CHAPTER XIX

THE MASQUERADER

"Can you do it, Lady Kate? *Can* you?" Clancy asked, when half an hour later they came away from the house of the banker.

"Of course I can do it," she replied with decision as he stood aside while she got into the black taxicab which Julius was to drive for them, for Katherine had lost no time in communicating with her faithful servitor that morning as soon as she had telephoned to Tom.

Clancy followed and seated himself beside her.

"It is a big undertaking," he said, shaking his head dubiously. "I tremble for you, Katherine."

"Nonsense," she retorted. "I will carry it off with flags flying and banners waving. There isn't a thing about it that I cannot do. I am quick at figures—I know how to handle money. Oh, I am not a bit afraid—I have been preparing for this opportunity for months."

"But your appearance, little lady. Do you really think that you can disguise that sufficiently well?"

"Certainly I can."

"I don't know about that. You are a mighty feminine sort of a woman. There isn't anything mannish about you at all. To be sure, your voice is a contralto, but it is very far from being a heavy one."

"Listen to it now," she said, dropping it to a much deeper tone—and then they both laughed.

137

"But your hair," he went on, in the effort to find more objections to the plan she had proposed that morning, and which he had now carried to a point where it would have to be fulfilled.

"I will have to sacrifice that, naturally."

"It's too bad. It is so beautiful."

"Nonsense. It will grow out again."

"And then"—he wondered if he was blushing, and decided that he was, so he half turned his head away—"there is your figure."

"Oh, I know how to fix that," she responded, laughing gaily, for the spirit of adventure was upon her. "I used to be quite a star at private theatricals. I have often taken masculine parts. I'm not a bit afraid that I will be discovered. I shall keep myself very much aloof from the others, for, to my mind, that will be the best way to find out what I want to know. It will be much better than to seek to ingratiate myself with them. Don't you agree with me?"

Tom nodded.

"One cannot help agreeing with you, Katherine, when you insist upon it. You would make a bully good crook yourself—you have such a taking way with you. Now, how am I to get the necessary papers to you? Your personal recommendations—I'll have the chief secure those—and the bonds and my letter to Chester, introducing you, which he will want to show to his directors?"

"You can do that by leaving your house to-morrow morning at half past eight o'clock and turning toward Columbus Avenue. You will find Julius waiting at the corner with this car. Engage him to drive you somewhere, and give the papers to him. That will be sufficient."

"You ought to be at the bank by nine—or a little before."

"I will be there," she assured him. "I was rather surprised, Tom, at the readiness with which Mr. Chester agreed to the arrangement."

"Well," Clancy said, "we had him dead scared, for one thing. For another, that play of Rushton's for the five thousand plunks sort of jarred him. It set him to thinking, too.

You see, lady, bankers are queer fishes when all is said. Once you arouse their suspicions, they will swallow the whole tackle—hook, line, bob, and sinker. It never occurred to Chester to doubt Rushton until he found that Rushton could be bought—and if there is anything on earth that a banker is shy of and hates constitutionally it is a man who can be bought. That conversation he had with Rushton jarred him so, that now he is more than half willing to believe that Rushton *did* frame up the case against Bing."

"Yes—I thought so, too."

"Only he has got to take time to think it over. If all men were bankers, Katherine, I would thoroughly sympathize with the Pharisee who went into the temple with the publican."

"Speaking of Rushton," she said, "just what are you to do this afternoon at three o'clock when he goes to the bank for that money?"

"I don't know yet. I haven't decided. I shall consult the chief before I do decide. But my impression is that we will have a warrant sworn out for him, and then have him pinched when he comes out of the bank with that marked money in his jeans. That is the way it looks to me just now."

"Don't you think that will be premature, Tom? And doesn't it weaken us a little bit with Mr. Chester? He would have to appear against Rushton, and that would mean giving the whole thing away. He would discover then that he had not committed such a great offense, after all. You know there was no official charge entered against me."

"Maybe you are right about that, Lady Kate. Anyhow, I'll talk it over with Redhead."

"Let me make a suggestion."

"Well?"

"Mr. Chester promised that he would have the bills marked that he is to give to Rushton. Very well, let Rushton carry them away from the bank with him—only have him trailed. He will deposit that money somewhere the first thing to-morrow morning—won't he?"

"Very likely."

"Well, one of the chief's men can follow him into the bank where he makes the deposit, and can step to the window the minute Rushton leaves it; and I believe that the bank, at the chief's request, will consent to lay aside those identical bills that Rushton deposits and to put an affidavit from the receiving teller with them, that Rushton did deposit them there. Why, Tom, if your friend should have five thousand dollars with him to reimburse the bank I think they would hand over those very bills—*with* such an affidavit."

"Lady Kate, I take off my hat to you. In purely classic phraseology you're a corker!"

"Thank you. And now I am going to drop you at the next corner. I have a great deal to do in order to make myself ready for to-morrow."

"That is no idle jest, I take it, Lady Kate."

"Tell me, do you think you will see Bingham to-day or to-night?"

"Give it up, little lady. I shall stop at the office of the chief on the way down, and I'll telephone to the top of the old warehouse from there. I assume that he will be there."

"You are not going to tell him—"

"Certainly not. That is understood."

"He would not consent to it, I know."

"Especially to your sacrificing your hair. I don't blame him. I wouldn't, either."

"Make him understand that he must not try to see me again until I send for him; for—don't you see—we must not meet while I am masquerading as a young man. He would spoil the whole thing."

"Again, I do not blame him. I would, too."

"Why? Don't you believe that I can do it?"

"I believe that you can do anything on earth that you start out to do."

"Then why—"

"Well, I expect it is because I admire you so much as you are. I don't like to think about the things that you may be up against in this undertaking. Do you know, I think it is rather tough that Bing should have seen you first—before I did, I mean."

Katherine laughed lightly as Tom opened the door to get out.

"It wouldn't have made a particle of difference," she said happily. "Bingham is my God of Abraham, Tom. He is my king. He is everything. And, oh, he *is* such a splendid fellow!"

"Isn't he, though? Well, here goes! So long, little lady!"

"Good-by, Tom!"

"Keep your eyes peeled when you go to work in that bank."

"I will."

Tom Clancy strode away in one direction—the cab rolled away in another.

That morning's work had accomplished much.

CHAPTER XX

THE HOUSE ON THE ROOF

Bing Harvard had been in the little house on the roof rather more than half an hour when the telephone rang. Remembering that it was the detective chief's private wire only that communicated there, he replied to it, and was delighted when he recognized Tom Clancy's voice.

"Hello, Tom!" he said. "This is bully—to be able to speak to you like this. Are you quite sure that there are not eavesdroppers on this wire?"

"Perfectly sure, Bing," came the reply. "Say, that was a pretty good joke you played on your good chief, Redhead, this morning."

"How is that? I don't understand. I am not aware that I have played any joke on him."

"Aren't you? He says that you are the only original combination of chain lightning and perpetual motion. You know, I suppose, that he has got one of his own men working on the regular force down at the bureau—a chap named Conner?"

"I think you told me as much, Tom."

"Well, last night he sent Connor to find out where they had taken Lady Kate after she was arrested by a detective named Hardner. Connor did find out and reported. This morning, bright and early, the chief beat it for the wilds of Queens, got there at eight o'clock, and—well, you know the rest. You got there first. That's the joke. Now, one more word, and then the chief wants to talk to you."

"Go ahead."

"Lady Kate telephoned to me this morning—after she parted with you. I had quite a long talk with her. She wanted me to tell you that she is all right, and to give you her love; *and* to say, with my own endorsement, that she has hit upon a theory and a scheme which she is going to work out right away. I am going to help her; so is Redhead, a little, and we both approve. *But* you are not to know about it at the present time, and are to ask no questions. I reckon she is the boss, and those are her orders. See?"

"All right, Tom; only I don't see—"

"You don't have to. The chief wants to talk to you now."

"I want to talk to him, too. I have something to tell him. I am dead tired. I feel as though I hadn't slept for a month. My inclination was to turn in the moment I got here this morning, but I had some papers that I took from Rushton's room when I made that call upon him; and some memoranda also. I want to tell him about all that."

"All right—"

"Say, Tom?"

"Yes?"

"I ran into Mordaunt this morning. He used to be one of my assistants at the bank."

"I know him. What about it?"

Then rapidly and concisely, Harvard related the incidents of the morning as we know them; and at the end of the story Clancy replied:

"Splendid, all of it, Bing. I have been holding the receiver so the chief could hear what you said. It fits in beautifully with something that he is going to do to-day; and he thinks that those papers and the memoranda you took from Rushton's rooms will help a lot, too. And now I'm going to turn the phone over to him. I am not going to try to see you to-night; but I will to-morrow night. Good-by."

"Hello, Harvard!" another voice called over the wire. "This is the chief speaking. We have not made each other's acquaintance as yet, but we soon will. You might give me a

bare outline of what those papers and the memoranda con-
sist, if you will. That will be sufficient for the present. After
that you can put them under a paper-weight on the table and
turn in. When you wake up you will probably find me sitting
there, examining them. I want to have a talk with you before
night."

"All right, chief."

"Now, what is that stuff? Give me just an outline of it."

"The memoranda I made were taken from bank books—
exchange and savings banks, both—that I discovered in
Rushton's desk. They were kept in cipher, and I have not had
time to work on that yet; but working out ciphers is a fad of
mine, and I have no doubt that I can read this one."

"All right so far. Go ahead."

"It is plain enough to see that the total amount of the
various deposits will go well into six figures."

"Good. Give me the names of the several banks, slowly,
so that I can jot them down as you call them off. I may want
to use that information before I have an opportunity to talk
with you."

Harvard called off the names of four exchange banks
and of two savings banks.

"Now, what about the papers you brought away with
you, Harvard?" the chief asked when that was done.

"They are mostly figures, made on scraps of paper; sums
added to other sums, with the dates jotted down. They are all
rather blind, but there is no doubt that they have reference to
the deposits—that is, to the receipt of various sums before
the deposits were made. In some instances there are initials
against the sums, which may indicate the sources of the re-
ceipts. In one instance there is a name—unknown to me. One
of the scraps bears my name, Harvard, plainly written, and
on that one there is more figuring; but it is done in lettered
cipher, like the bank books."

"Anything more?"

"Just a small package of vest-pocket memorandum
books, held together by a rubber band. Everything inside of
them is in cipher. I haven't yet had time to examine them
thoroughly."

"How many of these little books are there?"

"Six."

"That would be one for each bank you have mentioned."

"That's so. I had not thought of that."

"Is that all?"

"Yes."

"You are not going out on the streets to-day, are you?" the chief asked.

"I had not intended to do so."

"Well, don't—at least, not until after I have been there to see you; and I cannot say just how soon that will be. And now I want to congratulate you on that play you made in getting your wife out of the jail across the river. You have got the police department 'going' pretty nearly as badly as you did it before you went away, Harvard."

"That reminds me, chief; I wonder if Chester will get into any serious trouble on account of my leaving him locked up in that cell the way I did?"

"Not a bit of it, Harvard. There was no official record of the arrest of Lady Kate, and you can bet your life there won't be any now. Rushton got over there before I did, and he took Chester away with him. He tried to touch Chester, too, for a little graft. That is the lay I am on this morning. If I can get the 'goods' on Rushton—and it looks now as if I could—we won't do a thing to him, I don't think! Good-by."

"I say, chief!"

But the chief had replaced the receiver, and after a moment's thought Harvard decided not to call him again.

He was weary with his exertions and from lack of sleep, and it did not take him very long after that to throw aside his clothing and to seek the rest that he needed so badly.

In the mean time, Chief Redhead was as busy as a hive of bees.

The information that Clancy had taken to him, and that which Harvard had just given him to go with it, opened up a new phase of the case which was very promising.

And Harvard slept, blissfully unconscious that his wife was at that very time engaged in the preparation for the duties she was to begin the following morning, when, in the guise of a man, she intended to appear at the Centropolis Bank to begin her new duties as an assistant paying teller.

And she expected that great things would come of it—and great things did.

CHAPTER XXI

BAITING A TRAP

Mordaunt, the assistant paying teller at the Centropolis Bank, talked matters over very fully with his wife before he started down-town that morning, and they agreed, entirely, that the subterfuge which had been practiced upon the policemen at their home should not be continued at the bank.

"Suppose you do lose your position, Ben," his rosy-cheeked wife said to him at parting; "you will soon be able to find another one. We have got some money saved up to keep us going for a time—and I can't bear the thought of your telling lies. And it would not be fair to Bingham Harvard, either, for you to make it appear, even for a moment, that we have ever believed him guilty. He is back here to clear himself, and let us do everything in our power to help."

Thus it was that as soon as Mordaunt arrived at the bank he asked to see the president, who was usually in his place among the first; but Mr. Chester had not appeared, and when the clock pointed to a quarter of an hour before the doors would be opened for the business of the day Mordaunt sought the cashier.

"Mr. Cheever," he began, "I have got a confession to make. I hoped to make it to Mr. Chester, in person, but he has not arrived—and it is my duty to tell you what is on my mind before I begin my work for the day."

Cheever, the cashier, was a quiet, silent, taciturn man, past middle age, forbidding in a way, but, nevertheless, thoroughly well liked by every employee who came in contact with him.

He looked up keenly, under his bushy brows, at Mordaunt, and replied:

"The president will not be down till noon, Mordaunt. You may tell me what is on your mind, or you can save it until he comes, as you please. That is up to you."

"I think I would rather tell you about it than him, sir," Mordaunt replied, relieved.

"Well?"

"I met Bingham Harvard on the street near my home early this morning."

He paused, expecting some reply—but there was none.

Cheever was one of those rare men who never express surprise at anything. He merely nodded his shaggy head, and Mordaunt continued:

"I was honestly glad to see Harvard. I have never believed him guilty of that thing he was charged with. As soon as he understood that this morning he was glad to see me. I insisted upon taking him home to breakfast with me, and he went. There was, however, an officer trailing me, and—"

Mordaunt gave a clear and a full account of all that had happened at his house that morning, omitting nothing, so far as his knowledge went.

"Now, sir," he concluded, "if you think I had better keep out of the teller's cage until Mr. Chester has been informed of this matter, I am quite willing to do so."

"Nonsense, Ben," was the quick, almost savage retort, for that was Cheever's manner when he was very much in earnest. "Get into the cage and go to work. You did perfectly right. I am glad that you came to me, though, for already I have received a written report of all of it from the police."

"Thank you, sir," Mordaunt replied, and was turning away when a sharp word from the cashier stopped him.

"Your opinion of Harvard and mine exactly coincide," Cheever said shortly, fussing with some papers on his desk. "You may tell him that, if you should happen to see him again."

Mordaunt returned to his duties very much elated. Atkinson, the paying teller who had succeeded Harvard, looked up with a sneering smile and inquired:

"Business with the chief this morning, Mordaunt?"

"I merely told him something that he already knew about," was the reply; and the business of the day began.

Lieutenant Rushton strode into the bank at exactly five minutes past ten.

There was not an employee there who did not know him by sight, and more than one curious glance was cast in his direction as he made his way toward the raised office of the president.

But Badger, the watch, stopped him, and thrust out a huge paw of a hand—which Rushton, for some reason of his own, chose to ignore.

"Cheever, the cashier, told me to tell you to go straight to see him when you came in, lieutenant," Badger said; "so I guess you're expected, all right."

A moment later Rushton was listening to the message that Tom Clancy had telephoned to the bank from the library of Chester's house; and he was also scowling. It did not fit in exactly with his plans for that day.

"Is that all that Chester said?" he demanded. "Didn't he give you any directions about payin' me a bill he owes me?"

"Not a word, lieutenant," was the reply.

"Well, what does he want me to be here at a quarter past three for—the banks close at three? Didn't he say what time he was comin' down, himself?"

"The message was that Mr. Chester would be down about noon."

"Huh! Then what does he want me to wait till three for? Say—you just tell him when he gets here that I'll be back to see him between one and two; an' that I wanta close up that matter between us, right away, will you?"

"Certainly, lieutenant."

"I expect that mebby he was a little off his feed this mornin'," Rushton volunteered, with a grin. "However, that ain't neither here nor there. You give him my message, will you?"

"I will."

"Say, Cheever, did you know that the Night Wind—that guy Harvard—is back in town again?" Rushton asked suddenly.

"Oh, yes, I had heard of it," was the reply.

"Well, has headquarters notified you that one of your men here in the bank saw him and talked with him this morning?"

"Yes. I have been informed of that, also."

"Well, what are you goin' to do about it?"

"Nothing, lieutenant. It is a matter entirely for Mr. Chester to decide. The employee to whom you refer has already made his report to me about it."

"Huh! Well, *I* don't take any stock in his story about trying to notify the police that Harvard was in his house. He can tell that to Sweeney. You'd better keep an eye on that fellow Mordaunt. That's all. I'll be here between one an' two." And Rushton left the bank.

Shortly before twelve o'clock of that day Chester's limousine car drew up at the door of his house to take the banker down-town.

Ten minutes later Chester issued from the front door, and as he began to descend the steps a man with red hair and extraordinarily keen eyes and manner stepped quickly forward from nowhere in particular, and met him at the bottom of them.

"Good day, Mr. Chester," he said cordially. "I am a messenger from Mr. Thomas Clancy. He asked me to meet you here and to ride down-town with you in your car. Perhaps he mentioned my name to you? He usually refers to me as the 'chief' or as 'Redhead'."

The banker paused at the bottom of the steps.

"Yes," he replied. "You are, I understand, at the head of a detective agency. What do you want with me, sir?"

"I wish to arrange with you the plan for marking the bills that you are to pay over to Rodney Rushton some time to-day, Mr. Chester; and, also, to agree upon some plan by which those same bills may be isolated and identified at whatever bank Rushton may decide to deposit them. I know

150

of a plan by which that can be accomplished perfectly, but it will require your coöperation."

"Very well, sir; very well. You may get into the car."

"It is morally certain, Mr. Chester, that Rushton will not wait till three o'clock, as Clancy proposed, to go to the bank for that money. He will wish to deposit it in one of the banks where he does business this afternoon," the chief said as soon as they were in the car. "I have here a list of the banks he uses. He will deposit the five thousand dollars you will give him in one of them. You, of course, understand that the payment you make to him is in the character of blackmail?"

"Certainly."

"Well, sir, for many reasons I deem it unwise to proceed against Rushton, in any manner, to-day; and, therefore, I have thought out the following plan, which will be entirely successful at any time we may choose to spring the trap on him. But it will require your hearty coöperation."

Chester nodded; and then the chief recited in detail exactly what he wished to have the banker do in the matter.

A block away from the Centropolis Bank the chief said good-by to the banker and got down; but he hastened to the nearest telephone and called up Clancy, to whom he said, briefly:

"We have got him, Clancy, where he can't squirm—and we can nail him at any time we choose, after he has accepted that money and made the deposit. Chester is leaning very much our way now, although he doesn't quite realize it—yet."

CHAPTER XXII

A NET FOR RUSHTON

Sterling Chester, president of the Centropolis Bank, was deep in consultation with three men who, themselves, looked as if they might be bankers, when Lieutenant Rodney Rushton strode down the space between the screen and the outer windows toward the president's office at twenty-five minutes past one o'clock that day.

Rushton paused just outside the brass swing gate, and Chester, raising his eyes, saw him.

"Just a moment, Lieutenant Rushton," he said. Then, addressing the three men who were seemingly in consultation with him, he added, and so that Rushton could overhear him: "I will have to ask you to excuse me for one moment, gentlemen—if you will just step aside for a second. My business with the lieutenant will not occupy more than two or three minutes. Come inside, Rushton."

Rushton, with a scowl on his face, because it was habitual with him, but with no loss of assurance, passed through the gateway and seated himself upon a chair that one of Chester's callers had occupied—and which the banker indicated to him with a slight gesture.

Rushton's back was toward the three men who had withdrawn partly across the office space, but who, nevertheless, watched covertly all that took place.

Chester pulled open a drawer and took from it a package of bills, each of the denomination of a thousand dollars; and he counted them over slowly—five of them—on the desk.

"Here are the five thousand dollars you require of me, Rushton," he said, so that the others could hear him.

Rushton objected in a whisper. "You needn't talk quite so loud about this business. Who are them guys, anyhow?"

"Oh, those gentlemen? They are merely business acquaintances. I thought it best not to keep you waiting," Chester replied, still in a tone that the others could hear. And he added quickly: "As for the receipt—that is, of course, customary in business transactions."

"Well, I ain't goin' to sign no receipt," Rushton whispered sharply into the banker's ear. "Do I get that dough—or don't I? And you needn't tell anybody in the bank what your answer is, neither."

"Very well; very well, lieutenant," Chester replied, lifting his other hand away from the money. "But I hope—I sincerely hope that you will keep silent about what happened—you know. Here is the money. Take it, Rushton—and I hope you will not venture to make any more such demands upon me."

His voice was pitched quite low, and yet Rushton was not at all sure that it was sufficiently so for the others not to hear.

He took the money greedily and thrust it into one of his pockets. Then he leaned forward.

"Oh, I won't bother you no more about *this* affair," he said in a low tone; and raising his own voice a trifle he added: "This squares the present account to date, Mr. Chester. And I promise to have the rest of the work done without delay."

Then he went out of the bank, and without a glance to the right or the left as he did so.

The three men who had been in the president's office during the short interview stepped quickly forward to the desk, examined the receipt which Rushton had declined to sign, watched Chester while he made an endorsement on the back of it, after which all four placed their signatures under that endorsement.

Immediately after that one of the three strangers seated himself at the president's desk and did some writing on another sheet of paper, which each of the four persons likewise signed. And then the official notary public, who acted for the bank, was summoned, so that each man could attest his own signature.

Outside the building, when Rushton stepped from the doorway to the street, there were three more men who were interested in his movements.

They were posted at three of the four corners of the two streets; and it would have been apparent to anybody watching *them* that they were thoroughly versed in their occupations.

There is no man easier to trail in the streets of New York than a professional detective.

Besides, it probably never once occurred to Rushton that he was being trailed that afternoon. Least of all would he have suspected that the occupants of any one of the three taxicabs that kept within sight of him for the next half hour and more was particularly interested in him.

Nevertheless, when he entered a bank a mile further uptown, and after making out a deposit slip at one of the side desks, took his place in the line before the window of the receiving teller, one of those three men was directly behind him, also with a bank book in one hand, from the ends of which a package of bills could be seen protruding.

And another of the three had hurried through the bank to the cashier's desk, while the third one got into the line so that he was the third behind Rushton.

The cashier of the bank discovered (as soon as the second "shadow" spoke to him) that he had business inside of the receiving teller's cage, and went there; and he was there, with the receiving teller and the two assistants, at the moment when Rushton made his deposit and took himself off.

He was also there when the man behind Rushton pushed *his* book through the window.

154

That book contained fifty one-hundred-dollar bills; and after passing it through the window the man walked on to the cashier's department and waited; and in the course of time the cashier joined him and gave him a sealed envelope, which he carried away with him; and the envelope, fastened with wax, bore the official seal of the bank, with the attested date and hour added to it.

It would seem that the net which Chief Redhead had thrown around Lieutenant Rodney Rushton that day was a strong one, indeed, and would prove so when the time should come to draw it.

An hour later six men reported to their chief in the tall building down-town, and each party of three gave into his hands a large envelope sealed with wax, stamped with a bank seal, dated and attested; and these the chief presently deposited in an inner receptacle of a vault-like safe that was concealed behind one of the walls of his private office.

"There wasn't any hitch anywhere?" he asked of all of them generally.

"Not a one," came the reply from the foremost; and the others nodded their acquiescence in that statement.

"This envelope," one of the operatives announced, indicating to which one he referred, "contains the affidavits of Chester, Jocelyn, Butler, and myself, of all that occurred at the Centropolis Bank; and this one"—indicating the other—"holds the five marked one-thousand-dollar bills, with the affidavits of the deposit and the circumstances of it, made by the two receiving tellers who saw it, by the cashier, and by Holt, Harper, and Perry, of all that took place at the other bank. That is pretty clear and clean, isn't it, chief?"

"It's bully," was the hearty response. "Now, I shall put both of these envelopes into another, larger one, and seal it; and we will all make a short, joint, sworn statement on the back of it. That will be clinching the nails in Rushton's coffin, I think."

When the six operatives had gone the chief stepped into a closet and used a telephone that was there.

"Hello, Harvard," he said over the wire. "I thought I would call you up to tell you that I have got the goods on

Rushton at last. I have got a trap already to spring at any time we want to do it, and it will get him good and plenty, where he can't squirm out. Never mind what it is just now. I will explain it all to you in due time—who did it?"

"Oh, your wife did most of it, Harvard. She and Clancy really did it together. Surest thing you know, Harvard. That wife of yours is a wonder, as you will discover before long. What's that? Found it out already? Nonsense! You haven't found out half of it yet. No. Don't stir out to-day or to-night. That talk I had with you to-day helped me a lot. Stick to that cipher of Rushton's and work it out."

"I think you can do it, and it will, no doubt, prove of very great value in the end. All right. I'll tell Clancy what you say. He will go around to see you as soon as possible, but I think that you had better stick close to that roof until to-morrow night, anyhow. Good-by."

CHAPTER XXIII

WHEN LADY KATE MADE READY

That was Tom Clancy's busy day, too, and he gave very slight attention to his own business affairs.

First, he applied to the president of the Gibraltar Security & Casualty Company for the bond which was to guarantee the faithful performance of duty as a paying teller, of one Erin Caton—and because the said president was Clancy's particular friend he had no difficulty in obtaining it, particularly after he had guaranteed the company against loss by a hypothecation of some of his own securities.

Then he added to that bond over his own name, as he had promised Chester he would do, to satisfy still further the directors of the Centropolis Bank; and he prepared the letters and such other papers as were necessary to perfect the installation of the new assistant paying teller.

He could not deny to himself, all the time that he was thus engaged, that he had many misgivings concerning the propriety of the act that Lady Kate contemplated; but he went ahead with it, as he always did with everything that he undertook to do.

Late in the afternoon, approximately at five o'clock, he sought the office of the chief to tell him that everything was in readiness, and that he had the papers in his pockets, ready to deliver to Julius in the morning, as arranged by Katherine.

The chief heard him through without a smile; and then said:

157

"I think, Clancy, that you had better leave those papers with me and let *me* meet Black Julius in the morning."

"Why?" Clancy demanded in surprise.

"Because my operative, Connor, has told me enough of what they are up to over at the stone building, to render it pretty certain to my mind that you are not personally safe for a minute when you are on the streets."

"Aw, get off of the pony, chief—it's bucking. What's the matter with you?"

"It was all fixed up between a few of them down there to frame something on you, Tom, and they will do it if there is a ghost of a chance—particularly since they have got onto Connor and given him the cold mitt. His usefulness is past down there."

"So? Well, what of it?"

"Simply this: If they should pinch you somewhere— even if it should be for only a short time—they'd go through you. If it happened to-night they'd find those papers—and that would give the whole snap away."

"I'd like to know what they could frame up on me, chief. Why, they wouldn't dare—"

"My dear Tom, they will dare anything—now. Even I have received a delicate kind of a warning in a left-handed way to-day to keep my hands off. You give me those papers. I will pass them along to Julius. Hand them over!"

Clancy did so—reluctantly.

"I think it is all nonsense," he said, "but it is just as well not to take any chances when there is so much at stake. To tell you the truth, I wanted to have a look at Lady Kate in her make-up before she gets plumb inside of this job."

"I'll do that. She called me on the telephone an hour ago. I have got an appointment with her to-night. If there is an opportunity I will pass the papers directly to her at that time, instead of waiting to deliver them to Julius."

"Gee! I wish I could see her, too."

"Well, you can't."

"I have got to be doing something, chief."

"Then make yourself busy in keeping out of the clutches of Rushton and Coniglio and Masters. Those are the three men who are on your trail. Walk in the middle of the side-walk when you are on the street, stay indoors at night, and keep your eyes peeled for a few days, Clancy. They will get you if you don't."

Tom laughed, shook hands with the chief, and went out.

He descended in one of the express elevators and spoke to the man who operated it, who had once worked in the building where he had his own office.

That man remembered that the time was five-forty when Mr. Clancy left the building.

Outside, he walked to a station of the elevated road, because he preferred it to the subway, and it was just as convenient. At the corner where the station was located he encountered an acquaintance, and stood there talking with him two or three minutes.

That acquaintance happened to be one of the operatives of Redhead's agency, although the fact was unknown to Clancy; and *he* saw Tom begin the ascent of the stairway toward the station.

And right there Tom Clancy passed out of sight.

At nine o'clock that evening the chief called at Clancy's house, accompanied by a gentleman whom he wished to introduce to Tom—a man who bore the name of Erin Caton; but was informed that Mr. Clancy had not returned from his office, and had sent no word when he would be at home.

"It looks as if they had pinched him, in spite of my warnings, Mr. Caton," the chief remarked as they turned away together. "But we won't have to get as busy as we did in your case. There isn't quite so much at stake. All the same, I will have him traced from the time he left my office. It won't take very long to find him."

"And in the mean time—" his companion asked him.

"In the mean time he is a *man*, and it won't hurt him to swallow a little medicine."

"Nevertheless, I cannot help feeling anxious about him, chief."

"My dear young man, they won't hurt him—that is, it is not likely that they will. The 'System' is very anxious to get

159

him and a certain young woman of our acquaintance temporarily out of the way."

"They won't be able to get hold of the young woman now, because she has disappeared, and in a manner which renders it utterly impossible for them to get a trace of her. Clancy, it seems, they have got—at least that is the way it looks to me—but they won't be able to railroad him to prison without my knowledge—they dare not injure him, and it won't do any harm to anybody to let him rest for a while. So, for the present, we will let it go at that. Now, let us talk about yourself."

"There isn't any more to say, is there?"

"Only this, my dear sir"—and the chief chuckled—"As a new employee at the bank you will be watched and trailed very closely, every minute of the time while you are awake, by the regular detectives for the Bankers' Association. That is a rule that is never neglected."

"So, after to-morrow morning, when you go there to work, there must be no more meetings between us. Neither should you telephone to me, for a time, at least. Even letters would be unsafe for a week or so. Therefore, it looks to me as if you would have to play the game very much alone."

"And that is precisely what I most desire to do."

"But, all the same," he continued as if he had not noticed the interruption, "I shall wish to know at once of anything you may accomplish."

"I will find a way to keep you informed," Lady Kate told him—for, of course, we know that the chief's companion was Lady Kate. "If I make a discovery, which I think you ought to know about immediately, I will find a way to get the information to you."

"Very well. I will leave it to you. Now, one other point and we will part. What have you decided to do with Black Julius during the time you are located at the bank? You understand, of course, that it would be unwise to keep him about you?"

"Naturally. I shall send him to his brother, over in Jersey. He has a brother over there who practices medicine during the week and is a minister on Sundays."

160

"Julius is devoted to Mr. Harvard, is he not?"

"Absolutely so."

"Then I will suggest that you write a letter to your husband to-night, which you will give to Julius to deliver. Julius will come to me, and I will show him how to deliver it. In that letter you should explain to Mr. Harvard that you are going to keep very quiet, and also very much in one place, for a time, and that you will have no need of the services of the negro. I think that Harvard and myself—and possibly Clancy, if we find out what has happened to him—can make good use of Julius and his car."

"Very well—that is understood, then. I shall live in a boarding-house in Twenty-First Street," she replied, giving the number. "I doubt if I shall have occasion to go out at all, after dinner in the evening. If you have women operatives you might send one of them to call upon me from time to time."

With that understanding they parted.

But the chief turned after he had taken a few steps and stood watching Katherine as she swung along the street with the assured stride of a man whose years have accumulated a sufficient number to give him supreme confidence in his ability to face the world.

Her disguise was perfect, and the chief nodded his approval several times while he watched her.

Truth to tell he had until he saw her that night, doubted her ability to make the disguise sufficiently perfect to warrant the undertaking which she had set herself to do; but the moment he did see her he was satisfied.

Katherine had not made the mistake of attempting to pose as a very young man. She had adopted the middle course—that of a man nearing middle life, who still had the appearance of youth in his face.

And she neither wore a wig nor attempted to dye her own hair—unless a partial process of bleaching could be called dyeing it.

Directly over the temples she had bleached it white.

Above her forehead, where she brushed it straight back after parting it well down on the side, it was also white.

161

Spectacles, rimmed with tortoise-shell, altered, very considerably, the expression and naturalness of her eyes.

A very delicate, blue-black stain, lightly painted upon her cheeks and jaw and chin and upper lip, and put on with studied care, gave her face the appearance of having been shaved clean and close just a little while before. Her ears, fortunately, had never been pierced for ornamentation.

She wore a loose-fitting sack-suit of tweeds, well padded at the shoulders, and inside the shoes, which made her feet appear to be two or three sizes larger than they really were, she wore a pair of heelless house-slippers, from which she had cut most of the tops away.

A brown fedora hat, gloves, a cane, a striped shirt, and an unostentatious tie completed her outward appearance.

Katherine was a good actress, too.

There was nothing about her carriage or walk or in any of her motions to suggest that she was otherwise than what she appeared to be—a man who might be anywhere in the thirties, but who looked even younger than that, despite his gray hairs.

He was somewhat anemic and delicate from leading too much of an indoor life, and who was very slightly deformed, having the suggestion of the beginning of a hump on his back, between the shoulders, and being just a trifle chicken-breasted, to offset it.

"She will do," was the mental comment of the chief as he watched her go. "She would have been able to fool *me*, or anybody else who was not looking for a deception; and nobody will be expecting that—down at the bank. Her voice is all right, her motions are as correct as could be, her walk is perfect. *She will win out, too!*"

He turned away to start on again, and was startled into an exclamation of surprise when he discovered Bingham Harvard standing directly in his path, and only a few paces away—and the Night Wind seemed to have been waiting for him to turn around.

"Hello, chief?" he said, smiling. "Who is your friend?"

For once in his career the chief of the "best detective agency in the world" was thoroughly nonplused. He did not know how to reply, for he could not tell whether Harvard had recognized his own wife or not.

CHAPTER XXIV

THE NIGHT WIND'S CLOSEST CALL

Fortunately, perhaps, for all concerned, the Night Wind did not wait for a reply to his question, which had little interest for him.

He had merely observed that another man—one of small stature—was with the chief, and he had waited in an areaway, out of sight, until the chief was alone.

"I am on my way to pay a call," he announced smilingly. "Save for your call upon me to-day, I have slept the clock pretty nearly around. I am going to see Atkinson. He is the teller now, you know. He used to be my assistant."

"Where does he live? Near here?" the chief asked.

"No. In the lower edge of Harlem—a couple of miles north of where we are now. But the walking is good and I like it."

"Isn't it rather late to make such a call, Harvard? And isn't it risky, too?"

"It isn't late, because I happen to know something of Atkinson's habits. His mother and old maid sister will have gone to bed, and he will be working out mathematical problems in the back parlor of the old frame house where they live. That's his hobby—mathematical problems. As for the risk, I don't see that there is any in this visit."

"Why are you going there, Harvard?" the chief asked.

"Because I intend to make a call upon each one of that bunch who were so ready to believe that I stole that money,

164

and I thought I'd tackle Atkinson first. By the way, have you seen anything of Tom?"

"He called at my office about five," was the evasive reply. "I have just been to his house, but he isn't home yet."

"No? That's funny. Well—there comes a cop, chief. Good night."

The Night Wind wheeled in his tracks and was gone.

Thirty minutes later he pulled the knob of the old-fashioned door-bell at the frame house in Harlem where James Atkinson lived.

When the door was partly opened after a slight delay, Harvard stepped forward quickly, pushed it wider open and stepped into the lighted hall before the man inside could do aught to prevent the act; and at the same time he observed in the most casual manner, as if it had been his nightly habit to make just such calls:

"How are you, Jim? I thought I would drop around and have a chat with you."

Atkinson was made of different stuff from most men.

At the bank he was surreptitiously known as "Frozen-face;" and for all the emotion it ever expressed, the cognomen was quite apt.

Beyond a slight but sharp intake of his breath when he heard Harvard's voice and saw his face, he manifested no surprise at the presence of his former chief.

"Come in," he said, without expression; and, turning, he led the way through the hall, leaving Harvard to close the door.

Bing followed him very quickly, for all that. He was not entirely sure that Atkinson was alone, although there was no other person present when they entered the back parlor.

There, in the middle of the room, was a low table littered with pads and torn sheets of paper covered with figures, where Atkinson found his chiefest joys—or said that he did.

It all looked as if Atkinson had been busily engaged with his problems when he had heard the door-bell; and yet Harvard had the uneasy sensation that another person had been present in that room at the time.

165

Besides, there was the taint of cigar smoke in the air, and Harvard knew that his former associate did not smoke—unless he had acquired the habit within the last year.

Atkinson had not offered Harvard his hand; he did not do so then. Nor did he extend the courtesy of saying, "Sit down, won't you?" or words to that effect. He merely dropped upon a chair himself, and said, in his usual colorless tones:

"Well, Harvard, what do you want of me?"

Bing crossed the room and turned about so that he would command a view of the entire room and its entrances before he replied. Even then he did not sit down.

He had the feeling—without in the least knowing why he had it—that another pair of ears than theirs would be able to hear what was said in that room.

"I don't know whether Ben Mordaunt has told you or not that I saw *him* this morning, Atkinson," he said. "I came here to ask you if you believe that *I* took that hundred and thirty-six thousand dollars. But since your question to me, and the manner of it, I don't have to ask."

Atkinson shrugged his shoulders without replying; and Harvard, studying him with narrowed eyes, and bending slightly forward, said slowly, more to himself than to the other man:

"I wonder, Atkinson, after all, if *you* stole it?"

It was established then that Atkinson, *could* be roused out of that frozen calm, which was, after all, a pose.

He started to his feet, fury expressed in his eyes and upon his features. His lips parted, but he did not speak. Evidently he thought better of what he was on the point of saying.

Doubtless he suddenly recalled some of the startling feats of amazing strength that this man who faced him had performed. But he remained standing, and for a moment the two men eyed each other in silence. Then:

"I wish, Harvard, that you would go away," Atkinson said.

"I think, first, that I will, after all, insist upon an answer to the question I came here to ask of you," Bing replied. "Do you believe that I am guilty of that theft?"

"There was evidence enough to convince anybody, wasn't there?"

"That is not an answer."

"Would you have acted as you have done if you had been an innocent man?"

"Neither is that an answer."

"What more do you want, I'd like to know?"

"Do you believe that I took that money, Jim Atkinson?"

"Yes."

"Since when have you believed that?"

"From the first moment after the packages were missed; from the moment that *you* discovered the loss, if you must know."

"Since before the time when Rushton supplied the supposed evidence that I did take it?"

"As far as that is concerned, I do not know to this day what that evidence was—only in a general way. The old man has never told exactly what it was, more than in a general way, and that it satisfied him. But—"

"Go on, Atkinson."

"Well, I have never thought that *Mordaunt* took it; I know that I did not; and therefore it is quite apparent that you *did*. You are the only one who *could* have stolen it, if *we* did not. It was you who discovered the loss. When you did discover it you said nothing to Mordaunt or to me, but instead you went straight to Cheever, and with him to old Chester himself to report it."

"That showed that you were—then—quite willing to make it appear that one of *us* had taken it. It is a lot more logical for me to believe that you are guilty, *now*, than for you to have thought, *then*, that either Mordaunt or I was the thief."

It was a long statement for Atkinson to make. He was not given to them. Still, Harvard believed that he should justify his acts that Atkinson had mentioned. He passed a hand wearily across his brow and said:

167

"It did not occur to me then that the money had been stolen. I thought that it had been mislaid, or that an error had been made."

Atkinson shrugged his shoulders in a gesture which said as plainly as words could have done it: "You are lying now."

Harvard flushed under the wordless taunt.

"Jim Atkinson," he said slowly, "if I did not know that it was next to the impossible for you to have made away with those packages of bills, I should be of the opinion, after your words and manner to-night, that you are the thief."

He had taken a step nearer to Atkinson while he was speaking. Inadvertently he had turned his back toward the *portières* which were draped over the wide doorway between that room and the parlor in front of it.

He had forgotten for the moment his sensation that he and Atkinson were not alone.

But something in the expression of Atkinson's eyes made him turn, and he did so just as the huge bulk of a man of great size and weight came upon him with a rush and seized him with both arms around his body, holding him helpless for the briefest instant.

Even in that instant Harvard recognized the man, although he had never before seen him without his uniform of gray.

He knew that it was Badger, the giant watchman at the bank, who was supposed to be a Goliath in strength as well as in stature.

Never, in all of Harvard's experiences, had he stood more in need of his own great powers of muscle and physique than then, for the man who opposed him and who now attacked him so viciously stood five inches more than six feet tall, was built in proportion, and boasted that he carried not an ounce of superfluous flesh.

He was the guard outside the screen at the bank.

His huge arms, like the legs of an ordinary man, wrapped themselves around Harvard in a grip that made him think of a steamboat hawser around a snubbing post.

And even as the grip tightened he heard Badger call out to Atkinson:

"Use your telephone, Jim, and call the police. I'll hold this guy. He can't get away from *me*."

Could he not?

That boast of Badger's galvanized and electrified every muscle and nerve that Bing Harvard possessed.

His arms, held helplessly at his sides for an instant, began to swell with the strength that he forced into them. They twisted and writhed beneath the pressure that the giant forced down upon them.

He brought his hands up slowly but surely behind Badger's back until he could lock them together, and then he squeezed with all his strength, at the same moment lifting one of his feet and bringing his heel down heavily upon Badger's toes.

The shock was sudden and unexpected.

For the briefest fraction of an instant Badger's hold around Harvard's body relaxed with the pain of it; and in that instant Harvard jerked one of his own arms so nearly free that he was able to reach upward, around the watchman's shoulder, and to get the palm of his right hand beneath Badger's chin.

The advantage of the "hold" was now transferred to Harvard, and he forced the giant's chin upward and his head backward until he could feel the arms that were around him relaxing; and then, with a dexterous twist of a leg, Harvard tripped him.

The crash of two hundred and sixty pounds and one hundred and eighty odd falling to the floor together was some crash; but the hundred and eighty were on top.

Harvard, by main strength, forced his own body upward and backward out of the grip of Badger. And he sprang to his feet just as Atkinson rushed forward toward them from the telephone to take a hand in the struggle.

Harvard laughed in his face. It was an unpleasant and a dangerous laugh, too, and Atkinson stopped; and Harvard sprang past him, darted through the hallway, and passed outside into the street.

Then, as he went swiftly away, he thought, in unuttered words:

"That was about the closest call I have had yet!"

CHAPTER XXV

THE "SOCIETY OF CRIPPLED COPS"

In the mean time, it is quite necessary for the proper working out of the involved problems that we should know something about the things that happened to Tom Clancy after he had left the office of the chief in that tall down-town building, shortly after five o'clock that same afternoon.

For it was the ultimate focusing of the events of the twenty-four hours which began with the liberation of Lady Kate from the jail in Queens that finally uncovered the trail of the real thief.

Tom exchanged greeting with the man in the elevator, and spoke to his acquaintance at the corner near the stairs to the "L" road.

Two or three moments later, as he stepped past the box of the ticket-chopper, he heard his name spoken.

"This is Mr. Clancy, ain't it?" was the inquiry; and Tom nodded, not recognizing the man who addressed him, although the features were oddly familiar.

"You've got me guessing," he said. "Who are you?"

The man chuckled. "I have shaved off my mustache, and I'm without a uniform," he said. "I guess that's why you don't know me. I'm off the force, Mr. Clancy. I handed in my shield to-day."

"Still, I do not seem to remember you," Tom said, and turned toward the train that was pulling in at the station.

"Wait for the next train, Mr. Clancy," the man suggested. "There is something that I want to say to you—if you will let me. My name is Compton. The first time I ever saw you was also the first time that I ever saw the Night Wind; and that was nearly a year ago. Got me now?"

"Sure," said Tom, laughing. "Speaking of the Night Wind, didn't he take you out to the Bronx somewhere, and drop you, a night or so ago?"

"He did, sir. That is why I handed in my shield to-day. I'd have been called up for trial and I'd have got the worst of it, so I thought I'd just get out. I'm a joiner by trade, and a good one. I can easily get all the work I want. Why, I helped to do the inside work of that very bank where the Night Wind used to be teller; only that was nearly ten years ago."

They had withdrawn to the platform rail. Tom leaned his elbows upon it. Compton stood facing him.

"What is it that you wished to say to me, Compton?" Clancy asked.

The ex-policeman glanced warily around him before he replied. Then he said:

"This ain't just exactly the place to talk about it, Mr. Clancy; but—say! Have you got any idea how many cops Bingham Harvard has put out of business since he has been 'Alias the Night Wind'? Of course, he ain't hurt nobody since he got back; but I mean before he went away?"

"There ought to be quite a bunch of them," Tom replied, smiling with amusement.

"There are between twenty and thirty, counting in Brooklyn and the Bronx. I've got a full list of them at home, but that is a close estimate."

"Well, what of it? What about it, Compton?"

"That's what I wanted to talk to you about. A lot of them guys got together about a week ago, when they heard that Lady Kate was back again, and before they knew that *he* was; and—this is what I'm gettin' at—they have formed an association. We thought—"

Tom Clancy interrupted Compton by laughing aloud and with hearty amusement; and the ex-policeman, after watching him a moment, laughed also, although he remarked, a trifle testily:

"Maybe it is funny—only *we* didn't see it in just that way. Maybe you remember who Lieutenant Banta is—or was. Do you?"

"Yes. He was one of the three who made that first attempt to arrest Harvard at Chester's house when he was first charged with the theft. Banta was with Rushton and Coniglio. What about *him*?"

"He is off the force, too—same as I am. And *he* is the one who suggested organizing this association."

"The Society of Crippled Cops!" Clancy exclaimed, laughing again. "Is that what you call it, Compton—'The Society of Crippled Cops'?" and he laughed again.

"No, it ain't. But it wouldn't be no lie at that. But, say, Mr. Clancy, this ain't no joke that I'm talkin' about. I want to tell you right now, straight off of the reel, that Banta is as square as they make 'em, that he ain't got no use and never had any for any sort of a frame-up, and that *he* has just about made up *his* mind that the case against the Night Wind *was* a frame-up. And that's why he got the bunch together that has felt the weight of the Night Wind's hand. And you can just understand one thing about it, too, which is, that Banta hasn't included *all* of them—not by a long shot!"

"Rushton ain't in it, and Coniglio ain't in it, and there are a few others that ain't in it; and I only got into it myself since his nibs took me out to the Bronx and dropped me. And that society that you make such fun of ain't out for the Night Wind's gore, either—it is out for the purpose of helping him to square himself."

"That's what! And in helping *him* to square *himself* that bunch of cops and ex-cops means to square *themselves* at the same time. And they ain't doing it for any particular love that they feel for the Night Wind, either, but for the love that they do feel for the whole blooming police force of the city of New York, which is 'in' might bad because of this business."

"They just want to prove to the satisfaction of everybody that the *dis*honest cop is an exception, and that ninety-eight or ninety-nine percent of the police force is as fine a lot of men as ever walked a street or wore a uniform. And you can put that into your pipe and smoke it, Mr. Clancy!"

Compton had talked so rapidly and so excitedly, but, more than all else, with such genuine earnestness, that Tom Clancy's laughter stopped, the smile faded from his lips, and he bent forward to listen to every word that the ex-policeman uttered.

It was almost unbelievable; and yet Clancy sensed the truth of it all.

"Look here, Compton," he said soberly at the close of the statement, "I would like to see that man Banta and have a talk with him."

"That is exactly why I wigwagged you, Mr. Clancy. I thought maybe you'd like to do that very thing."

"*Can* I see him?"

"Surest thing you know, sir."

"When?"

"To-night—within a few hours—if you want to go with me to do it."

"Where?"

"There is to be a meeting to-night of part of us—as many as can get there. I ain't at liberty to tell you just where it's at, but you'll find out when you get there. We will have about a dozen of us present, I guess. Are you on?"

"Am I *on*? You bet your sweet life I'm on, Compton. I wouldn't miss it for a farm. And, say, I want to shake hands with you." Then he hesitated a moment and added: "But what I cannot understand is this—just why the very chaps that Harvard has laid up or maimed or put down and out should be the ones to do this thing. I'm not onto those curves; not yet."

"Maybe there are a lot of reasons, when all is said, Mr. Clancy," Compton replied a trifle thoughtfully. "Lieutenant Banta says that we all ought to be thankful that the Night Wind didn't lay us out cold when he had a chance, considering the fact that it was us that always tackled *him*, and that he never lit into any of us at the start."

174

"He says, too, that there are about nine chances out of ten that the Night Wind is innocent, because he claims that no guilty man has ever acted just as he has done. And he says that Rushton is a crook, anyhow, and Banta knows it, although he can't prove it. But the whole bunch of reasons boiled down into one is this—that the honest cops want to square themselves, and they want to make it so uncomfortable for the *dis*honest ones that they'll get off the force. And there you are, Mr. Clancy."

"That's bully, Compton—perfectly bully. Here comes another train. Shall we take it?"

"Not if you're going with me, sir. We will go in another direction. I only chased you up the stairs to tell you all of this."

"Which way, then?"

"We will take a surface car across the bridge and walk a little ways after we get to the other end of it. But there's a couple of hours yet before we get together."

"Good. Then we will go somewhere and have dinner. Do the others know that you are to take me to their meeting?" he asked as they descended the stairway to the street.

"Nope. The idea has been suggested, but was never acted upon," Compton replied. "What they would like to do would be to have the Night Wind himself show up at one of their confabs. And that is what I thought that maybe you could arrange when I made up my mind all in a minute to tackle you."

"Eh? Harvard himself?" Clancy stopped stock-still in the middle of the sidewalk. "Why not?" he added.

Then he turned and faced Compton, and there was a dangerous look in his eyes as he said slowly: "Compton, if there is anything like a trap to catch him about this business I *know* that I will live long enough to kill you for it. *I know it*."

Compton smiled reassuringly.

"I have been wondering why you didn't raise that objection, Mr. Clancy. It is the most natural one in the world under the circumstances, and you haven't got anything but my word to go on. But you ain't nobody's fool, and if you'll just look me straight in the eyes while I'm sayin' all this I guess you'll believe me."

Clancy did stare into Compton's eyes for several seconds; then he said:

"You go ahead over to Brooklyn, Compton. Wait for me in the office at the Clarendon Hotel. We will eat there. I will be there inside an hour and a half." And he turned and ran back to the elevated station, leaving Compton gaping after him.

He rode only a few stations. When he descended he speedily found a "vacant" taxicab, and in a very short time abandoned it in the middle of a block where he ordered the driver to wait.

Ten minutes after that he entered the door of the "little house on the roof," where he had hoped to find Bingham Harvard.

But Harvard was not there. As it happened, he had gone out into the streets only a short time before Clancy arrived, and there was no telling where he had gone nor when he might return. So Clancy seized upon a sheet of paper and wrote:

> DEAR BING:
>
> If you see this in time meet me exactly at midnight, at the corner of Congress and Adams Streets, in Brooklyn. If I am not there in fifteen minutes, don't wait. It may be important and it may not. If I think I am followed I won't show up. A new wrinkle has developed. It looks all right, but it may be a plant.
>
> TOM

He found Compton awaiting him at the Clarendon when he got there, and they went into the café for dinner.

"Is that meeting-place of the Crippled Cops anywhere near here?" he asked while they were at the table.

"Yes," Compton replied. "It is between here and Fulton Ferry; and that is all I can tell you at the present time. Banta will tell you everything about it when you get together."

There was little more said between them until they left the table and started for the outer door; but then Clancy remarked soberly:

"Compton, I'm trusting you a whole lot if anybody should ask you. I have sent word to the Night Wind since our talk. Maybe I will see my way clear to bring you together. I don't know yet. But—if any funny business develops, that society of Crippled Cops will be a society of dead ones before we are through with you."

CHAPTER XXVI

FOR THE HONOR OF THE SERVICE

"I am going to ask you to stroll slowly down the street while I skip on ahead and let the bunch know who's coming," Compton remarked before they had traversed a block together. "What do you say to that?"

"You are asking me to put a heap of trust in you, Compton," Clancy replied slowly; "but I don't think anybody would want *me* for anything—and, besides, I'm taking chances to-night. Go ahead. As long as I am in the game I'll play the limit."

"Keep straight ahead on this side of the street until I meet you, if it takes you all the way to the old ferry," Compton called back as he started.

But Clancy had not gone more than half that distance when he saw Compton returning; and he was all eagerness when they met.

"It's all right," he said. "Banta is there, and he's mighty glad you are coming. He says it'll be the first chance he has had to put himself right—though just what he means by that I don't know. It is only a little way farther now."

"Did you tell Banta what I told you about the Night Wind—that I had sent word to him?" Tom asked.

"No. I thought I would leave that to you. You can suggest it or not, as you choose, after you have seen enough of the bunch to satisfy yourself that we are on the level. You

178

can bet your bottom dollar that *I* am on the level, Mr. Clancy."

"I somehow believe that, Compton, although I do not see exactly why I should do so, at that. Hello! Is this the place?"

"Yes. Up two flights. Denton, one of the Brooklyn cops—the Night Wind busted an arm for him once—lives here. He hasn't got any family—only a brother who works nights in the composing-room of a newspaper; and they keep house for themselves and get their grub outside, I guess."

It was one of the old-fashioned three-story brick houses which may still be seen in the lower part of Fulton Street, Brooklyn.

A door stood open at the top of the stairs, and as Clancy approached it, slightly in advance of Compton, Lieutenant Banta appeared at the threshold.

"You are Mr. Clancy," he said, extending his hand. "I have seen you often, although I don't suppose you have ever noticed me. I used to be at the Oak Street Station in the days of Ed Sleven. I knew you when you were a youngster around your father's office."

"Glad to renew the acquaintance," Tom replied, accepting the proffered hand.

He glanced around the room into which he was drawn and smiled grimly. Counting himself and Compton, there were exactly thirteen men present, and every one of them save himself had experienced the mightiness of Bingham Harvard's strength of muscle.

Banta conducted him around the room, introducing him to each man in turn and making some appropriate comment as he did so, such as:

"This is Maddox, Mr. Clancy. He used to be stationed at Coney Island. He hasn't much to complain about—only a crushed toe, which was well long ago. This is Denton, our host to-night; he had a broken arm. And this is Morris; he got a black eye when the Night Wind slammed Conover's head against it. It broke Conover's nose, as you can see, for this is Conover sitting next to him."

179

And so on throughout the list. The names and what happened to each one are not necessary. Only it was funny—or at least Tom Clancy thought so, for he wore a wide grin all the way around the group.

"Banta," he said when the introductions were over, "if I had been suddenly taken up in an aeroplane and dropped down into the tree-tops of Timbuctoo, I wouldn't have been half so much surprised as I am at this minute. Why, these chaps seem to be actually proud of their—er—what-you-may-call-ems."

"Call them experiences, Mr. Clancy. They are. They learned something. We are not regularly organized, understand. We have simply got together in a common cause; and that common cause is to square ourselves *with* ourselves—and incidentally, of course, with Mr. Bingham Harvard, if he is, as many of us believe, innocent."

"He is, Banta. I *know* it," Tom replied with feeling.

"And I believe it. The reason why I believe it is manifold. Principally it is because I have had a long experience with criminals and crooks of all descriptions, and I have yet to know of one who would conduct himself exactly as Harvard has done since the beginning of this affair."

"The next most important one is that I know Rushton and Rushton's methods, and while I do not *know* anything to *prove* that he framed up that case against Harvard, I do know that he is quite capable of doing it."

"We will get the goods on him before we are through with him, Banta," Tom replied.

"And this bunch here, every one, will help—if there are 'goods' to be delivered," was the instant reply. "All the same, some of us are not entirely satisfied that Harvard did not get that wad; *and—we would like to have a straight talk with him in person.* How does that strike you?"

"I can see no objection—provided, always, that Harvard can be convinced that you are playing fair."

"If he is the man I think he is, it won't be a very difficult matter to convince him of that, Mr. Clancy."

"I am not so sure. His opinion of the police is somewhat severe just at present."

"Naturally. That is what we want to remedy. Do you think that you can induce him to come here to see us?"

"When?"

"At any time you will fix. To-night—now, if he is within summoning distance."

"I will hear more of what you have to tell me before I make up my mind to summon him, lieutenant," Tom replied.

"Suppose you question me, then? What is it that you wish to know further?"

"This, first of all: what is the real reason for this organization? It is not for any especial interest you have in the affairs of Bing Harvard. When all is said, you chaps don't care a whoop whether he is guilty or innocent. So, what *is* the real reason?"

"It is for the individual honor of every honest cop in the city of New York," was the straightforward and emphatic reply. "This getting together was my idea in the first place. I found that the others fell for it on the spot. We don't care a picayune whether Bingham Harvard is Bingham Harvard or John Jones; but we do care if we have been put into the position of hunting down an innocent man, if our superior officer knew all the time that he *was* innocent."

Tom nodded.

"I understand all that," he said. "Here is another thing: Compton tells me that he turned in his shield to-day and quit. He says that you have quit also. If all that is true, what interests have you still in the police department?"

"Compton can answer for himself; or perhaps he has already done so. As for me, I have served my twenty years, and I have long intended to retire when that was done. But I love the 'force' and a lot of the men who are on it. I have got just as much respect for the rank and file as I ever had."

"And—here is the point, Mr. Clancy—there isn't any doubt whatever that a good many 'frame-ups' have been worked on innocent men and women in the past; but, within the knowledge of these men here, there never has been a probable or even a possible frame-up that has attained the celebrity of this Bingham Harvard case. Don't you see the point I am making?"

"Go ahead—I'm all attention."

"If the Harvard case *was* a frame-up, and it can be proved that it was, and if the man who did the 'framing' can be nailed and punished as he should be, it will put the ever-lasting kibosh on any more such practices in the New York police department. And it is to the distinct personal interest of every cop in New York to assist in bringing that very thing about. Do you get me now?"

"Yes."

"Do you think that the Night Wind—Harvard—will be willing to meet us and to reply to a few questions we would like to ask him to his face?"

"I do think so; yes."

"Will you undertake to arrange such a meeting, Mr. Clancy?"

"I will put it up to Mr. Harvard himself."

"That is all that we can ask. You see, there are several things about the affair that get our goats, so to speak."

"What, for example?"

"Well, for one thing, before he went away he had to spend a lot of money. Where did he get it to spend, if he didn't have that dough that was swiped from the Centropolis Bank? The—"

"Wait a minute, Banta."

"Well?"

"I was going to say that *I* could reply to that question for him; but, on second thought, I'll let him do it for himself. But I know this much: *I know that what he did spend was his own money!*—and that it was merely an accident that he happened to have a large sum with him in cash that night when he made his getaway from you and Coniglio and Rush-ton."

"That sounds all right, only we would like to hear *him* explain it, Mr. Clancy."

"Of course. And if you have got any more such questions, keep them under your hat until I bring him here before you, just so you won't think that I could post him about what to expect."

"That's all right. We wouldn't think that. Don't forget we are all cops, and that some of us are detectives as well. We think we know something about men, too. Do I understand that you will bring the Night Wind here to us?"

"Yes."

"When?"

"Soon after midnight, I think—if he receives a message that I left for him. That is, if you and the others can wait till then," Tom replied.

Banta looked about him.

"Four of this bunch will have to go before that," he said; "but there will be several others here by that time to take their places. He will have about the same number present as are here now. It is now nine o'clock. I will expect you back here between twelve and one. Is that correct?"

"Entirely."

Clancy left them soon after that.

Once outside, he decided that he would not await the appointment at the corner of Congress and Adams Streets, but would return to the "little house on the roof" of the old warehouse, in the hope that he would find Harvard there, and so hasten the hour for the appointment.

And so it happened that when the Night Wind returned from his somewhat exciting call upon Atkinson he found Tom Clancy awaiting him with an eagerness that was very quickly explained.

Nevertheless, when Clancy made known all that had happened, Harvard shook his head in grave doubt.

"It looks all right on the face of it, Tom," he said; "but I haven't much confidence in the police, and it is just as likely to be a 'plant' as not. However, since you approve of it, I will go there with you. But, old chap, if it *is* a put-up job—if it *should* prove to be a trap—I'll give that bunch such a run for their money as they never dreamed of in all their lives."

* * * * * * *

It was twelve o'clock precisely—a trifle earlier than he was expected—when Tom Clancy rapped upon the door beyond which he knew that Banta and the others were awaiting the Night Wind.

And for the first time since the arrangement was made Tom had misgivings of his own.

CHAPTER XXVII

THE GOOD THAT MEN DO

Former Lieutenant Banta was standing expectantly beside a small table near the middle of the room, and fourteen policemen—a few of them in uniform, but the majority in citizen's clothes—were seated in various attitudes around it when Tom Clancy entered in response to the summons "Come in!"

Tom was alone, and the face of Banta expressed some surprise; but one glance around that room and at the faces of the men who waited there satisfied Harvard's friend that there was nothing to fear. He half turned about and called out:

"Come ahead, Bing!"

Bingham Harvard, alias the Night Wind, stepped across the threshold and halted there, facing them all.

Every man of all of them had anticipated that moment and was prepared for it, and yet it came in the nature of a surprise, after all.

There is no doubt that each one had wondered what he would do or say when the Night Wind should actually appear—and the remarkable thing about it was that for a brief space nobody moved or uttered a word.

And then it was the Night Wind who broke the odd silence.

"It strikes me, gentlemen," he said, "that this is rather an unprecedented event."

185

Banta stepped forward quickly, with enthusiasm in his face and eyes.

"Mr. Harvard," he said in his deep and resonant voice, "this is one of the most satisfactory moments of my entire career as a policeman. Every question that we would ask you is, in effect, answered by the fact of your presence. None but an innocent man would have ventured to come here to face us. I want to shake hands with you."

As they stood so for a moment, with their right hands clasped together, while they looked earnestly into each other's eyes, Banta remarked, half whimsically and with a friendly smile:

"Those fingers you are holding, Mr. Harvard, are the same ones that you crushed for me, up at Chester's house, that time when Rushton and Coniglio and I attempted to put you under arrest. Perhaps it will please you to know now that not one of them is a bit the worse for that experience."

"I am very glad of that," Bingham replied simply.

"And there is not a man here who has not some personal recollection of you of the same sort," Banta continued. "Of course, they are not *all* here. There are others who are on duty and could not come."

Harvard nodded. It was a trying moment. He did not know just what to say.

"I think," Banta went on, "that all who *are* here would like to shake hands with you as well as I."

"I am sure that I will be mighty glad to shake hands with *them*," Harvard replied instantly and looking smilingly from face to face, "and to ask one and all of them to try to forgive me for the injuries I have done them."

"*Forgive you!*" Cregan of the Bronx exclaimed, stepping quickly forward, while the others crowded around him. "Why, I'm *proud* of that collarbone you busted up for me; and there isn't a guy in this bunch that don't brag—on the quiet—of how he got *his*."

"You wished to ask me some questions, Lieutenant Banta," Harvard said as soon as the general hand-shaking was over and the men had resumed their seats.

Banta nodded.

"The necessity for the replies to them has passed now," he said. "It has become merely a matter of perfunctory duty. The very fact that you are here, and the manner in which you have come among us, *satisfies every man here as to the main fact.*"

"Nevertheless, lieutenant, I prefer to hear the questions, and to answer them."

"All right. Here is one: where did you get the money that you have used—and you have spent considerable—since you became an outlaw and a hunted man? I have got to ask these questions straight from the shoulder, you know," he added, half apologetically.

"I much prefer that you should do so, lieutenant. It was my own money that I spent. Perhaps all of you have been informed that I do not know who my parents were. I was a foundling."

"Mr. Sterling Chester took me in and cared for me. He gave me the privileges of a son. He was always extremely kind and affectionate to me. I loved him; I love him now as well as if he were my own father. Wait, please; let me finish in my own way."

"From my early youth he gave me an allowance. As I grew older he increased it. I was never a spendthrift, nor extravagant in my tastes and desires. I saved much of that allowance. Later, after I left college—where Mr. Clancy here was my chum—I went to work in the Centropolis Bank, and as I progressed and was promoted from one position to another my salary was increased. I saved a great portion of it."

"Such sums as I had laid by I invested from time to time in real estate in the outlying sections of the city. Then, just before this thing happened to me, I had arranged to take up all of those investments, save one or two small ones, and to group them all together into one big one—at least I called it a big one."

"It happened that my agent telephoned for me to go to his office after banking hours that very day that Mr. Chester asked me to go to his house in the evening—that afternoon before the evening of the attempted arrest at his house, in which you participated, lieutenant."

Banta nodded. The others were paying the closest attention.

"I went to the office of my agent as soon as I was free from the bank that day. He gave me the money that was due me in cash, as is often the whim and habit of real-estate dealers. It was in bills, contained in a large envelope, which I put into the inner pocket of my coat. It was still there, lieutenant, when you and the others attacked me in the library of Chester's house. The amount was twenty-eight thousand four hundred and sixty-nine dollars; and it represented very nearly all the savings as well as the accrued profits of my life up to that day."

"It was almost as if fate had directed that you should have that money with you, Mr. Harvard," said Lieutenant Banta.

"I attribute it to a much higher power than mere fate, lieutenant," Harvard replied with a smile. "What is the next question?"

"All of the others are unimportant; possibly attributable to curiosity and interest rather than to the case itself."

"Nevertheless, ask them."

"What, in your own opinion, did become of those packages of bills that were lost or stolen from the bank?"

"Concerning that I am as much in doubt as any person in this room."

"But—you have suspicions?"

"If I have such, they have been formed since my return to New York. I had not one before I went away."

"Are you willing to tell us those suspicions?"

"No. They are not sufficiently direct; and my own experiences demand that I shall not divulge them until I am very certain that they are, in the main, correct."

"Are you now engaged in an effort to discover who the real culprit is?"

"Yes. That is why I returned."

"We are here to assist you in that effort, Mr. Harvard."

Bingham Harvard raised his head proudly. His eyes shone, and there was a suggestion of moisture in them as he replied with deep feeling:

"I thank you, gentlemen. This moment, and what it brings to me, repays me for all that I have suffered. It does more, for it restores my confidence in my fellow men and my belief that justice must finally triumph. I want to say now that I regret more than I can express the physical injuries I have inflicted upon so many policemen—for here before my eyes I can see the living proof that the New York City policemen are the finest and the best lot of men who were ever enlisted under one direct command."

Everybody was silent for a moment after that; then Harvard asked:

"Are there more questions, lieutenant?"

"I'd like to ask one!" Officer Casey exclaimed from the background. "I'd like to know how the blazes you do it, sir?"

"Do what?" Harvard inquired smilingly.

"Well, you chucked me down some elevated steps once on a time, an' then you went up in smoke or something; annyhow, you disappeared mighty suddint. Rushton is called the strongest man on the force; Coniglio ain't far behind him, and Lieutenant Banta could handle anny two of us if he set out to do it; yet you wance put all three of thim guys in the soup at once. How'd you do it? That's what *I* wanta know."

"I don't know. I was born that way. The strength is inherited from my unknown parents. I only know that I have it, and that I am sometimes afraid of it myself. It is a gift—in just the same way that some persons can sing while others cannot; some can paint pictures and others cannot."

"Just in proportion, Casey, as you are stronger than the average man you meet on the streets, and as Rushton, Coniglio, and Lieutenant Banta are stronger than you are, so have I been given more physical strength than they possess."

"How did you get from Boston to New York, once, when there wasn't any train to bring you?" Brainard of the Forty-third asked. "That was the time when you took my gun and stick away from me at the corner of Park Avenue and One Hundred and Twenty-Eighth Street. How did you do that?"

"I came on the fast mail, which carries no passengers. I rode all the way over between the engine tender and the first car, which was 'blind.' That was easy, although it *was* uncomfortable."

"How did you get here, the other day, from the steamship *Golgotha* when she was somewhere between Fire Island and Sandy Hook?" Lieutenant Banta asked, smiling. "I confess that that has puzzled *me*."

"I was not aboard the *Golgotha*, lieutenant. I left the other side two days after Mrs. Harvard sailed. I came on the *Pretoria*. I arrived here four days after she did. That cablegram that I showed to the inspector, if you know about that, was faked for the purposes of that little joke. So, you see, there is nothing supernatural about it after all."

"Well, Mr. Harvard, we have done with the questioning. We are all in line to help you to square yourself, because we want to square *ourselves*. There are some of us here who are going to work on the *inside* of that thing that you call the 'system' to that end. I am one of them; and, now that I have retired, I am in a position to do perhaps more than I otherwise could. Are you willing to keep in touch with us—with me?"

"Most certainly. I—"

"Hold on a minute, Bing!" Tom Clancy interrupted him. "I have held my breath so long that I'll bust if I don't let it out."

He turned toward Banta.

"I have been thinking of a plan since this confab began," he said. "I have decided to stick with Harvard from this out until the game is finished. I need a vacation, anyhow."

"I'm going to let a few friends of mine worry about me, thinking that I have disappeared. *I* will keep in touch with you, Banta, and I will put some others in touch with you, too. We won't lose any tricks, either. How does that strike you?"

"Very favorably, Mr. Clancy," was the reply.

"All right. Then I'll give you a pointer. You get busy down at headquarters, and find out exactly the method that Rushton used in that frame-up. And *you* can do it. And if you can get anything on the inspector in the mean time—get it!"

CHAPTER XXVIII

THE GREAT WHITE LIGHT

"Say, Chester, who is that new guy you've got inside of the payin'-teller's cage?"

Rushton had walked into the bank and through it directly to the office of the president, shortly after one o'clock on the second day of Lady Kate's incumbency as an assistant teller under the name of Erin Caton.

He had barely glanced toward the cage as he passed it. One would have supposed that he had not noticed the presence of a new employee there. Nevertheless he seemed to be thoroughly aware of the fact.

The thing that Chester noticed concerning him, however, was an utter absence of the half reluctant and partly respectful formality with which Rushton had addressed him heretofore. Since the experiences in Queens County and the payment of the five thousand dollars the lieutenant's manner toward the president of the Centropolis Bank had undergone an entire change.

"He is the new assistant paying-teller," the banker replied. "We have been short-handed since the Harvard affair. Why do you ask?"

"Oh, nothin'. Only you wanta look out that he don't get into you for a wad, the same as Harvard did. That's all. It ain't always safe to put a new man into a responsible job like that, is it? I thought you boosted 'em from one place to another."

"We do, as a rule. However, Mr. Caton is very highly recommended."

"Caton's his name, eh? Why don't you call him in here and let me look him over?"

"That would be quite an unnecessary proceeding, lieutenant. Why should you want to look him over, as you express it?"

"Oh, just to take his measure. If I am going to keep tabs for you on things down here, it's just as well to start in right, you know."

"But I was not aware that you were going to perform any such service for me, Mr. Rushton."

"Wasn't you?" Rushton grinned. "I guess if you think about it a minute you will remember that we made that arrangement the other mornin' when we took that ride together. You don't mean to tell me that you have forgotten it, Chester?" he demanded in mock surprise.

"I haven't the slightest recollection of—"

"Say, now, look here, what's the matter with you? Of course you remember when you stop to think about it. I was to keep tabs generally on everything that's doin' around the bank and to give you all the spare time I could from my regular duties down below, and act as a sort of 'specially privileged detective right along, and you was to pay me the small sum of twenty-five hundred a year for doin' it. See?"

Chester could only stare his amazement.

His wit was nimble enough so that he instantly comprehended that Rushton was indulging in another form of "touch," cloaked although it was in a pretense of a previous business arrangement.

There were so many emotions in his mind at the moment that it would have been difficult even for himself to have told which one was uppermost—disgust, anger, or outraged dignity—that he should be compelled into juxtaposition with such a character as Rushton was fast proving himself to be.

If Rodney Rushton had put down on the desk in front of Chester the proofs of his own "frame-up" against Bingham Harvard they would not have been more convincing to the exact mathematical mind of the banker than the revelation of

Rushton's true character as it gaped him in the face at that moment.

And, oddly enough, it brought him the first sense of real relief, the first emotion of joy, that he had experienced during all the year and more since his loss of faith in Harvard.

He raised his eyes slowly to Rushton's face, and if they had been X-ray eyes the banker could not have seen more clearly into the fleshless skeleton of the police lieutenant's character.

Sterling Chester, according to his own methods of business life, was as shrewd and deft in the manipulation of affairs as anybody. Given a proposition which required only the exercise of his own judgment for a decision, it was a rare thing indeed when that judgment was wrong. It was only when he was forced to rely upon the judgments of others—as in police matters, or anything extraneous to his own business, for example—that he erred.

The condition at that moment—and it all came with the suddenness of a flash of light—was as if Bingham Harvard had been standing before him covered from head to feet in a cloak of guilt and Rushton had sprung into the room and torn the cloak aside. And yet the steady calmness in the mildly cold eyes of the banker never wavered for an instant while he looked into the police lieutenant's eyes.

Rushton saw nothing, realized nothing, of what was passing in the banker's mind.

Not once, in all the effort that Bingham Harvard and his friends were making to establish his innocence, had so great a step forward been made as that one which Rodney Rushton inadvertently compelled the banker to take at that moment.

Sterling Chester suddenly *knew* that Bingham Harvard was innocent.

It was not belief merely; it was knowledge.

As one may gaze upon a moving picture while it is thrown upon a screen before one's eyes, so Chester saw revealed the moving drama of his own misjudgments of his foster-son as they had been enacted during the past year; and yet not a trace of all this showed upon his face or in his eyes.

Nor, in spite of all this explanation that has been given here, was there a noticeable hiatus in the conversation between the two men.

If the banker appeared to hesitate while he searched for a reply to Rushton's remarkable statement, it was but a natural hesitation under the circumstances; or, at least, the lieutenant so regarded it.

When the banker did reply it was with the calm directness which might be expected of him.

"Let me understand you perfectly—if that is possible, Rushton," he said coldly. "I will make no pretense of recalling a conversation which never occurred between us; but I do hear, and understand also, all that you have just said. Stated as a plain, cold fact, the situation is this: In order to avoid the unpleasant possibilities which might arise if you choose to reveal the circumstances of my call at the jail in Queens County, I must henceforth pay you the sum of twenty-five hundred dollars a year for some sort of pretended service which you will be supposed to perform for me at this bank or in connection with it. Is that correct?"

Rushton never batted an eye.

"Oh, I will perform the services right enough, when there are any to perform," he replied.

"Nevertheless, in the main my statement is correct, is it not?"

Rushton nodded, and there was a perceptible sneer on his face.

"You have just received five thousand dollars from me to pay for silence on your part. I had supposed that that ended the matter. Now you come here and demand an additional sum which amounts, approximately, to fifty dollars a week. How long a time will it be before you make further demands upon me, lieutenant?"

"Aw, there won't be any more, Chester. That five thousand was a retainer. This here twenty-five hundred a year is to be my regular salary—and I'll earn that; you see if I don't. Only, it's got to go, and that settles it."

"Very well. If I must, I must, I suppose. How do you want it paid to you?"

194

Rushton's eyes gleamed avariciously. He had not antici-pated quite such an easy victory as this was. The very ease of it should have warned him, but it did not.

"You just now arranged for that part of it when you said something about payin' me fifty a week," he replied.

"Then, if you come here every Saturday—"

"Make it Mondays, Chester."

"Very well; if you come to me here every Monday I will pay over to you the sum of fifty dollars. Is that understood? And also that there will be no further demands made upon me?"

"Sure."

"Because there is a limit to my endurance. And now, if you will glance behind you, you will discover that there are two gentlemen outside the rail waiting to see me; so I will ask you to excuse me."

"Oh, I'll go in a second or so. Don't you want me to take a look at that young fellow you call Caton first?"

"No. It is not necessary."

"All right. Just as you say. I'll take a squint at him through the window of the cage as I pass outside. That'll do just as well." Rushton got upon his feet. "I guess we'd better shake hands on it, Chester," he said, extending his own, which the banker pretended not to see. "Shake hands, Mr. Chester," Rushton repeated, and there was a suggestion of menace in his tone. "There's a few guys lookin' this way, and it won't do no harm to have 'em see us part real friendly."

Chester rose to his feet. For an instant he permitted his right hand to rest limply upon Rushton's. Then, as the lieu-tenant went from the office, the president turned and actually hurried into his private lavatory, where he let the cold water run upon his hands for several minutes.

The dispatch with which he transacted the business of those waiting men was unusual with him; and they sensed that there was something new and eager in the banker's manner and attitude. There was a new light in his eyes, an unusual alertness in his methods, which they regarded as un-usual. Had they but known it, Sterling Chester had not been

195

so happy as then for more than a year; because—*he knew that Bingham Harvard was innocent.*

As soon as the business of the moment was dismissed Chester pressed a button beneath the edge of his desk and directed that the new assistant paying-teller be requested to come to the president's office immediately.

Then he leaned back in his chair and waited, and there was an unusual—and unreadable—expression upon his kindly face that had been absent from it for a long, long time.

Lady Kate, when she received the summons, experienced a thrill of consternation. She had seen Rushton pass into the bank and out of it again. She knew that he had stopped near the window in going out and had stared long and hard at her through the screen of steel. She wondered if he had penetrated her disguise.

"Don't be afraid of the old man, Caton," Mordaunt cautioned as she started away. "His bark is worse than his bite—as a rule."

Nevertheless, she entered the private office in some perturbation; and the first remark addressed to her by the president was not calculated to allay her uneasiness.

"Mr. Caton," he said, leaning back in his chair and putting the tips of his fingers together, as was a habit with him when he was very much in earnest, "certain matters have just been brought to my attention which renders it necessary for me to question you somewhat closely concerning yourself and your employment in this bank. I must know, and at once, exactly who and what you are, and precisely what you expect to accomplish while you are here with us. Be seated, Mr. Caton."

CHAPTER XXIX

FINDING A BANKER'S HEART

Lady Kate gasped—inwardly; but she stuck to her guns just the same.

"I supposed, sir," she replied coolly, notwithstanding the fluttering that was going on inside of her, "that the letter I brought to you, and the other papers, sufficiently explained all that."

"For your purposes as they stood an hour ago, and for my own part they did," he went on mildly. "But things have happened in the last half-hour or so which entirely change my attitude toward you and your reason for being here. You are, as I was led to understand, a detective. Is that correct?"

"In the main it is. I am acting in that capacity, sir. Of course, you were made fully aware of that fact before I came here at all."

"Naturally. I was forced into receiving you here as an employee. I deeply resented that fact, although I was power-less to prevent it. Just now I find myself inclined to be glad that you *are* here."

Katherine was more puzzled than ever, but she wisely kept silent.

"As I look at you closely," the banker went on in that same mild tone, "I find a suggestion of familiarity in your features, although I cannot for the moment place it. But it really makes no difference. I assume, for reasons well known to each of us, that you are more or less well acquainted with Mr. Thomas Clancy. Is that correct?"

"It is."

"And—with Mr. and Mrs. Bingham Harvard as well? You need have no hesitation in answering."

"Yes, sir."

"Could you communicate with either of the two persons I last named?"

"Yes."

"Will you undertake to convey a message to one or both of them from me?"

"Yes—as soon as it may be convenient and expedient to do so."

"Please say to them, then, that I have this day become absolutely convinced of the entire innocence of Bingham Harvard in the matter of those missing three packages of money."

Lady Kate started to her feet. For the moment she forgot utterly the part she was playing; and yet she did not betray herself.

"*Oh!*" she exclaimed and sat down again.

The banker continued in that same low, even tone of finality which left no doubt in the mind of Lady Kate of his entire sincerity:

"It is not necessary that I should explain now just how this certain knowledge has come to me. I doubt if I quite understand it myself. In fact, I believe that in my heart I have known it all the time, and that I only needed a shock of some sort to uncover it. But it has been given to me to-day to see it all very clearly. I realize the sad mistakes I have made—the almost inexcusable misjudgments of which I have been guilty. And I will not attempt now or here to excuse them. I have called you into my private office to say to you that I now stand ready to give you every aid in my power in discovering the real thief or thieves. Is all that quite clear to you, Mr. Caton?"

Lady Kate nodded. She could not have spoken just then to save her life.

"Will you undertake to convey to Mr. and Mrs. Harvard the full purport of all that I have said on this subject?"

She nodded again, and still she found it difficult to reply in words. She wanted to leap to her feet, to throw her arms around the old man's neck and kiss him, to rush from the bank and fly to her husband, to tell him the wonderful news of the miracle that had been wrought—and yet she had to sit calmly in her chair in her masculine character, while every feminine impulse within her struggled to reach the surface.

She did not know that her face flushed, and then grew pale, only to flush up again with the succeeding instant.

She did not realize how intently the banker was regarding her; how he bent forward in his chair to get a closer and a better view of her face and eyes; and she thought it strange that he left his chair, crossed to the door of the directors' room, and called to her to follow him.

He closed the door as soon as they had passed beyond it. Then he turned and faced her.

"This information has been too much for you—as it almost was for me," he said, with a kindly smile on his face. "It has made you betray yourself, Mrs. Harvard. You are a brave young woman, indeed, to undertake such a task as this. Bingham might well be proud of you—as I am also."

He extended his hand, and she grasped it with both of her own; and so they stood for a passing moment or two in silence. Then, with a whimsical smile on his face, which had become oddly transfigured since the door was closed, he said:

"I shall be glad to welcome you as a daughter whenever it shall please you to come to me—although I must confess that you have not much the appearance of a daughter just now. Your disguise is perfect. But for the emotion which you could not hide I would not have penetrated it."

"Please tell me what has happened to bring about this miracle," she asked, smiling happily.

"I cannot. I don't know. As I said a little while ago, I think I have known it all along, but would not admit it even to my inner consciousness. Rushton has laid bare his true character. I have looked upon it, stripped of all concealment.

Bankers are mathematical creatures. Two and two make four with them always—never more nor less. That very fact is possibly my excuse—if there can be one—for the attitude I have persevered in so long. The mask was suddenly pulled aside from the searchlight of truth, and I saw it revealed. I am happier at this moment, Mrs. Harvard, than I have been for more than a year. You and Bingham must come to my desolate home at once and make it your own. I will straighten out this tangle—"

"You forget, Mr. Chester," she interrupted him, "that the thief has not been found."

"We will find him in good time. Just now—"

"Bingham can never appear in the open; he can never again hold his head high among men until his innocence is established to all the world. There are others than yourself to be convinced, sir."

"Yes, yes, that is true. I was forgetting all that."

"But you must not forget."

"No. You are right." The banker was silent a moment, then: "Will you tell me what you expected to accomplish by your presence here in the bank?"

"Yes," she replied, and her eyes took on a dreamy expression as she raised them toward the embossed and figured and ornately decorated ceiling over their heads, in an effort at concentration. That ceiling was a continuation of the one outside which canopied the greater room of the bank proper.

"Well?" Chester asked her.

"I expected," she answered slowly, "to find out *how* those three packages of bills were removed from the paying teller's cage. I hoped to be able to discover *the method* by which they were taken. I have believed all along that if that much were made clear, the next step—that of finding out who did it—would be a simple one."

"You have been here two days, very nearly. Has anything developed yet?"

"Nothing."

"Do you know of any way in which I can be of assistance to you—without making that fact apparent to others—to the guilty party or parties, for example?"

200

"No. Just at this moment I do not. But, now that I am assured of your aid, all things are made possible."

"Have you in mind any plan by which—"

She started eagerly, and he stopped with the question incomplete.

"Well?" he said.

"Your words suggested something to me, Mr. Chester. I wonder—Can you tell me when this building was erected?"

"Certainly. Ten years ago."

"Were you here then? Were you president of the bank at that time?"

"Yes; I have been its president a much longer time than that."

"A moment ago you made use of the word 'plan,' although with a different meaning than I will now apply to it. Have you got in your possession now, or can you procure for me, the architect's plans—all of them—elevations, sections, everything—that were finally accepted and approved for the construction of this building in every detail?"

"Most assuredly. They are—"

"It does not matter where they are. Will you get them for me and let me have them in my possession before I sleep to-night?"

"I will take them to my home with me when I go there after the bank has closed. You may come there if you will this evening at any hour that best suits your own convenience. I should perhaps inform you that there are certain secrets connected with those plans which are known only to myself as the president and to a few of our most important directors—secrets which the cashier does not know—which no man who is employed on the main floor of the bank is aware of. It is so with all banking institutions of the first class which have erected modern buildings."

Katherine nodded. "That is exactly why I wish to study them," she said; and added: "I probably will not go to your house alone, Mr. Chester."

"If you will bring Bingham with you—" he began, but she interrupted him.

"I am not sure that I can do that. I have not decided. He does not know of this disguise of mine. He has no suspicion of what I am doing. I would ask Mr. Clancy to go with me if I were sure that I could find him in time. All of that will depend upon circumstances. But there is at least one man who I will want to have with me. I refer now to—" And she mentioned the name of the man whom we have identified through these pages as Chief Redhead.

"Bring whomsoever you will," Chester replied. "And come to the house whenever you will after eight o'clock and before midnight. And now, Mr. Caton"—he smiled happily—"I think it is time that you returned to your duties. You may tell Mr. Atkinson that I want him in my office, if you please."

"Surely, Mr. Chester, you do not intend to confide in him, or in anybody, regarding what has passed between us?" Katherine exclaimed in sudden alarm.

"Indeed, no. I shall tell him that I have had a long talk with you, and that I believe you are going to serve us well; but that I wish him to keep rather a sharp lookout upon you for a time, for all that. Afterward I shall send for Mr. Mordaunt and tell him the same thing. Otherwise they might regard this extended interview between us as unusual, to say the least."

At the door Katherine paused and addressed the banker again.

"How shall I ever thank you enough, Mr. Chester?" she asked, with a suggestion of moisture in her eyes.

"By inducing Bingham to find it in his heart to forgive me, by assuring him that I am hungering for his old-time affection for me—and by trying for yourself to give a little love to an old man whose heart is in the right place, even if his head does go wrong sometimes," the banker answered promptly.

CHAPTER XXX

THE CIPHER

It developed that Lady Kate was obliged to go quite alone to the banker's home that night, and thereby hangs not one but several tales.

She recalled for one thing the caution that the chief had given her in regard to using the telephone during the first days of her incumbency.

Also, when she came away from the bank after her duties for the day were over, she was deeply concerned to discover the ominous presence of Rushton, who had posted himself at one of the opposite corners, and who, she did not doubt, was awaiting her appearance.

An encounter with Rushton had been the one thing which she most dreaded when she undertook to impersonate a man at Chester's bank, for Lieutenant Rushton, with all his crookedness, was shrewd and keen and able.

Katherine had not a doubt that if she were compelled to stand face to face with him he would see through her disguise at once. She had known enough about him when she was down at headquarters to be aware that he possessed in no small degree that talent which is known to the police as the "camera-eye."

She trembled inwardly lest he would cross the street and attempt to speak to her; but he did not do that. He contented himself by merely trailing along after her—and for what reason, or why he should take it upon himself to watch her at all, she could not attempt to guess.

She went directly to her boarding-house in Twenty-First Street, and, although she was not able after that to see him from any of the windows, she was nevertheless certain that he was on the watch, or that he had arranged for another man to do the watching for him.

Twice she went to the telephone with the intention of calling up the "chief," but each time abandoned it; and at last she determined to remain quietly in her own room until ten o'clock, or about that time, and then to summon a taxi and have herself driven boldly to the banker's house. She would get possession of the plans in that way, and would trust to the opportunities of the morrow to pass them along to the chief.

In the meantime, as it developed later, the chief would not have been at his office to receive a message had she sent one, because a little before three in the afternoon he had been called on the telephone by quite another person, and had gone out soon after that.

His first destination was the "little house on the roof" of the warehouse, and when he had climbed to it and tapped against the door he did not seem at all surprised to find Tom Clancy, as well as Bingham Harvard, apparently awaiting him.

"We thought you would do one thing or the other, chief"—Tom grinned at him—"telephone or come here yourself. You were so dead certain that I would be gobbled up by the cops, and have something framed on me and be sent away, that I thought I'd let you sweat for a while over my disappearance. This is why I persuaded Bing not to say anything about my being here when you called up at noon to-day. What's on your mind?"

"I have been talking on the telephone with Banta," he replied, as he settled himself on a chair and lighted a huge black cigar.

"Oh—then you are wise to the game, are you?"

"Partly. I want you and Harvard to tell me the rest of it. I would like to know everything that occurred. But, first, I will tell you this: Banta told me that he has seen and talked with

204

both of you. He says that he is working now in Harvard's favor—and he says a lot more which it is not necessary for me to repeat. The main point is this: He wants me to meet him and a retired cop named Compton in room 1046 of the Hotel Mammoth at half past eight o'clock to-night. Get that?"

"Yes."

"Harvard, I'll take your judgment rather than Clancy's. Banta says that he has got something of vital importance to tell me—something that Compton has told *him*. *Now*, in your opinion, how far can I trust that chap Banta?"

"To the limit, I should say," Harvard replied without hesitation.

"You mean that?"

"Yes. Listen!" And the Night Wind recited in detail the story of the "society of crippled cops" and of his interview with them in Brooklyn.

But the chief shook his head in doubt, even after he had heard the story through.

"That's a foxy bunch," he said. "The whole thing has a sound that is too good to be true. The inspector is a long-headed proposition, and it would be just like him to put up this sort of a job. Anyhow, I am going to room 1046 at half past eight to find out what this wonderful news is about."

"I would like to hear it, too," Harvard said. "Why not send word to Banta and Compton to come down here instead?"

"And give away your hiding-place?"

"I will trust both of them, chief, to the limit, as I said a moment ago."

"All right. I'll take a chance if you will. You have seen them and talked with them; I haven't. Say, Clancy?"

"Well?"

"Suppose you chase yourself up to the Mammoth and find them? They were in that room when they telephoned to me, and are probably there now. If they are not you can wait around until they show up. You can bring both of them down here as soon as it is dark."

"Are you going to stay here yourself until I get back?" Tom asked, rising.

"Yes. I want to go over that cipher memoranda of Rushton's that Harvard has been working on. I'll slip out presently and bring in something to eat; and, anyhow, we will have enough to talk over to keep us busy. Don't bring them here till after dark; that's all."

As soon as Tom was gone Harvard brought out the cipher upon which he had been working and spread the papers on the table. From among them he selected one sheet which he had captioned at the top with the word "Recapitulation."

"You can put all the others in your pocket, chief," he said. "I'm not going to bother you with the details. You can go over them at your leisure. The cipher is very simple and easy to work out, save for a few arbitrary signs; and those arbitrary signs in each case refer to the names of persons without a doubt."

"Go ahead," the chief replied. "Give me the summary of it all."

"First, then: Within ten days after those packages of money were taken from the Centropolis Bank Rodney Rushton made significant deposits of cash in four different banks in this city—the banks that you already have a list of."

"All right. Fire away, Harvard!"

"The four deposits were made two days apart—the first one was two days after we lost the money, the last one was ten days after it. Those four deposits were in sums of seventeen thousand dollars each. Four times seventeen are sixty-eight, and sixty eight is one-half of one hundred and thirty-six. The amount of money lost in those three stolen packages was one hundred and thirty-six thousand dollars. Does that mean anything to you, chief? Does that suggest anything?"

"By jingo, Harvard, I should say so!"

"It looks to me, chief, as if Rodney Rushton knew that that money was to disappear before it was stolen. It looks to me as if he claimed half of all of it as his share of the theft. How does it look to you?"

"It looks good to me, if anybody should ask you. Rushton got the money; that's a lead-pipe cinch. Anyhow, he got half of it and soaked it away. But, Harvard, it is a sure thing that *he* didn't *steal* it out of the cage. Who did that?"

Harvard referred to his "Recapitulation," and replied:

"A person who is referred to here as 'Z. G.' got eighteen thousand, a person known as 'K. N.' got twenty-five thousand, as also did another individual who is entered under the letters 'S. X.'"

"And you have no idea as to whom those initial letters may refer?"

"None. They are evidently used arbitrarily."

"Do not any of them suggest to you the name of any person who is employed at the bank?"

"No."

"What else have you got there on that sheet of paper?"

"Oh, records of other deposits that Rushton has made from time to time. He has evidently been grafting in all directions. Here, take it and put it in your pocket with the rest of them. We are not much nearer the real goal than we were before—unless I should pick Rushton up in my arms some fine night and carry him off to a secluded spot and *make him talk*. I might scare him into telling me the whole thing."

"No. You could not do that. I have got a list of all the employees at the bank at my office. I will go over it when I get a chance. These initial letters have some, more or less, direct reference to names. They would not be entirely arbitrary."

"Here is a list that I have made from memory," Harvard said. "Suppose you light a fresh cigar and sit over there in the corner and try it out now."

* * * * * * *

It was ten minutes to nine o'clock that evening when Clancy reappeared, and he brought Banta and Compton with him. The Night Wind and the chief had used up the intervening time in going over and over Rushton's figures and memoranda—and also in eating heartily of food which the chief went outside to procure.

"My suggestion may or it may not impress you as important, Mr. Harvard," Banta said as soon as the preliminary greetings were over. "But here it is for whatever it proves to be worth:

"Compton, here, was a joiner by trade, and an expert one, before he became a cop. He has told me—he says he told Mr. Clancy also—that he worked several weeks on the inside of the Centropolis Bank Building when it was put up ten years ago. He says that there is a space six feet high between the ceiling over the bank, and another ceiling over that one. He says that the underceiling is littered with what he calls 'watch-holes,' where, at any one of them, a man who is stationed there for the purpose may sit or lie at his ease and observe every slightest motion that takes place beneath him in the bank. Do you get me, chief?"

Redhead nodded. "I know of a dozen banks between here and Frisco that are equipped in that manner," he said. "I confess that I had not thought of the Centropolis in that connection. But the idea is full of possibilities, Banta—and we cannot settle a single one of them here by ourselves. I understand perfectly what you are driving at. Are you game—you and Compton—to go with me right now to Chester's house and to stand by me when I put this whole question up to him?"

"That is what we are here for, chief."

"You see," the chief remarked, half to himself, "if Chester's bank makes use of those watch-holes right along every day in the week, this discovery won't amount to much; but if it should happen that they haven't been of much use, and have been therefore practically abandoned, except perhaps on payroll days, like Saturdays, we will be, I should say, on the track of one of the mysteries. Come along, Banta. Come on, Compton."

"Can Bing and I go along, too, chief?" Clancy asked.

"No. You two stay where you are. You are both like red rags to a bull when Chester sees either of you," and he led the way out of the little house on the roof.

Harvard stretched himself and yawned after they had gone. Then he seized his hat.

"Come on, Tom," he said. "I need exercise. We will trail along and keep tabs on the outside of Chester's house while they are inside. I feel just as though something had happened, or was going to happen mighty soon. Anyhow, I need the air. Come on."

At approximately the same time Lady Kate came out of the boarding-house in Twenty-First Street and entered a taxi-cab that she had ordered by telephone.

Her destination, as we already know, was Chester's house. Lieutenant Rushton, in another cab that he had summoned as soon as he saw the fist one appear, followed—for, while Rushton did not suspect that Erin Caton was Lady Kate, he had discovered the resemblance between them with his camera-eye, and he suspected relationship.

He was convinced that Erin Caton would lead him to Lady Kate.

CHAPTER XXXI

IN FRONT OF CHESTER'S HOUSE

Katherine got there first. She dismissed her cab, telling the driver to return in an hour.

Chester opened the door for her himself, and did it before she could ring. He had, in fact, been watching from one of the windows for her arrival; and he had taken the precaution to send away the servants who would respond to a summons at the door, though just why he had done that he could not have told.

He would have greeted Katherine with too apparent eagerness if she had not observed instantly who it was that opened the door and warned him.

"Be careful," she cautioned. "I am afraid that I was followed," and she passed inside and the door was closed.

Outside, half a block away, Rushton thrust his head out of a cab-window, saw what house Lady Kate had entered, and muttered:

"I wonder what in thunder that means? What does that guy mean by goin' there to Chester's ranch?—for if he ain't some relation to Lady Kate I'll eat a raw dog for *my* next meal!"

He called to his chauffeur to stay where he was till further orders, then lighted a cigar, and settled himself to the enjoyment of it while he waited and watched.

Ten minutes later three men swung around the corner nearest to him and walked rapidly up the avenue to Chester's

210

house, where they hurried up the steps; and Rushton, observing them closely as they passed him, opened his jaws to swear his astonishment again—only this time he made no sound.

"Banta, by all that's sizzlin'! And with Redhead at that! And them goin' to Chester's house! And together! Now, what do you know about that? And who's that other guy? He looked like a cop in plain—*I've* got it! That was Compton—the boob that turned in his shield the other day! Say, Rod, old man"—addressing himself audibly—"what kind of a stuss game are you up against, anyhow?"

He waited and watched, wondering the while why the banker did not admit the three men, for, although the minutes passed and they continued to press the button at the door, nobody responded.

Rushton could see that the three men on the doorstep were as greatly surprised as he was that nobody answered their ring, and he chuckled to himself.

"I guess maybe I don't know just how to read this riddle—not all of it," he told himself. "The first part of it is easy enough, unless I'm *clear* up a tree. Lady Kate has fixed it up somehow so's her brother, 'r cousin, 'r whatever he is, could go to work in the bank, and now they're trying to bring old Chester around to seein' things their way. Much good it'll do 'em. *He* don't see nothin' down there about that Harvard business that *I* don't point out to him."

Down the avenue, a block farther away, and hence behind Rushton, so that he did not observe them, two men sprang over the park wall at the opposite side of the thoroughfare; and one of them said to the other as they hurried to get to where the trees would hide them from view:

"I guess Chester must be out, Bing."

"There would be somebody there to answer the bell, even if he is out," Harvard replied.

"Then he has seen them from a window, recognized who it is, and won't admit them."

"That sounds more like it."

"Tell you what I'll do, Bing; I'll bet a house and lot against a steamboat that Redhead will stay right where he is until he *does* get inside. Oh, I know *him*, all right!"

"Who do you suppose is inside of that taxicab?" Harvard asked, after a moment.

"Give it up, old chap. Nobody, most likely."

"There is somebody inside of it, all the same. My eyes are accustomed to seeing things in this half-light, and I just saw tobacco smoke coming out of the window of it."

"The chauffeur is smoking, likely enough, while he waits for his fare."

"He *is smoking*—a cigarette. I can see him. The other smoke came out of the window."

"Well, what of it?"

"Nothing; only I'd like to know who it is, Tom. I have got a hunch that it is somebody who is watching Chester's house."

"Maybe it is your bosom friend, Rushton," Tom Clancy said, and laughed. He had not the least idea in the world that he had guessed correctly. Neither had Harvard. "Hello!" Tom said, a moment later. "Redhead is camped out."

"Banta and Compton have seated themselves on the steps, and the chief is still pushing the button. Ah! There you are, Bing! The door has been opened. There they go, all three of them, inside. Now, what, I wonder?"

"I would give a pair of old shoes to know who is inside of that cab over there," Harvard said, in reply. "For a nickel I'd go across the avenue and find out."

Calmly, deliberately, and with a broad grin on his face, Tom Clancy took a nickel from the change pocket of his coat and offered it to Harvard.

In the mean time, inside of the house, Katherine had followed Chester into the same library which had already been the scene of so many incidents in the career of the Night Wind.

The banker had already prepared the plans for her to see. They were on the library table, and he had been poring over them himself while he awaited her coming.

212

"There they are," he said. "There are quite a number of them, as you will see. I have been looking them over myself. Look!" He selected one of them and spread it open on the table. "Here"—he indicated with his forefinger—"is one of the secrets I referred to to-day. Nothing ever came of its use, however. We never use it, only on Saturdays, when our depositors are drawing large sums in small bills and in coin to pay off their help."

"What is it?" Katherine asked, bending down over the plan.

The banker laughed lightly.

"We call it the observatory," he replied. "It is a space, six feet high, above the ceiling over the banking room and beneath the floor of the next story. The bank proper, as you may have noticed, is very high, made so for proper ventilation. It takes in two full stories."

"But what is it used for?" Katherine insisted, puzzled; "that space between the ceiling and the floor above it. What use do you make of it?"

"Almost none at all, as a matter of fact," he replied. "All the same, it is a cleverly devised means for observing all that goes on within the bank, without the observers being seen or their presence suspected. Many of the larger banks have arrangements of the same sort—and make constant use of them; to keep watch on their own employees, for the most part. It was used originally in one of the Western cities," he explained.

"But I do not understand, Mr. Chester. How is the watching done?"

"Oh, there is a system of holes cleverly arranged so that they cannot be seen from the bank below. They are everywhere. There is one for every bookkeeper, every teller, every employee. There are others which command more extensive views, taking in several of the positions below at once. And they are so arranged that the one who is watching may sit at his ease, may even lie down at full length, if he cares to do so, while he sees everything that is taking place beneath him. He can move about at will without making a sound to betray his presence—and so forth, and so forth. You see—"

213

The ringing of the door-bell interrupted him.

"Now, who can that be?" he said. "At all events, I shall not answer it; and I have taken care that there is nobody else here to do so."

"It may be some person who followed me here," Katherine suggested.

"Hardly. Such a person would scarcely ring for admittance."

"Probably not; unless—unless it should be Lieutenant Rushton, and he has recognized me in spite of the disguise."

"Rushton? Rushton? What would *he* be following you for?"

"I don't know. He was waiting in the street when I left the bank this afternoon. He followed me, I am sure, to my boarding-house. More than likely he remained on the watch, and has pursued me even here. Listen. It is ringing again."

"Well, let him ring—if it is Rushton. There is no reason why I should admit him."

They attempted to give their attention again to the plans, but the persistent ringing at the door disturbed them both; for the chief, outside, was perfectly satisfied in his own mind that somebody was at home, and that before long somebody would come to the door.

"I wonder if that *is* Rushton?" the banker remarked, when the constant ringing of the bell was beginning to get on their nerves. "I think I will try to find out who it is."

"You won't open the door if it is Rushton, will you? Please don't."

"No. More than likely I will not open it at all. But from the drawing-room windows I will be able to get a view of the greater part of the steps. Wait here, Mrs. Harvard, till I return."

She waited, pacing impatiently up and down the room in the mean time. Chester came back very soon.

"There are two men on the steps whom I do not know, but they seem determined to wait until somebody opens the door. They were just about to seat themselves on the steps as I looked out at them. There must be a third one who is ringing the bell. It is possible—it is just possible that there may be something wrong—that I really should go to the door," he said rapidly.

"Wait," she said, beginning to gather the plans into a roll. "I will take these away with me, if I may. I will study them when I get to my room at the boarding-house."

"But—are you going? I wish you would not. There is so much that I wish to say."

"Really I think I must; and it is late. I will step into the reception-room while you open the front door. Then, if you will direct your callers to this room, I will slip out as soon as they have entered here. By to-morrow evening I will have studied the plans thoroughly, and will have had time to think, too; and if I may, I will come here to see you again."

She gave him her hand, and he bent gallantly over it, like the gentleman of the old school that he was, and touched his lips to her fingers, entirely forgetful of the fact that she was garbed as a man.

Katherine passed swiftly through the foyer and into the reception-room at the south side of it. Chester waited until she had partly closed the door and then threw wide the front entrance.

"Please pass right through into the library, gentlemen," Chester said at once, "and then perhaps you will explain to me the reason for this persistent ringing of my door-bell."

Lady Kate heard the voice of Banta reply to Chester with some casual remark, and she recognized it; and, knowing nothing of his change of heart and condition, she had not a doubt that one of the other two men who were with him was Rushton.

She heard the library door close behind them, and knew that Chester had done that to guard her escape from the house; and so she glided from the obscurity of the reception-room, opened the outer door silently, passed outside, closed it again, and ran hastily down the steps.

Down the avenue, half a block away, she saw a taxicab, and supposed it to be the one she had ordered back again in an hour. It was exactly like it, she thought. At all events, it was a cab.

She gave a sigh of relief and started toward it, little thinking that her arch-enemy Rushton was seated inside of it, patiently awaiting this very opportunity.

CHAPTER XXXII

LADY KATE'S DISGUISE UNCOVERED

It will be remembered that Tom Clancy offered the nickel to the Night Wind a moment only after the "chief," followed by Banta and Compton, were admitted to the banker's house.

Of course, Harvard's expression that for a nickel he would find out who was inside of the cab, and Clancy's tender of the coin, was mere banter on both sides; and yet the mood was upon Harvard to carry out his end of the offer, and so without more ado he started forward through the shrubbery and leaped the park wall at the very moment that Lady Kate, in her guise of Erin Caton, came out of Chester's house.

Neither Harvard nor Clancy had any idea that the cab was standing idle where it did for any other purpose than to await some customer who was calling at one of the houses near Chester's.

But *we* know that Rushton was inside of it; we know that he had followed the supposed Erin Caton to Chester's house, believing that that person was a man who was related to Lady Kate and would lead him ultimately to her.

We know how puzzled Rushton was by the coming of the chief and Banta—who had formerly been one of Rushton's side-partners—and Compton.

217

While he sat inside of the cab and smoked and waited and watched, he had eyes for nothing save what was going on at that house and on the steps of it; for his mind had been busily engaged in putting two and two together while he waited, and he had already figured it out that the entire circumstance, taken as a whole, was not exactly promising to himself.

That Erin Caton, the new teller at the bank, should visit the home of the president at ten o'clock at night, and apparently in secret, instead of transacting such business as he might have at the bank and during banking hours, was of itself ominous; but that he should be followed there by no less a person than the head of the most important private detective agency in New York—*and* by Banta!—it all looked to Rushton as though they were getting something "on him."

Thus, when Lady Kate came out of the house at almost the same instant that Harvard leaped the park wall, Rushton had eyes only for the figure on the steps, and he did not turn his head to discover that a man was crossing the avenue toward him from the direction of the park.

Harvard always moved with that incredible swiftness which had in the past helped to cloak him in so much mystery.

He was close to the rear of the cab before Katherine had covered half the distance between it and Chester's house; and he peered through the small, square window at the back, prompted, as we know, merely by curiosity.

Rushton was bending forward with his head close to the cab door, which he had opened a few inches, watching the approach of Erin Caton, otherwise Lady Kate. His profile was clearly outlined against the lights of the street—and Harvard recognized him instantly.

Harvard had given no thought to the person who came out of Chester's home. He had not seen that person enter; he supposed—if anything at all—that it was merely an acquaintance of the banker's who had called upon him, and was now going away.

Harvard drew back quickly and stepped around to the street side of the cab.

218

His idea in doing that was twofold; he wished, if possible, to keep out of sight of the person who had just come from the banker's house, and whom he had no doubt would pass on—and he determined in that instant to have a word with Rushton.

In the mean time Lady Kate mistook the waiting cab for her own hired one that had returned.

She approached it rapidly. She stopped beside the chauffeur and addressed him; and when Harvard, waiting at the opposite side of the cab, heard the voice, he gasped with amazement.

Lady Kate had not neglected to deepen it, in accordance with the disguise she wore—with the character she was playing; but the ears of love, as well as the eyes of love, are hard to deceive.

Bingham Harvard, during the last seven months, had listened to that voice in every tone and cadence it could express. He loved every murmur of it. He knew every modulation of it, as Liszt knew every tone of his violin.

Can you imagine the thrill that ran through him when he heard it—when he realized who it was who was drawing near to that cab, and remembered who it was who waited inside?

"I am glad that you returned so soon, chauffeur," Lady Kate began—and stopped. A closer look had developed the fact that the man was *not* the chauffeur who had taken her there; and before he could reply she supplemented the remark by adding: "Excuse me. I see that I have made a mistake," and she would have passed on.

Rushton, however, pushed the cab door wide open and stepped outside, confronting her; and she started back, and then stood stock-still in her tracks, not knowing for the moment what to do.

Rushton had noticed the voice, too; but he had not recognized it as Harvard did. His mind was too intent upon the masculine personality of the one who used it. There was not the magic understanding of Love to identify it. Harvard, in the mean time, found an opportunity to peer through the cab at the two figures, for he could not understand how the voice of Katherine could proceed from the mouth of a man.

"Excuse me, sir," Rushton said in his politest tones. "If you are in need of a cab, I can let you make use of mine."

"Thank you," Katherine replied in the most masculine voice she could assume. "It is not at all necessary."

She made an attempt to pass on her way then, but Rushton stepped quickly in front of her and barred it; and as he did that he also threw aside the mask of courtesy.

"I guess I'll ask you to use it whether you want to or not," he said with a half laugh, at the same time throwing back one side of his coat and displaying his official shield. "You'll get inside of that cab and take a ride with me, mister, or I'll throw you into it. Take your choice."

The "mister" reassured Lady Kate. It told her that Rushton had not recognized her—as yet.

"You have no business to speak to me in that manner," she retorted, trying to bluster, and making rather a poor success of it; and she would have made another attempt to pass him had she not realized that he would seize her if she did so; and she knew that if once his hands should rest upon her the secret would be out.

Rushton chuckled.

"Ain't I?" he jeered. "I ain't followed you ever since you left the bank this afternoon for nothin', Mr. Erin Caton. I'm onto your curves. It's plain enough to me, even if some others don't see it, that you're a relation of Lady Kate's. And that's what I'm here for. You are going to take me to see her—right now. See? She's the gazabo that I wanta get next to. Climb inside of that cab or I'll chuck you into it!"

He stepped forward toward her threateningly.

She darted backward out of his reach and away from him and turned to run. But she ran plump into the outstretched arms of Tom Clancy, who appeared at that instant, running likewise, from the opposite side of the avenue.

Rushton leaped after her when she started to escape from him—that is, he attempted to do so. But he did not take even so much as one jump; he only started to make it.

A hand fell heavily upon his shoulder from behind. Resistless fingers grasped his collar and jerked him backward. A foot dexterously thrust forward tripped him, and he found himself lying upon his back on the pavement, looking up into the eyes of Bingham Harvard, alias the Night Wind, who was bending over him.

Rushton's sensations in that instant of discovery can better be imagined than described. Instinctively he realized that it was up to him to remain perfectly still, and he did so.

Lady Kate was no less startled, in one way, than Rushton.

There is no doubt that the moment might have proved a tragic one for the lieutenant had it not been for the irrepressible humor of Tom Clancy; for Rushton had affronted Katherine, and Harvard had heard it.

But Clancy saw the funny side of it all, and laughed. That laugh of his saved the situation.

Katherine laughed also—a bit nervously, perhaps—and the ripple of it that Harvard so greatly loved to hear brought a smile to his own face. His quick wit, also, brought him to an instant understanding of the situation.

Almost at the same instant the chauffeur of the cab had a hunch that that immediate vicinity was unhealthy for him. He knew that his fare was a fly-cop and had been suddenly attacked by two men who had appeared from the other side of the park wall. He had visions of gunmen getting square on squealers.

He jumped down from his seat the minute the incipient row began, cranked his engine, sprang back, and the taxicab sped away from the four persons on the sidewalk as if it were shot out of a gun.

Nor did any one of them attempt to stop it. The effort would have been useless at best, and it was unnecessary.

Harvard frisked the lieutenant for his weapons and relieved him of them. Then he jerked Rushton to his feet. But, nevertheless, his eyes stared past the detective toward Erin Caton, while a slow smile appeared again upon his countenance.

"I heard you addressed as Mr. Erin Caton just now," he said with a half drawl in his tone. "This person here, who thinks he is some detective, seemed to want you to conduct him to the presence of Lady Kate of the Police; so I guess it is up to you, Katherine, to decide what we will do with him now that we've got him."

"I think we had better keep him," Katherine replied instantly. "He has had rope enough; and his race is almost run. Wait a moment. There is a taxicab coming around the corner. Perhaps it is the one I used, returning."

Then they were treated to another surprise, and a most welcome one. The approaching cab drew up at the curb near to them, the driver of it jumped down—and Katherine uttered an exclamation of pleased surprise.

The chauffeur was Black Julius, and the cab was not the I. T. O. A. taxi that Katherine had used, but her own car that had been made over in imitation of one.

"I disobeyed you, Miss Kitty," Julius explained rapidly. "Instead of doing what you told me to do, I was afraid that you would need me near you, and so I waited outside of the house when you sent me away. And, Miss Kitty, I didn't carry you around in my arms when you was a baby and I didn't watch you grow up to what you are now for nothing, or to be fooled by any disguise, either. I hope you will forgive me, Miss Kitty, but I haven't been very far away from you any of the time."

"But how do you happen to be here now, Julius?" Clancy asked him.

"Why, sir, I just hired that chauffeur to let me take his place when he went to the house in Twenty-First Street, where I was watching, to get Miss Kitty; and I kept my head turned away and my face covered when she gave the order to bring her up here. And then when she told me to come back in an hour I thought she'd be safe for that long, and so I took the other cab back, and went and got Miss Kitty's. You see, sir, I don't like to have her playing the part of a man. It isn't safe. And so I have kept watch."

"Faithful Julius," Harvard said, resting one hand for a moment upon the black's arm. "You are on hand, as usual, when you are the most needed. You always keep rope and cord in your tool-box. Have you got some there now?"

"Yes, sir."

"Get it. We will tie up this thing we've got here that was born a man and turned into a snake. We will gag him, too, if necessary. Then, Tom, you will get into the cab with him and take him to the 'little house on the roof' and keep him there for the present. Katherine and I are going to ring the bell at Chester's house again, and we are going inside to find out what is happening."

"Oh, Bingham—" Katherine began and stopped.

She would let the revelation of Chester's change of heart wait just a little longer.

CHAPTER XXXIII

THE WAY THE MONEY WENT

"Who is at the door now?" Chester exclaimed impatiently.

Then he started quickly to his feet, for it occurred to him that it might be Katherine returned; and now, since the talk he had already had with the chief and his two companions, the banker wished for nothing better than that she should be there to hear it.

"I will go to the door with you," the chief said, rising; and so, when Katherine pushed forward into the foyer as soon as the way was open, and was closely followed by Bingham Harvard, the meeting was a mutual surprise all around.

But if three of the four persons who confronted each other were mildly surprised, the fourth one was amazed into utter consternation for the moment by the reception that was accorded him.

For no sooner had Harvard stepped across the threshold, and Chester discovered who it was, than he rushed forward with his arms outstretched—and Harvard found himself the recipient of a convulsive embrace, the genuineness of which could not be counterfeited.

"My boy! My boy! My boy!" the old man exclaimed over and over again, with a sob in his voice, but with a joy that was unmistakable. "Forgive me, Bingham; I was wrong; all wrong. I know it now; it is all plain. I have been a fool—

224

oh, such a fool—my boy! But say that it is all right now. Say that you will forgive me, Bingham. I want you to love me again, just as you used to do. And I want Katherine to love me, too. I want you both. Oh, I am blessed indeed, for now I shall have a daughter as well as a son! And *such* a daughter, Bingham!"

He talked so rapidly, so joyously, so contritely, so earnestly, that there was no stopping him; and Bingham, reaching out both hands and resting them upon the old man's shoulders, looked earnestly into his eyes as he replied:

"Dear old chap! Dear old gov'nor! That is what I used to call you when I was a boy. I knew it would come out all right, sir. I knew that your heart was kind and good and just. My love for you has never faltered, sir; and—maybe you will have almost as much to forgive as I."

Katherine stepped forward quickly and threw her arms around Chester's neck, and there was not one of them who remembered in that moment the garb she was wearing.

"I will love you, too, Mr. Chester—very dearly, if you will let me," she said, and she kissed the old man on the lips.

"Why," he exclaimed, stepping back a pace away from her, "I feel like a boy again! I never expected to be as happy as I am at this moment. Chief, why don't *you* say something, eh?"

"I will," the chief replied, running his fingers through his red hair. "I think we had better get back to business. Banta and Compton will be wondering what has happened."

"There is one thing that I ought to tell you at once," Harvard said as soon as they were all in the library together and greetings had been exchanged. "Clancy and I, with the assistance of Black Julius, have just tied up Rushton good and snug, and Clancy has taken him to the little house on the roof. I thought, chief, that seeing as we had him, it would not be a bad idea to keep him. What do you think about it?"

"I think it is splendid, Harvard. When we get through here we will give Mr. Rodney Rushton a hearty mouthful of one of his own favorite practices."

"What is that?" Katherine asked.

"They call it the 'third degree,'" was the significant reply. Then the chief turned abruptly to Harvard.

"You came at the right moment," he said. "We have arrived at a point where we need your personal help. Do you know anything about the so-called observation-room directly above the bank?"

"No," Harvard replied, and glanced inquiringly toward the banker. But Lady Kate put forward the roll of plans that she had carried from the house with her and from which she had not relinquished her hold throughout all the scenes that had been enacted.

"Good," said the chief and unrolled the plans, selected two of them, laid them down side by side, and bent over them. "Here we have it," he added presently. "Now, Harvard, come here."

"I am here already."

"Well"—the chief indicated locations on the plans with the point of his pencil—"this is the so-called observation-room over the bank. This part is the floor-plan. Here and here and here and here—all of these marks—are the watch-holes through the ceiling of the bank."

"Why, gov'nor, I never knew anything about this!" Harvard exclaimed, turning his eyes toward Chester.

"Never mind that fact now," the chief said. "Watch *me*. Compton, who helped to fit up the observation room, has explained it to me in detail, and since my talk with him and Mr. Chester these plans make it all very clear. Got that?"

"Yes," said Harvard. They were all grouped closely around the table by then.

"This," the chief went on, indicating another of the plans, "is the finished floor-space of the bank itself; and right here is the cage of the paying-teller."

"I see," Harvard said eagerly. "I understand."

"Well, if we place these two plans so on the table they fit, one above the other, just the same as to position as the observation-room fits over the bank. Now, here is a foot-rule; here is the teller's cage; and here, according to a drawing that you made yourself and which Mrs. Harvard gave to me, is the spot where the three packages of bills that were stolen disappeared from. So, we put the foot-rule down here, so that it reaches from one plan to the other. We follow along the edge of it from the spot where the packages of bills were lying to this spot in the floor of the observation-room; and—Do you see, Harvard, what we find?"

Bingham nodded, intent upon studying the plans.

The chief continued:

"We find that by exact measurement the largest of all the watch-holes in the floor of the observation-room is directly over the cage of the paying-teller; and we find, by reducing it to scale, that the watch-hole is on a plumb-line exactly over the spot from which the packages of bills disappeared."

The chief straightened himself where he stood and pushed the plans aside. He addressed the banker.

"Mr. Chester," he said, "do you use the 'in' and 'out' checking system for your employees at the bank? I mean, if one of them has occasion to pass outside of the screen for any purpose—to go to the wash-room, or to your own office, even—is there somebody who takes note of that fact and who marks down the time of his going and the time of his return?"

"Certainly," Chester and Harvard both replied as one, and Chester added: "In an institution like ours that is quite necessary. The time of every man must be accounted for to the exact minute. Not that the time is important to us of itself, but—as in a case like the loss of that money—it may become necessary that we should know the location of every man at a certain moment during the day; that is, whether he was actually in the bank and inside the screen at a specified minute."

"Exactly. Harvard, how nearly can you approximate the minute of the day when that money was taken?"

"I cannot approximate it at all. The packages of money were not missed until the closing hour."

"Was there any time that you recall during that day of June 13, more than a year ago, when one of the clerks in the bank might have slipped into the cage and out of it again without your knowledge?"

"We talked that aspect of it over—Mr. Chester and I—before I was charged with the theft," Harvard replied, and the banker winced, but smiled bravely. "There were possibly, but not probably, two such intervals. One was of two minutes or less; the other was of two or three minutes, but by no possibility more than three."

"What occasioned those intervals? Do you remember?"

"Perfectly. They happened, in fact, very close together."

"At what time of the day?"

"At about half past two."

"What was it that happened to occasion those two intervals? You have not told me that yet."

"One—the first one—was caused by three successive explosions in the street in front of the bank and quite near to the door. They sounded like pistol-shots. I never knew if they were so or not. But they startled everybody inside of the bank, and naturally everyone there raised his head and craned his neck, and took his eyes momentarily from his respective duty to discover what was happening or had happened. I figured that interval as not exceeding two minutes at the most while the attention of the employees of the bank was distracted."

"What was the other incident?"

"It followed almost immediately after the first one—within a moment or two or possibly a little more. It was a fight between two men. One man struck another one and they clenched and fell to the floor."

"That happened inside of the bank?"

"Yes."

"Were the two men who fought known at the bank?"

"I think not. Badger, our watchman, sailed into them immediately. He hustled them both outside—literally threw them into the street, I believe. He is a powerful man. I do not know whether they were arrested or not. My impression is that they were not."

The chief turned back again to the banker.

"Mr. Chester," he said with slow emphasis, "those three packages of bills were removed from the teller's cage while those two men were fighting and while Badger was putting them outside. They were taken by means of a slender but stout cord, probably black, which was lowered through that largest watch-hole in the floor of the observation-room."

"The first diversion that happened—the pistol shots in the street—was done to excite the nerves of your employees generally and to make them all the more ready to give attention to one that would follow. They would naturally associate the two."

"One of your employees—a bookkeeper or any other clerk—who was an accomplice in the theft must have gone outside of the screen just a few minutes before either of the two incidents described occurred. He knew about the observation-room, and he made his way to it. At the right moment he dropped the cord, weighted at the end, through the hole, which is large enough to pull the bills up through it, notwithstanding the fact that it is so cleverly concealed that it is not visible to the eye from the floor of the bank."

"Another of your employees—Harvard or Mordaunt or Atkinson, or another clerk who slipped inside of the cage at the right moment—snapped a heavy rubber band around those packages of bills and inserted under it a hook that was attached to the end of the cord. While the fight was going on, while Badger was putting the men outside, the money was pulled up out of the teller's cage through the hole in the ceiling, and the deed was accomplished."

"Now, the fight was a fake, of course. Harvard tells me that he called at Atkinson's house the other night and found Badger there, and had a fight with him; so, in my opinion at least, it is a safe proposition that Badger was in the game, and that Atkinson is the man who attached the cord to the packages of bills."

"We do not know yet who lowered the cord through the hole in the ceiling, but your records showing who was absent from behind the screen in the bank at just that time will establish who that was—and I will be at the bank at nine o'clock in the morning to get him along with Badger and Atkinson."

"There is just one more thing that we do know, however, and that is that Rodney Rushton received for his own share one-half of the amount that was stolen; and if I don't make him and Badger and Atkinson give up the whole story to-morrow morning I am very much mistaken."

"Harvard, I advise you and Lady Kate to stay right here with Mr. Chester to-night and to go to the bank with him in the morning. Mrs. Harvard can send for her dresses and things, I suppose."

CHAPTER XXXIV

TAKING THE "THIRD DEGREE"

Bingham Harvard, Lieutenant Banta, Tom Clancy, Compton, President Chester, Chief Redhead, Black Julius, and Lady Kate were seated together in the little house on the roof at eleven o'clock the following morning.

Outside on the roof, under guard of three of the chief's operatives and handcuffed together, were Atkinson, Badger, and a bookkeeper from the bank whose name was Seixas— for his name had been the one discovered as the absentee from the interior of the bank at the crucial moment of that Thursday in June more than a year before.

Over in a corner, bound hand and foot, with a bandage over his eyes and a towel fastened tightly around his jaws, helpless, soundless, beside himself with rage but utterly powerless, was Rushton.

He was receiving, and was still to receive, a practical demonstration of an art that he had often practiced upon others—a demonstration of the third degree.

The chief began the proceedings, speaking in cool, even tones, addressing the others generally.

"It was this way," he said. "Rushton planned the entire affair. Badger, I find, used to be a cop, but was dismissed from the department three years ago on charges. He had been an apt tool of Rushton's, and it was partly through Rushton that he received his appointment at the bank from you, Mr. Chester."

The banker nodded.

"James Atkinson has a passion for so-called mathematical problems; but his problems are, when studied, found to be 'systems' for gambling—systems which he makes no use of directly, but which he prepares and sells to gamblers, who are the most superstitious people in the world. In order to perfect those systems to a selling point he often visited gambling-houses and race-tracks, although he has never been known to gamble himself. For that reason the bank detectives let him alone."

"But Rushton made his acquaintance, followed him up, found that he was selling so-called systems, and used the fact as a lever and finally won Atkinson over to the point of becoming an accomplice in this theft—and in others that would have followed it before very long."

"In Rushton's memoranda, taken from his room by Mr. Harvard on a memorable occasion, we discovered by working out the cipher that one-half of the stolen one hundred and thirty-six thousand dollars—sixty-eight thousand dollars, to be more exact—went to Rushton, and was deposited by him in four banks in sums of seventeen thousand dollars to each one."

"We found that eighteen thousand dollars was paid over to a man who was entered in the memoranda as Z. G. I find that Z is the most prominent letter in Alonzo and that G takes the same prominence in Badger. Alonzo is Badger's given name; so Alonzo Badger got eighteen thousand dollars of the stolen money."

"Twenty-five thousand dollars went to each of two men—one represented by the letters K. N., the other represented by the letters S. X. You will readily see that K. N. bears the same relation to the name Atkinson, and S. X. to the name Seixas, that Z. G. does to Alonzo Badger."

"Still, we had no proof—save only the deciphered memorandum-books of Rushton's; and they were hardly sufficient. But I discovered that the man Seixas is a weak proposition. This morning, an hour ago, when I made it plain to him that we had the goods on him, and after I had made him think that Rushton had given up the whole story, he broke down and confessed; and now I have his signed and sworn confession in my pocket. He swears that Rushton cooked up the entire affair."

Rushton could be seen vainly struggling under his bonds, but nobody paid the slightest attention to him.

"Atkinson, confronted by the confession of Seixas, and by the further assurance that we had the goods on Rushton—and being told, also, Mr. Chester, of Rushton's attempt to blackmail you, and of how we have the marked money that you paid him, and affidavits from both banks to go with it, so that he is bound to be convicted and sent away on that—became defiant and abusive, and finally made a confession, also in the presence of witnesses, although he would not swear to one."

"Badger, that great hulk of a man, was easy. He seemed glad to tell the whole story about Rushton and Rushton's methods, and he knows enough of the back record of Rushton to cause his indictment a dozen times over."

"As a matter of fact, all three of those men are sore at Rushton for taking the lion's share of that stolen money when he did nothing but plan it, and they took all the risk and did all the work. Rushton was not anywhere near the bank when the money was actually stolen."

"Now, there is one more important thing—the *frame-up*."

"Rushton told Badger all about that. Badger actually assisted him by procuring the stamped paper-slips that are used for wrapping packages of bills at the Centropolis Bank; those scraps of paper that Rushton showed to you, Mr. Chester, at the time he succeeded in so nearly convincing you of Harvard's guilt."

"Those scraps were charred and scorched and partly burned at Badger's home, and he was present with Rushton when it was done. That explains the frame-up; and that, Lieutenant Banta, is what *you* have been most interested to know about."

"That's no dream, chief," Banta responded.

"Now," the chief continued, "just one moment, if you please."

He went to the door to the roof and threw it open. He signaled to his three operatives who had Badger, Seixas, and Atkinson in charge, and the three men were brought silently into the room.

Then the chief stepped swiftly behind Rushton, and almost with one motion stripped the bandages from the lieutenant's eyes and jaws; and Rushton, blinking, saw those three men standing in line directly in front of him.

It was a dramatic moment—a perfectly prepared climax—and it worked.

The bottled-up, repressed wrath of Rushton was uncorked.

The tirade of abuse that he heaped upon those three men with his tongue defies description. It could not be repeated. It could not be half told; but, in still another corner of that room behind a screen, an expert stenographer took down every word, profane or otherwise, that he uttered.

And when he did at last stop for breath there was nothing more to be desired in the way of a confession from him.

The names that he did not call his accomplices were few indeed.

The incidents that would convict him, that he did not refer to in words, were *nil*.

He damned them, one after another, to all kinds of perdition to the end of time; and when he had quite finished, and he was breathless, Atkinson replied to him calmly by saying:

"You seem to have told it all, Rushton. I had not confessed to anything; neither had Seixas. Badger had, of course; but there would still have been a fighting chance for us maybe if you had kept your mouth shut. But you are only a common yellow dog, anyhow." He turned to the chief. "Take me away from here, please, and I will write out a full description and confession of the whole thing," he added.

"And you, Seixas?" the chief asked.

"Oh, I'll sign it," was the reply, given with a laugh.

"Badger, how much of that stolen money have you still got in your possession?" the chief asked.

"All of it," was the reply.

"How much have you, Atkinson?"

"About fifteen thousand of my share."

"And you, Seixas?"

"Not a cent. I blew it all in on the ponies."

"Well, Mr. Chester, we will recover about a hundred thousand dollars of it at that," the chief said, with a smile. "This is a pretty good morning's work."

There was a general hand-shaking all around after that—that is, after the four prisoners had been sent away—for you may be sure that the chief had everything in preparation for that interesting event.

"I have arranged an appointment for you, Harvard, at my office," he said a little later. "It is for one o'clock. I want you and Lady Kate, Clancy, and Banta to go with me."

CHAPTER XXXV

THE AFTERMATH

Lady Kate looked very *chic* indeed with her closely cropped, boyishly trimmed hair and her tailor-made, perfectly fitting suit of gray as she sat in the chief's office with her husband and his friends, awaiting the return of Redhead, who had gone for a moment into another room.

Presently the chief came back, and he beckoned to Harvard and Lady Kate and to Banta and Clancy to follow him.

In that other room which they entered a man was seated, with his face turned toward the window, and he did not look around until the chief spoke to him.

But then he got upon his feet and turned about so that he faced them, clinging to the back of the chair upon which he had been seated.

What they all saw was, in one sense, pathetic, for it was the inspector who faced them—the inspector who had been made a slave of that "system" which has ruined so many perfectly well-intentioned men.

They were all silent. Not one of them could think of anything to say. It was the chief who spoke first.

"Tell these friends of ours what you have to say to them, Aaron," he said.

Again there was a moment of silence. Then the inspector spoke in a low tone and very quietly.

"I want to congratulate you, Harvard, on the happy ending of your difficulties," he said. "I should have known it—

236

and I did know it without knowing it. I might have known by implication that there had been a frame-up, but I refused to know it. I am sorry."

"Lady Kate, if I may still so address you, I congratulate you also. You have a splendid and a good man for your husband, one whom I have learned to honor and respect. I wish to assure him through you that the commissioner has agreed with me already that there will never be any notice taken of the acts of Bingham Harvard in his defiance of police authority; and I ought to tell you both that the commissioner's principal reason for that attitude is owing to a signed petition that he received yesterday—signed by every man except Rushton, who has felt the weight of Harvard's hand."

"Mr. Clancy, we have had misunderstandings in the past. I have forgotten them, and I hope you will do the same."

"Banta, old friend, this is a tough moment. We have always liked each other, and I am more glad than ever now to have called you my friend. Chief, you cannot do better than to take Banta on with you. You couldn't have a better man."

"He is on already—since last midnight," the chief replied.

"Then I have just one more word to say, and it is addressed to all who are here. I have resigned from the department, and my resignation has been accepted. It takes effect immediately. The chief, who has proved himself to be my very good friend, advised it; the commissioner approved of it—so there it ends."

He bowed, reached for his hat, bowed again at the doorway and was gone.

"Now, what do you know about that?" Clancy exclaimed. "I suppose there are some people who would say that he ought to have got it in the neck, but I'm satisfied as it is. Eh—what?"

* * * * * * *

At the home of Banker Chester that evening there was a select dinner-party, at which, upon the insistence of Mr.

237

Chester, Bingham Harvard presided at one end of the table and Lady Kate graced the other one. We need not mention the names of those who were present, save only that Black Julius waited upon them at the feast.

It was the banker who offered the first toast of the evening. He arose in his place, and lifting his glass of light wine on high, said:

"To my son and my daughter, for so I regard them! God bless them always!"

Then it was that Lady Kate left her place, crossed to a door, threw it open, and admitted a distinguished-looking gentleman with a lady on his arm.

"My friends," she said, "this is my father, Senator Maxwilton, of Kentucky; and this is my dear mother. We had a misunderstanding once because my father wished me to marry a man I did not love; but, now that I have found one, and married one whom I do love with all my heart and soul, we are all content."

"Gee!" Tom Clancy exclaimed in an aside, "can you beat it?"

www.ingramcontent.com/pod-product-compliance
Lightning Source LLC
Chambersburg PA
CBHW050516260626
47157CB00004B/1342